PRAISE FOR

BEFORE THE FALL

"[A] surprise-jammed mystery that works purely on :
character-driven terms...Mr. Hawley has made it ve:
easy to race through his book in a state of breathless suspense."
—Janet Maslin, *New York Times*

"BEFORE THE FALL is a ravishing and riveting beauty of a
thriller. It's also a deep exploration of desire, betrayal, creation,
family, fate, mortality, and rebirth."
—Michael Cunningham, Pulitzer Prize–winning
author of *The Hours*

"Noah Hawley really knows how to keep a reader turning the
pages, but there's more to the novel than suspense...exposes the
high cost of news as entertainment and the randomness of fate."
—Kristin Hannah, *New York Times Book Review*,
"Notable Book of 2016"

"A book that combines a thriller's tight structure and addictive
narrative with characterisation and thematic richness reminis-
cent of Jonathan Franzen."
—*Sunday Times* (London), "Thriller of the Year"

"Imagine that Agatha Christie had set a closed-room mystery on
an airplane and included Wall Street and entertainment executive types in her lineup of suspects. Now imagine that airplane
crashing into the Atlantic before the story even gets going...Mr.

Hawley, the expert TV showrunner, obviously had the skills to pull this off." —*New York Times*, "The Top Books of 2016"

"I started and finished BEFORE THE FALL in one day."
—James Patterson, #1 *New York Times* bestselling author and winner of the National Book Foundation's 2015 Literarian Award

"A masterly blend of mystery, suspense, tragedy, and shameful media hype...a gritty tale of a man overwhelmed by unwelcome notoriety, with a stunning, thoroughly satisfying conclusion."
—*Publishers Weekly* (starred review)

"A pulse-pounding story, grounded in humanity."
—*Booklist* (starred review)

"A multilayered, immersive examination of truth, relationships, and our unquenchable thirst for the media's immediate explanation of unfathomable tragedy."
—Karin Slaughter, #1 internationally bestselling author

"Cathartic...BEFORE THE FALL is about the gulf that separates perception and truth, and the people who fall into it."
—Sam Sacks, *Wall Street Journal*

"BEFORE THE FALL kicks ass. A surefire summer read."
—Justin Cronin, *New York Times* bestselling author of *The Passage* and *City of Mirrors*

"Like the successful screenwriter that he is, Hawley piles on enough intrigues and plot complications to keep you hooked."
—*Kirkus Reviews*

"This isn't just a good novel; it's a great one. I trusted no one in these pages, yet somehow cared about them all. BEFORE THE FALL brings a serrated edge to every character, every insight, and every wicked twist."

—Brad Meltzer, bestselling author of *The President's Shadow*

"Highly entertaining...Hawley invests the same care with a soupçon of dark humor into BEFORE THE FALL as he does on the TV series *Fargo*." —The Associated Press

"A remarkable and memorable accomplishment by any standard...BEFORE THE FALL is brilliantly constructed and wonderfully told...a tale that will haunt you long after you read the last page, even as you wish the narrative was twice as long, for all the right reasons." —*Book Reporter*

"Essential reading this summer for anyone who likes a good story well told...You won't read a more thoughtful page-turner anytime soon...irresistibly cinematic." —*St. Louis Post-Dispatch*

"Remarkably fun to read, filled with suspense, memorable characters and incredibly visual scenes...a compulsive experience."
—*Austin American-Statesman*

"Compulsively written and involving, BEFORE THE FALL is a stunning inquiry into human drive and desire...A powerful and genuinely surprising work." —*The Saturday Star*

"Abundant chills and thrills...Noah Hawley's novel grabs you by the throat and won't let go...BEFORE THE FALL is storytelling at its best, as Hawley presents a range of diverse characters with rich histories...Seeds of doubt are cast in what is sure to be the summer book you won't want to miss." —*The Missourian*

"In the hands of a writer like Noah Hawley, who knows how to build tension from mundane moments, it is a remarkable thriller that most readers will find difficult to put down...it moves toward a breathless ending." —*Washington Times*

"A complex exploration of human nature in an age of celebrity."
—*Pittsburgh Post-Gazette*

"BEFORE THE FALL won the hearts and minds of *The Post* staff. We're certain it will be the big talker of the summer."
—*New York Post*, "Summer's Hottest Reads"

"[The] thriller of the summer." —*Baltimore Sun*

"The crash and the flashbacks recall *Lost* and Thornton Wilder's Pulitzer Prize–winning novel, *The Bridge Over San Luis Rey*, and Scott's travails are the lot of every hero in a conspiratorial thriller going back to *The 39 Steps*." —*Slate*

"A thoughtful and compelling page-turner...Hawley's writing is taut and clear, his characters richly developed...Readers may be moved to stand up and cheer." —*New York Journal of Books*

"Noah Hawley's BEFORE THE FALL isn't a typical mystery. Perhaps that's why I couldn't put it down." —TheAtlantic.com

"Fast-paced, mysterious...reads like a great episode of TV."
—*The Tennessean*

THE PUNCH

THE PUNCH

A NOVEL

NOAH HAWLEY

GRAND CENTRAL
PUBLISHING

NEW YORK BOSTON

Copyright © 2008, 2018 by Noah Hawley
Cover design by Jason Heuer
Cover photographs: Mïnden (cloud background); Shutterstock (tree); Alamy (brownstones)
Cover copyright © 2018 by Hachette Book Group, Inc.
Hachette Book Group supports the right to free expression and the value of copyright. The purpose of copyright is to encourage writers and artists to produce the creative works that enrich our culture.

The scanning, uploading, and distribution of this book without permission is a theft of the author's intellectual property. If you would like permission to use material from the book (other than for review purposes), please contact permissions@hbgusa.com. Thank you for your support of the author's rights.

Grand Central Publishing
Hachette Book Group
1290 Avenue of the Americas
New York, NY 10104
grandcentralpublishing.com
twitter.com/grandcentralpub

First published in hardcover by Chronicle Books in 2008
First Grand Central Publishing Edition: October 2018

Grand Central Publishing is a division of Hachette Book Group, Inc.
The Grand Central Publishing name and logo is a trademark of Hachette Book Group, Inc.

The publisher is not responsible for websites (or their content) that are not owned by the publisher.

The Hachette Speakers Bureau provides a wide range of authors for speaking events. To find out more, go to www.hachettespeakersbureau.com or call (866) 376-6591.

ISBN 978-1-5387-4653-0 (trade paperback)
ISBN 978-1-5387-4655-4 (ebook)

Printed in the United States of America

LSC-C

10 9 8 7 6 5 4 3 2 1

For Tom

FOREWORD BY NOAH HAWLEY

1.

Is there any word more human than *redemption*? The sea otter has no concept of karma. Birds do not seek forgiveness. Spiders never feel regret. Human beings are the only animals that live their lives based on an idea, that make choices based on *how we feel*, the only species that holds a grudge. Our flaws are human flaws: arrogance, insecurity, addiction.

There is no tragedy in the animal kingdom, but humanity is rife with it. All the roads we should have taken. Things said that can't be taken back.

2.

Think of this book as a wildlife documentary, filled with every human flaw. Parents and children. Brothers and sisters. We should love each other, but we can't. We should help each other, but we don't. We should forgive the ones we love the most, so why are they the hardest to forgive?

3.

The word *absurd* is defined in the following ways:

Adjective: utterly or obviously senseless, illogical, or untrue; contrary to all reason or common sense; laughably foolish or false.

Noun: the quality or condition of existing in a meaningless and irrational world.

Like redemption, absurdity is an idea that is uniquely human, because human beings are the only species on Earth that believe our lives should *mean something*, even as we realize how "laughably foolish or false" this idea is. What does the word *meaning* even mean? Viewed in this way, humanity becomes an Abbott and Costello routine, in which we are both the setup and the punch line. We are the birds who forgive, the regretful spiders.

4.

They say comedy is tragedy plus time.

5.

Another word for this would be *family*.

THE PUNCH

THE EMERGENCY ROOM is decorated for Valentine's Day. Plastic roses sprout from metal bedpans. Glitter sawdusts the floor. Overhead, colored streamers ribbon out of paper hearts like veins, all the bright colors blown flat by the hospital fluorescents. Love, it seems, is alive and well at St. Vincent's Hospital in New York City. Inside the waiting room, the sick and wounded sit in orange bucket-bottom seats, cradling the parts of themselves that ache or bleed, consoled by friends and relatives. Their moans mix with the piano music of the man in the tuxedo T-shirt sitting in the corner. He's playing electric keyboard and singing sentimental love songs: *Your love is lifting me higher . . . You are so beautiful to me.* It has to be one of the worst gigs in history, right below the band that played while the *Titanic* sank.

Time is elastic in emergency rooms under normal circumstances, but the usual slow-motion syrup of minutes and hours becomes surreal when given a soundtrack. Right now the clock says 6:15 P.M. In the back of the room, two men sit on hard-bottomed chairs, side by side. They are both in their mid-thirties, both wearing suits. One has his head back. He holds an ice pack to his broken nose. The other clutches ice to his broken hand. They are brothers, Scott and David Henry, but they don't speak to each other. They won't even look at each other.

A broken nose.

A broken fist.

You do the math.

And yet, despite the clear antipathy between them, and though there are plenty of empty chairs in the emergency room, they sit side by side.

Looking at them, you might think you understand what they've been through—a routine spat, words that escalated— but you'd be wrong. This was no simple brawl. No petty disagreement over inheritance or who said what to whom. These brothers—David the older, Scott the younger—have traveled thousands of miles together in the last few days. They've confronted death and strippers and the sudden life-altering emergence of God. They've drunk too much and sprinted into oncoming traffic.

Worse, they've had to spend time with their mother. Far, far too much time.

A white-gowned orderly emerges from behind a dirty yellow door.

"Hernandez?" he says. An elderly Latino man gets to his feet, assisted by a young woman, probably his daughter. Following behind is her son, playing a Game Boy. They disappear behind the door. The brothers go back to waiting.

With his chin tilted up at a forty-degree angle, all Scott can really see is the ceiling and the top eight inches of the walls. This is where most of the decorations hang, tacked up in a moment of seasonal zealotry by some love-struck orderly. The hearts have pithy sayings on them—*True love is blind, Love is a many splendored thing,* that sort of thing. It doesn't seem so far off, this decorating schematic. All of them there, the bloodied and cramping, the sneezing and moaning, could just as easily have stumbled in off the street following some love-related mishap. They could be heartbroken, starved for attention, crushed by rejection.

Scott considers mentioning this to his brother, but the time for words between them has passed, swallowed by a black-hole acrimony familiar to combatants in most of the planet's age-old ethnic conflicts. The Jews and Arabs, the Hatfields and McCoys. From here on out it's broken bones or nothing.

In the last few days Scott has learned that sometimes in life you land on your face instead of your feet.

David has learned that he is the kind of person who sees a cliff coming and speeds up.

The orderly emerges, calls another name. A woman who has been vomiting into a plastic bucket rises weakly to her feet and shuffles forward. The brothers watch her go, ice melting, to the tune of "Wonderwall" by Oasis. They're beginning to wonder if their time will ever come.

Speaking of time, there is a theory of time that goes like this: Chronological time is just a concept invented by animals. It is our way of understanding the universe. Sentient life could not exist without it. How would we navigate a universe in which things didn't happen in some kind of order, in which there was no beginning, middle, or end? Empirically, however, says the theory, all events exist simultaneously, and the entire span of time is just one infinitely dense dot exploding all at once.

Time, in other words, is subjective. There is no such thing as past, present, or future. And if there is no such thing as past, present, or future, then the fight that divided these brothers is still happening. And because it is still happening, they feel no shame about it, no guilt or remorse. Because it is still happening, it does not color the rest of their lives one bit. Without time, you see, there is no memory. Memory exists exactly because time is linear, because the past recedes. The human brain collects the things you do and see and feel and hear (both good and bad) and chases you with them into the future. But without time, events would never recede into the past because there would be no past. People would not be forced to relive their mistakes over and over again, the things that haunt them.

And yet, because they are animals, Scott and David see time in a narrow linear light. They believe their lives have a beginning, a middle, and an end. They believe the things they've done, the choices they've made, have led them to this place of physical, emotional, and (most likely) economic bankruptcy.

A punch was thrown. A nose was broken, and (at the same time) a hand.

And so now, as a result, two brothers sit side by side in a New York City emergency room. They will not speak to or look at each other, but both find something reassuring about the closeness of the other.

Because, the truth is, each is all the other has left.

PART ONE

CAGES

JOE HENRY IS dead. In his prime he was a tall man, fat around the middle, with a red beard. He had a smile like a pirate. Now his ashes are stored in a garage in Portland, Oregon, zipped up in a plastic bag, sealed inside a cheap wooden box. He lived for sixty-eight years, which in the age of the pony express and the steam engine would have seemed like a good long time, but now, with our modern medicine and cutting-edge technology, seems like a gyp. Joe was born in Ohio and died in Oregon. He spent most of his life in New York City. He was a soldier in the army during the Korean War (though he never fired a shot). At different times in his life he was a copywriter, an industrial filmmaker, and a salesman. And for the last seven years of his life he was a very sick man. He had what the literature refers to as multiple organ failure—heart, liver, kidneys. Because of this, he went to dialysis three times a week for four hours a day. There they literally drained the blood from his body, stripped out the toxins, and fed it back to him. What a thing to watch— your own blood flowing out of your body into a machine, the sight of it, hot and red, draining from your arm through a clear, shallow tube (does the machine suck it out, or is there a dis- comforting feeling of evacuation, of your blood rushing out, escaping?). It is like something fundamental about you is being rewired right before your eyes. How many days did he sit there wondering *Am I still me without my blood, without the impurities they strip out?*

Joe died with a huge zipper scar running from his clavicle to his belly. This is where the heart surgeons opened his chest and spread his ribs. He had smaller scars on his arms and legs where veins had been extracted and arteries bypassed. There was a shunt is his right arm, taped closed, and a strange subterranean bulge in the suicide vein of his right wrist, tubes lurking just under the surface. His teeth floated in a glass by the bed. A mess, in other words. He was a mess. He had never been a particularly healthy person. He smoked and drank. He never exercised, never went to the doctor. At sixty-one his heart, liver, and kidneys faltered. Over the course of the next seven years he went from hospital to nursing home, losing body mass, folding inward. He contracted liver cancer, a tumor the size of a walnut that was removed by surgeons with a glowing poker.

But still he kept going.

Then he was diagnosed with lung cancer, which, if you think about it, leads you to one of two conclusions: Either (A) there is no God or (B) God must have really, really wanted Joe Henry dead. Joe Henry must have owed God money or slept with his sister or something, because say what you want about heart failure, liver failure, and kidney failure, lung cancer is a motherfucker. Which is why, just three months later, Joe Henry died, restless and mumbling fitfully in his nursing home bed.

Now he is what you might call a *passive character.* The sum total he can contribute to the world is this:

Zero.

By coincidence, zero is also the current level of confidence Joe's son Scott has in the girl he has been dating since his father's death. As our story begins, Scott is drunk and seated in the VIP area of a San Francisco strip club. He is watching a woman in a thong give a lap dance to Kate, the girl he's dated for the last two months. The two of them are in the club as part of a foursome (though, in truth, it is more of a threesome, with Scott just along for the ride). It is the end of a long night of drama and humiliation. Certain truths have come to light (details of Kate's extracurricular activities, unflattering information about her character) and Scott is exhausted, emotionally, physically. He is beginning to think he isn't in Kansas anymore, by which he means he is off the map, has sailed past all known landmasses over the lip of the page (past the signs that read THERE BE DRAGONS HERE). It is all blackness now, and fog.

He orders another tequila, another beer, and watches as the man who brought them here, a fifty-three-year-old captain of industry, negotiates price with a blonde, top-heavy stripper. Scott watches as the Captain takes his girlfriend's hand and retreats with the stripper to a back room for a private session, which Kate tells him will involve actual penetration (Kate and the Captain and his girlfriend come to this place often, it turns out). The VIP area is smoky, filled with the thundering confusion of electronic beats. It is two o'clock in the morning. They have already been to two gallery openings and a party. Kate leans over and tells Scott that the last time she was here with the Captain and his girlfriend, she made three hundred dollars lap-dancing for strangers. She says it with a smile on her face, pride in her voice. She is hot the way a knife is hot when you hold it over a fire, then press the blade against an open wound. When she looks at Scott, he feels like an egg cooking on the sidewalk. His dad has been dead for twelve weeks. All he wants is to be loved like a puppy. Instead he is locked in some kind of twisted dating deathmatch. He feels dizzy, a hot electric coil in his stomach frying up his guts.

No one ever told him there was so much sadness in the world. It is a smothering syrup that coats the land and sea, a cherry-red sludge you can't escape. The catch is, you can't see it all the time. When things are good, when the world is normal, the varnish of sadness is almost invisible, but then, when you least expect it, like an egg, the world cracks open and sadness coats your hair, your clothes. It comes in the mail. It seeps into every electronic transaction, a binary sadness of ones and zeroes. It pours out of the faucet when you brush your teeth, fills the air like pollen, reddening your eyes, making your nose run.

Right now what fills the air is the smell of pineapple and coconut, artificial, cloying. It's the smell of cheap perfume the strippers carry in their boxy purses, like little cans of Mace. Food, they smell like food.

Seven hours from now—after the strip club, after a long cab ride home, after they tumble into bed, and Kate herself smells like food, like coconut and pineapple (like a stripper)—he will tell her she has to go. That she's killing him. And right in the middle of his speech he will break down crying, feeling at once humiliated and liberated, because finally it's all coming out, all the grief and anger, seven years of suffering and regret (heart failure and liver failure and kidney failure and liver cancer and lung cancer, Jesus Christ!). Death. He will be crying because of death. *I just want to be happy,* he'll say pathetically, and she will hold him like she cares (stroking his hair, whispering soothing words), but she doesn't. It is a lie. A beautiful lie. And he will tell her to get out, will throw her clothes at her, push her out the door, then lie on the bathroom floor panting, dizzy with booze and loss.

In case you haven't figured it out by now, this is not going to be a love story about Scott and Kate. The truth is, she is just another in a long series of crazy ladies, narcissists. *Same bullet,* he will say later. *Different gun.* She is like a shirt you keep trying on because it looks great on the rack, but on you it is misshapen, hideous. The colors are not your colors. The cut makes you look ridiculous. But you can't walk away from it, can't stop trying it on, because in your mind you think, *This shirt is so cool!* It is a shirt that looks profoundly stylish on a shaved-headed Italian soccer player modeling in a Dolce & Gabbana ad. And looking at it, you think it should look good on you, too, but it doesn't. On you it looks like a clown costume. It is the same with these women. They are the perfect girls, yes, but for someone else.

Scott sits in a dark, humid strip club watching as a topless Asian dancer presses her tits against Kate's face, as she spreads Kate's legs and rubs her naked thighs against Kate's denim-clad groin. Seeing this, Scott closes his eyes and for one overwhelming moment thinks, *I miss my dad.*

I miss my dad.

Or maybe the story begins here, at six A.M. in a house in Portland, Oregon, where Scott's mother, Doris, emerges slowly from her bedroom, checking the hallway for signs of life, moving furtively, sneaking into the kitchen to pour herself another glass of wine before anyone else is up. She is having anxiety attacks these days, experiencing shortness of breath, feelings of panic and hopelessness. Her husband of almost forty-two years has been dead for three months, and his ashes are locked in a cheap wooden box in her sister-in-law's garage, and the idea of this—the knowledge that all she has to show for four decades of having and holding, loving and obeying (though let's face it, she was never that good at obeying), is a box of human kitty litter—keeps her up at night, makes her feel like an elephant is sitting on her chest. The deep-organ certainty that he will never again call her at eight in the morning from his nursing home and tell her his pancakes are cold, will never again kiss her forehead, hold her hand, and call her *beauty,* makes her want a cigarette, two, six, ten. But because of the emphysema she isn't supposed to smoke, isn't supposed to light up, close her eyes, and inhale that deep, chemical sense of calm. And yet, give me a fucking break. If there was a big glass case on the wall with a pack of cigarettes inside and a sign that read DO NOT BREAK EXCEPT IN CASE OF EMERGENCY, now would absolutely be the time to smash it open. Because if not now, then when? The man is dead, for God's sake. All the information stored in his meaty gray brain has been returned to its original sources. All those memories, all the history books he used to pore over, now may as well have been unread. It is thoughts like these that drive Doris into the kitchen to uncork a bottle of Merlot at six o'clock in the morning.

Or maybe the real place to start this story is in Los Angeles, at the home of Doris's other son, David, the eldest, the family man who, on a cold, unforgiving Valentine's Day, will break Scott's nose. He is a tall man with sandy brown hair and straight white teeth, a sales executive for a major pharmaceutical company. As our story begins, it is six-thirty in the morning and the kids are awake, running amok—Christopher, ten, and Chloe, eight, and the new baby, Sam—and it is time for brushing and dressing and eating. Time to pack lunches and buckle up. His wife, Tracey, isn't a morning person and so David rises with the first rustle and herds the kids through their routines. He makes their breakfast, ties their shoes. His days are scheduled down to the millisecond. He has meetings to go to and sales strategy memos to write. His father has been dead for three months. He is stressed out and overwhelmed but has no time to deal with it, so he tells himself to man up. At this point, with a new baby and a full plate at work, grief is a luxury he can't afford. Since his father died there hasn't been a single moment to stop and take it in, to cry or scream or punch a hole in the wall, and it doesn't look like there will be a moment in the foreseeable future. So he locks it away and steps into his underwear. Yesterday his brother, Scott, called and laid out this long, rambling monologue about some girl who'd broken his heart, the latest in a series of obviously unreliable lunatics, and it was all he could do not to tell him to shut up. Not to tell Scott to call back when he had some real problems—kids who need braces or a mortgage that needs paying.

David's wife shifts under the covers, murmurs something encouraging, like *Have a nice day* or *I love you*. David knots his tie, unravels it, knots it again until the dimple is perfect. This is what he needs, for everything to be perfect, to be just so. But the truth is, David's life isn't perfect. Far from it. In fact, he has a secret. A big one, and the secret is this: He has a second wife in New York City. He never meant to have a second wife in New York, or anywhere else for that matter. It just sort of happened. He met a girl on a business trip last winter (Joy. Like how could you not fall in love with a girl named Joy?), and had a fling, and somehow she got pregnant. She wasn't supposed to get pregnant, but she did. And when she told him, he found himself asking her to marry him, heard the words coming out of his mouth, even as this polite, semi-English-sounding voice piped up in his head and said, *Excuse me, sir, but aren't you already married?* Like a butler was reminding him of some minor engagement he was late for, instead of the reality, which was HE WAS ALREADY MARRIED. He had two kids and a third on the way. He couldn't get married again. There were laws against that kind of thing, not to mention all the moral implications. And yet there he was, proposing. And the next day he and Joy went to City Hall and stood before a justice of the peace—a foppish man with a comb-over—and Joy floated an inch above the floor, beaming, while David swayed on his feet, sweating, tugging at his tie. And now there is a baby boy, also named Sam. (He tried to stop her. Sam was, coincidentally, Joy's father's name. Like what are the odds?) And so in just twelve short months, David has turned into one of those *Montel Williams Show* subjects (Next up on *Montel:* Bigamy!). But it's not his fault. He swears. He never meant for any of this to happen. Things just kind of... escalated.

But that's not even the worst of it. The worst of it is, in three days his mother and brother are going to arrive carrying a cheap wooden box of ashes. They're going to show up with all their chaos, their alcoholism and tragic love disorders, and turn his life upside down for two days. And then, as if that wasn't bad enough, the four of them (David, Scott, Doris, and Joe's ashes) will wing to New York City for Joe's memorial service (big party, historic location, towers of shrimp). After which, if they manage to survive, the four of them, exhausted and cranky, will pile into a rental car and begin the seven-hour drive to Bailey's Island, Maine, where on a rocky, winter beach they will open the box and spread Joe Henry's ashes into the sea.

It's enough to make a grown bigamist cry.

THERE WAS AN article in the *New York Times* recently about a survey given to scientists around the country. In it they were asked to answer the following question: *What do you believe is true even though you can't prove it?*

Kenneth Ford, a physicist, wrote, "I believe that microbial life exists elsewhere in our galaxy."

Roger Schank, a psychologist and computer scientist, said, "I do not believe that people are capable of rational thought when it comes to making decisions in their own lives. People believe they are behaving rationally and have thought things out, of course, but when major decisions are made—who to marry, where to live, what career to pursue—people's minds simply cannot cope with the complexity."

Scott Henry is an expert on the complexity of life's decisions. He knows these kinds of choices—who to marry, where to live, what career to pursue—are not easy. In his job, he hears a lot of waffling. Scott is a spy. A corporate mole. When you call customer service for any one of a dozen companies, he is the one who monitors the calls. *Quality assurance*, they call it. Day after day he sits in a cubicle in Emeryville, California, surrounded by other spies in cubicles. They all wear headsets and listen in real time to the conversations of others. Standing in that room, surrounded by bodies, one hears nothing but the collective breathing of a hundred eavesdroppers.

Right now Scott is at the Oakland airport waiting to board a flight to Portland, Oregon. He is going to see his mother. This is the first stage of his dad's final trip, the four-city tour (like his father's ashes are some kind of rock band: *Hello, Portland! Hello, Los Angeles! Hello, Madison Square Garden!*) that will put to rest his father's physical remains. Scott wants to do this as much as he wants to take an electric drill and bore a hole in his head. He remembers reading an article about people who do that, who drill holes in their heads. The rush of air on their exposed brain tissue is supposed to get them high. He wonders if any of those people ever called customer support while he was listening. If, as they were on hold waiting to speak to a friendly, conscientious salesperson about a faulty microwave they bought online, they revved up the old Black & Decker and set the drill bit to their temples. It wouldn't surprise him.

His phone rings. It's his brother, David, calling from L.A.

"Are you there yet?" David asks.

"I'm at the Oakland airport. I'm considering drilling a hole in my head to relieve the pressure. What do you think?"

He can hear his brother typing at the other end of the line. That's the thing with David. You never have his full attention.

"I'm supposed to tell you that we have plenty of room if you want to stay here once you reach L.A.," David says.

"Supposed to?"

"Tracey thinks it's the right thing to do. To have the family all together."

"Is she crazy?"

"That's what I wondered, but of course you can't say that kind of thing out loud. Not to my wife."

Scott watches a woman wipe chocolate off a toddler's face.

The toddler is the size of one of those yoga balls you roll around on to stretch your back. Outside the window, his plane looks like nothing except a giant, passenger-laden missile. Not for the first time in the last few years Scott longs for a simpler era, the 1980s or '70s, when terrorism was someone else's problem and hijackings were quaint, semicivilized political acts, the start of a conversation. He remembers reading a survey of common passengers' responses to hijackings back in the mid-'70s. The answers people gave were straight out of *Leave It to Beaver:*

1) "History is being made and I'm part of it."

2) "Gosh, I wonder what I'll see in Cuba."

3) "If they put us in a hotel, will there be any women?"

Scott hunkers down in his seat. He says, "You can have Mom if you want, but I'm staying at a hotel. Something hip and fabulous. I think I've earned that. I think I've earned starlets in bikinis drinking screwdrivers poolside."

"You're going to put Mom at a hip L.A. hotel?"

"Oh, no. Once we get to L.A. she's your responsibility."

In his six years listening to other people's phone calls, Scott has overheard all kinds of dialogue. He once listened slackjawed as a technical service question from a bored housewife to an Internet provider turned into a multiorgasmic phone-sex session. *What kind of operating system are you using?* Windows 2000. *What are you wearing?* A camisole, some pedal pushers. *Do you know what I'm doing to you right now? I'm fucking you.* Oh, God. Don't stop.

"Do you still have that drill handy?" his brother asks.

"Very funny," says Scott. "I'm serious. I'll be in Portland for three days and then we're coming to you, and once we get there I expect to scrape her off at your house and go to my hotel for a very large drink."

"Fine. I'd put her up here, but she can't do the stairs, which

I told Tracey, but she says, Can't you carry her? Like this is what I want to do, carry my sixty-five-year-old mother up and down the stairs for three days."

"Sixty-three."

"What?"

"She's sixty-three."

Silence. Scott worries he has lost his brother's interest entirely. In fact, David has just gotten an instant message from his second wife in New York, Joy. MISS U. CALL ME. *This is what happens when you don't deal with things head on,* he thinks, deleting it, erasing the trail. When you don't nip problems in the bud.

On the other end of the line, Scott hears David crumple up a piece of paper and throw it in the trash. This is how fine-tuned Scott's hearing has become in the last six years: He can tell that the paper is a sheet of eight-and-a-half-by-eleven laser-printer paper, not a piece of newspaper. He is like one of those submarine sonar men who can differentiate between thirty kinds of whale farts.

"Are you there?" he asks.

"Just a second. Okay. What was I saying?"

"The stairs."

"Right. I'll put her up at the Hotel Bel-Air or something swank."

"She'll hate it."

"She hates everything."

"At least we know we're talking about the same mother."

A flight attendant comes over the PA to announce the preboarding of Scott's flight. He panics. He sees the world now for what it truly is, an uncontrolled assault. How is he ever going to survive the next two weeks? He needs more time, more time to prepare, to get his head together. The flight is too short. Why couldn't his mother live in Boston instead of Portland?

Why couldn't she live in Florida? Japan? Scott checks the clock on the wall. Barring an act of God or some kind of mechanical failure, he will be in Portland in two hours, pulling his rental car up to his mother's apartment—a soulless condo in the Pearl District—fumbling in his pockets for change for the meter. Standing by the front door, his suitcase at his feet, he will take a deep breath and pray silently (not to God. He doesn't believe in God. But to some kind of fickle, punishing fate. He will stand there for ten minutes, eyes closed, begging the Universe for a break. *Just one break. Come on. You owe me*) before ringing her bell, before beginning the elevator ride that will finally and irrevocably prove beyond a shadow of a doubt that his father is dead. Not just dead, but cremated and stored in a Ziploc bag inside a cheap wooden box in his aunt's garage. At the airport, Scott feels the egg of sorrow crack open, feels sadness seep down slowly over the crown of his head. Sitting in the terminal, he prays for engine failure, for faulty landing gear, a crucifix-shaped crack in the wing.

"That's my plane," says Scott. "I gotta go."

He joins the line snaking its way slowly onboard. He has never been the kind of man who drinks on planes, but right now he's wondering how many beers he can consume before the landing gear descends and he finds himself in Oregon, as if that isn't bad enough, being in Oregon, without a dead father and a clingy, punishing, drunken mother to contend with.

AT SIX P.M. Scott parks his rental car outside his mother's apartment building. It is misting out, a classic, gray Pacific Northwestern winter dusk. His luggage is on rollers, and the wheels make a steady thrumming drone as he walks around the block for the sixth time, trying to get up the courage to go in.

"Didn't you just come by here?" asks a woman with a stroller sitting outside the Starbucks on the corner.

"My suitcase needs the exercise," he tells her.

In his job he has heard every personal detail you can imagine about strangers: their dates of birth, Social Security numbers, their wives' maiden names, how much money they have in the bank, which communicable diseases they suffer from. He eavesdrops while people are on hold, cataloging the private interactions of the average American household. People mumble to themselves on hold. They sing. He has heard men batter their wives while waiting to make flight reservations, has heard women shout at their children and punish their dogs. One woman, calling in to the headquarters of a home-pregnancy-kit manufacturer, spent her time on hold talking to a woman in her kitchen about how the baby's father was, in fact, her own father, and what the hell was she supposed to do about *that*.

The operators he monitors live in all parts of the world. He has eavesdropped on technical services personnel in India, has overheard inmates in federal penitentiaries in Wyoming take telephone orders for cookwear from people in Hawaii. He listens to customers in New York talking to operators in Frankfurt. He scores operators on their openings, grading them on the friendliness of their greetings. He flags annoying habits, redlining operators who speak in monotone or use run-on sentences. He black-marks operators who transfer callers without asking, blackballs those who purposefully give out faulty information.

He cannot begin to quantify the number of angry callers he has heard since he started the job, the sheer volume of verbal abuse, the death threats. Profanity, forget about it. After six years on the job, he knows how to say *motherfucker* in twenty-one languages. People lose their minds on hold. They go crazy talking to machines, pressing 2, pressing 3, speaking their account numbers, answering questions asked by robots. They curse and belittle. They fume and gnash their teeth.

Scott Henry believes but cannot prove that, at heart, people are inherently rotten.

Riding up in the elevator, he checks his reflection in the mirrored doors. *Not bad,* he thinks. He is thirty-five, medium height, hair thinning slightly on top, but basically handsome. He works out, goes to the gym. His stomach is pretty much flat. Things could be worse. Except that the two beers he had on the plane have now worn off entirely, and he's not sure how he feels about this. On the one hand, it seems morally and strategically dangerous to face your alcoholic mother drunk. On the other hand, it does take the edge off.

He takes a deep breath, rings her bell. He hears footsteps. The door opens. A strange man is standing there, mid-fifties, bald on top with hippie hair hanging down from the back of his head. Scott doesn't know what to say. He thinks maybe he got off on the wrong floor, but then the man, who Scott now notices is wearing glasses and a tattered green army jacket, says, "You must be Scott."

Scott manages a nod.

The man turns around, leaving the door open.

"He's here," he says, retreating inside.

Cautiously, Scott enters the apartment. His mother is sitting at the kitchen island, a glass of red wine in front of her, a thin plastic oxygen line looped over her ears and positioned under her nose.

"Here he is," she says, smiling.

Scott gives her an awkward hug. She feels like a bag of sticks. The man has taken a seat on the sofa and is reading the paper.

"Who is that?" Scott asks, voice low.

"Oh, that's Joe," she says. "He's my roommate."

"Your roommate."

She sips her wine.

"I told you about Joe."

In the past three weeks she has, in fact, referred to Joe on numerous occasions, but since Joe was also her dead husband's name (Scott's father's name), Scott assumed she had simply lost her mind and was hallucinating. That in her grief-stricken, al-coholic haze she imagined her dead husband going grocery shopping twice a week and running downstairs every afternoon at three to get the mail. Now Scott sees that there actually is a Joe, and he's some kind of aging hippie who's living with Scott's mother, probably stealing every penny she's got every time he goes to the ATM.

"Doesn't he have a middle name or something?" Scott wants to know, leaning in, lowering his voice. "I can't call him that. Dad's name."

She turns to Joe.

"Do you have a middle name?" she asks.

Joe looks up from the paper.

"Roscoe," he says.

Roscoe? thinks Scott. *Wasn't that the sheriff's name on* The Dukes of Hazzard?

"Roscoe," says his mother, "this is my son Scott."

Roscoe gives Scott a gap-toothed smile and winks, returning immediately to the paper.

"Can I talk to you for a minute?" Scott asks his mother.

"What?" she says.

He glances at Roscoe, takes his mother's arm, pulls her into the bedroom, the thin, clear oxygen line dragging on the floor behind her.

"Who the hell is this guy?" he wants to know.

"Who? Joe? He's Cindy's father. You knew that."

Scott thinks about this. Cindy is the home-health aid who takes care of his mom three days a week.

"Her father?"

"He's a documentary filmmaker, a little down on his luck."

Scott feels a tic start up in his right eye.

"As opposed to all the documentary filmmakers buying tuxedos at Barneys."

"What?"

"Nothing. Just, what do you know about this guy?"

"What do you mean, *what do I know?* He's harmless."

"Maybe, maybe, but how do you know? Did you check his references?"

"What references? He's Cindy's father."

"That doesn't mean he's, you know, on the up-and-up. Does he know your PIN number?"

"Of course. He has to get me money."

"Mom, no. You don't just—you can't go around giving

everybody this very important, this very secret number. Believe me, I listen to a lot of calls, people who've been ripped off, had their identities stolen."

"Oh, please. Roscoe's not going to rip me off. He's not that bright. And he voted for Nader. People like that don't lie or cheat or steal. That's why this country's being run by Republicans."

Scott rubs his face. He's been here ten minutes and already he's wishing he'd drilled a hole in his head when he had the chance. That way this pressure wouldn't be building up behind his eyes at such an alarming rate.

"Is he staying here?"

"He sleeps in the guest room. I figured we'd put you on the couch."

The thought of sleeping on his mother's couch for three nights while Roscoe luxuriates in the guest room makes Scott want to take a belt sander to his own face.

"I could go to a hotel," he says. As he says it, the words give him a shock of pure happiness. It's perfect. If he went to a hotel he could control his exposure, come over around lunchtime, stay till dinner, then head back to the hotel, or better yet, out to find a beautiful woman who would make him forget his dead father, his alcoholic mother, his emotionally absent brother, the girl who doesn't love him, his dead-end job. Right now he feels like he needs that more than anything, to press his head against a woman's breast, a sweet, freckle-faced girl who'll stroke his hair and tell him everything's going to be okay. He's willing to pay a lot of money to hear this lie. It has nothing to do with sex. If he were a little more clued in, a little more objective, he would realize that what he really wants in this time of ultimate despair is his mommy. He wants creamed carrots on a spoon, a mother's cool lips pressed gently to his fever-hot brow. He wants a note excusing him from school, from work, from life. And yet the mother he has is just not the reassuring type. She's not about to make him cocoa or scratch his back. *You feel bad? What about me?* This is more her speed.

"No hotels," she says. "You're staying here and that's final."

He sighs. It would never occur to her to make Roscoe sleep on the sofa. A strange man she met three weeks ago. He gets the guest bed, while her own son will have to fold into the deep slouch of her old sofa.

Scott believes but cannot prove that whatever maternal instinct his mother once had dried up sometime around 1990, when he went off to college.

"Open another bottle of wine for me, would you?" she says.

He goes back into the kitchen and gets the corkscrew. He's been opening wine bottles for his mother since he was tall enough to reach the counter. Cutting the foil from the bottleneck, he has that familiar muscle memory, feeling before it happens the slow corkscrew bite as it grabs. He remembers being a kid, fetching wine for his mother, getting his dad another beer from the fridge. Picture a ten-year-old boy, laden down with booze, walking slowly, tongue jutting from the corner of his mouth, trying not to spill. Black Label, that was his dad's brand. A couple of shots, Jameson, neat. Scott's mother would drink Johnnie Walker Red, or, as the years went on, Merlot.

When Scott was thirteen, his parents started sending him to the corner store for cigarettes. Camel unfiltered for his dad, Vantage Blue for his mom. He would watch them rap the virgin pack against their wrists, tamping down the machine-packed leaves. Somehow the cellophane wrappers always ended up on the floor and the cat would chase them around, batting them. It seemed funny at the time, but then all their cats had to be put to sleep before they were nine, giant tumors protruding from their bellies, their hips. At camp, when other kids were making coffee mugs for their parents in ceramics class, Scott was molding ashtrays. This is how early the training starts. You know the cigarettes are killing them, but when they ask, you run to the store to buy another pack, anyway. In this way, Scott feels he has not been so much a son as an accomplice.

Every summer their father would rent a car and they'd make the seven-hour drive up to Bailey's Island, Maine, the windows closed, air-conditioning on. Scott and his brother would spend the entire ride ducked down in the backseat footwells, trying to stay under the smoke.

When Scott's dad got sick, when his liver went, he had to stop drinking, but he still smoked. Even after he was diagnosed with lung cancer he smoked. On the last day of his life, when he had to be carried to dialysis on a stretcher, when he had only eight hours to live, Joe made the orderlies stop in the parking lot so he could have a final cigarette. He was on liquid morphine at this point, a skeletal lump shivering under a blanket, but he asked them to stop, and they did, and the two orderlies stood patiently in a misty drizzle, waiting while Scott's father smoked one last cigarette. When Scott thinks about this he feels something like pride at what a tough guy his father was. This was a man who believed in controlling his own death. Fuck the doctors. Fuck the government with their ban on smoking indoors. You could have put a skull and crossbones on the front of the pack next to a picture of a withered, blackened lung and his dad still would have smoked.

And then Scott thinks, *That doesn't make him tough. That makes him weak.* He was an addict. He *needed* that cigarette. He was powerless against the yearning. Each cigarette was a mile marker on his father's scenic road to death.

Maybe that's why they decided to cremate him. Why men

in overalls took Joe's sixty-eight-year-old corpse, put it in a big cardboard wrapper, and smoked it. Because what was Joe Henry in the end but a giant cigarette?

When Scott's mother was diagnosed with emphysema, she had to quit smoking. What once she and Joe were able to achieve alone—that smoky, boozed-up hum—they now needed each other to manage. She inhaling his delicious secondhand smoke, he trying to build some kind of contact high from her dark, grapey breath. Together they made one fully dysfunctional person.

Scott finishes pouring his mother another glass of wine, then excuses himself and goes to the bathroom. Inside he checks his phone to see if Kate has somehow called and he missed it. She hasn't. He sits pants-up on the toilet and thumbs through his contact list. He has one of those PDA phones where you can take pictures of your friends and the pictures come up onscreen when they call. He goes through his directory and finds Kate's picture. Looking at it calms him. Her slim, aquiline face, the seductive crazy of her eyes.

Almost as soon as it starts, the calm recedes, replaced by panic, by the deep-marrow certainty that she was his last chance at happiness. That from here on out all he has to look forward to is rejection and loneliness, and the only woman in his life is going to be his mother. She will move down to San Francisco and they will get a place together. He can open wine bottles for her around the clock, and every morning she can needle him about when he's going to get a real job.

His fingers are itchy. He wants to push SEND, wants to dial Kate's number, but what would he say? This girl is no good. She's poison. His father is dead, for God's sake, and all she can think about is herself. She is the boxing glove he's been using to punch himself in the face. And yet the need in him is so strong, the sharp Neanderthal craving. Maybe this is his addiction, all these lunatic women. The drama they carry with them in their cute little handbags, the crazy, idealistic, romantic rush they exhale with every breath, like smoke. He imagines himself laid out on a stretcher on the last day of his life begging the orderlies for just one more promiscuous blonde.

Please, he will say. *Just one. For old times' sake.*

"Are you okay in there?" his mother asks, knocking on the door.

"Just a minute."

He stands, flushes, throws water on his face. It is seven in the evening. He has another sixty-four hours in this godforsaken place. Looking at himself in the mirror, he has no idea how he's going to make it, and yet what choice does he have? You do what has to be done.

He emerges from the bathroom running a hand through his hair.

"So I figure I'll drive over to Aunt Barbara's place tomorrow and pick up Pop's ashes," he says. His mother is back on her barstool at the kitchen island, sipping her wine. This is where she always sits, like her apartment is just one big bar where they never use the words *Last call.*

"Oh, they're already here," his mother says. "Barbara brought them over this morning."

She points to the coffee table. There, in the center, is a small pine box, about the size of an encyclopedia. Scott stares at it. For a second all the sound in the room disappears and there is only the beating of his heart, the sound of his own breathing. *How can she be so nonchalant about it?* he wonders. *To leave them sitting out like that, next to a potted plant and that crazy* Wizard of Oz *cookie jar she bought at a tag sale for eighty-nine cents.*

"They're heavier than I thought they would be," his mother says.

When she says this, Scott has this impulse to go over and pick up the box, to open the lid and look inside, but he doesn't. It feels rude somehow, disrespectful. There is no more naked a person can get, no more vulnerable than when they're dead. After they've lost the ability to protect themselves, to speak up *(hey, put me down)*. You don't want to mess with somebody's corpse, his ashes. It's bad juju. And yet he wonders what it would feel like to open the box and unzip the bag, to run his fingers through his father's ashes. Would they be smooth like sand? He's always heard a person's ashes are coarse, that there are still pieces of bone and stuff inside. He thinks of all the movies where the grieving widow opens her husband's ashes on a windy bluff and tosses them into the breeze, only to have the ash blow back in her face, get caught in her hair, inside her mouth. What would his father taste like if Scott dipped his finger into the rocky gray and touched it to his tongue? Like a cigarette, probably. Camel unfiltered.

"I was thinking Chinese for dinner," she says. "Joe can go get it."

"Roscoe," says Scott.

"What?" his mother asks.

"Nothing. Chinese is fine."

At this, Roscoe rises to his feet. He is like some strange hippie butler. He gets the menu from its spot and they look it over. Decisions are made.

"And pick me up another bottle of Merlot," his mother says.

Roscoe opens a kitchen drawer, takes out a few twenties. Scott watches him, trying to discern whether the amount he took is commensurate with the expense of the dinner, the wine.

"I'll be back," says Roscoe and leaves.

They sit there for a minute in silence, listening to the gentle applause of raindrops on the windows.

"So, how are you really?" he asks.

"I'd kill a nun for a cigarette," his mother says.

"I know, but it's not gonna happen."

His mother sips her wine. She has the beginnings of an old-lady mustache. Fifty years of cigarettes have made her face craggy, weathered.

"How's your lady person?" she wants to know. "What was her name?"

Scott goes to the cupboard and gets himself a glass, pours himself some wine. He has been resisting on principle, but if they're going to have this conversation, he needs a drink.

"Kate," he says. "She's crazy."

"You like them that way, I thought. Crazy."

"Well, yes, but this one took the prize."

He imagines the prize, like a page in the high-school year-book, a picture of Kate under the heading *Most Likely to Develop a Fear of Intimacy So Profound It Makes Her Incapable of Carrying on a Real Relationship*. He could special-order a plaque, some kind of trophy, a bronze-and-plastic statue of a woman in high heels, holding a tiny bunny over a pot of boiling water. They could hold a ceremony, an awards dinner. He pictures Kate crying onstage, trophy in hand, thanking her third-grade drama coach.

"She can't be crazier than Georgia," his mother says, "or that girl from college. What was her name, the blonde?"

"Kris."

"That girl had a screw loose. Why can't you meet a nice, normal girl?"

He considers telling her there's no such thing. *No offense, Mom, you unhinged nutjob, but I should know. At thirty-five I've dated a lot of women. It's always the same story in the end.* Scott believes but cannot prove that all women will leave you eventually.

When things get tough. When something better comes along. Look at his mother. She talked about divorcing Scott's father when it became clear his illness would be chronic, terminal.

"Are you sleeping much these days?" Scott asks her.

She shrugs. "As well as ever. I'm up and down all night."

"Anxiety?"

She shrugs.

"Do you take the pills the doctor gave you?"

She adjusts the oxygen line under her nose. Wearing it, she looks like a little girl, eyes wide under giant glasses.

"They scare me," she says.

"They're there to help you sleep."

"I know, but I'm not supposed to take them when I drink."

Then don't drink, he wants to tell her, but doesn't.

"One thing is medicine. The other thing isn't."

She makes a face.

"Don't beat up on me. It's not easy, you know. You get to go home. You have your life. I'm here in the middle of nowhere."

"I'm not beating up on you. I'm just saying. You get anxious. It makes you short of breath. The booze doesn't help. It probably makes it worse."

"I don't drink that much. Just a couple of glasses."

An hour, he wants to say, but again bites his tongue, because what's the point? She'll just play the victim, turn him into the bad guy. He's never known anyone so reluctant to help herself, someone who goes to such lengths to justify her most self-destructive choices.

"They scare me," she says, "the pills. You remember what happened last time."

He sighs. She's talking about her "suicide attempt," the time last year when she had to be placed on a respirator.

When he got the call, Scott took the red-eye to New York—

this was when his parents were still living there—and went
straight to her apartment. Inside he found the chaos the paramedics had left behind—empty syringe casings, paper bandage
wrappers, medical trash discarded in haste, the bedding thrown
to the floor, and there, on the table beside the bed, a handful
of empty pill bottles lying on their sides, white powder spilling
out, and a couple of empty glasses, red wine stains ringing the
bottom. Scott stood in her bedroom stunned by the wreckage.
Deep down he believed but could not prove that his mother
was too much of a coward to take her life. But maybe he was
wrong.

He hurried over to the nursing home and found his dad
up and dressed, sitting in his wheelchair. As always there was
that disconnect between the father he remembered—the broad,
bright-eyed bear with the hard belly—and this man—the
drawn, scowl-faced recluse whose dentures now looked too big
for his face, and whose clothes hung on him (worn brown cor-
duroys too wide in the hips and leg, faded blue oxford, loose
in the chest, covered with a stained knit cardigan [now that
he was underweight, Scott's father was always cold. He rarely
undressed, even to sleep. At the same time he was tremor-
handed and prone to spilling, and his sweaters absorbed the
brunt of every egg sandwich, every wobbly Styrofoam container of wonton soup]. He had stopped taking his socks off
a couple of years back, stopped bathing except under extreme
duress. Like an earthen cheese, Scott's father went through
phases of stinking and being unsettlingly odor free. He had developed infections on his legs and feet, wounds that wouldn't
heal. The nurses now came by once a day and berated him into
letting them clean his feet. His sneakers had Velcro fasteners,
which he left closed, slipping the shoes onto his swollen feet
with a slow grinding motion. He was stubborn. His sickness

had become another part of his life he didn't want people med-dling in. His wounds were *his* wounds. His infections were *his* infections. On top of the dirty sweater he wore a blue wool peacoat that was too heavy for him. Once he put the coat on, he was barely able to stand under its weight. His legs, after all, were splinters. Any ass he'd ever had was long gone. Muscle tone was just a dream of youth. To top off the outfit, he wore a faded wool baseball cap, swag from some corporate promo-tion a decade past, its logo promoting a company that no longer existed. The whole ensemble, taken together, had a kind of shopping-cart-lunatic circa 1999 feel to it. [For a few months the year previous, after he had refused to trim his beard, cabs had stopped picking him up, assuming he was homeless.]).

This was the sight Scott found when he showed up sleepless and jittery on that blustery winter morning, his father vibrating in his wheelchair, antsy to get to the hospital and see his wife.

"Hey, Pop," said Scott. His face was numb. His lips were chapped from the cold. He bent for a hug, feeling the unnatural protrusion of his father's shoulder blades. *Shouldn't there be meat on those? Muscle?*

"Where have you been?" his father said. "It's almost eight."

As soon as the wheelchair reached the street, Joe had a cig-arette lit, the smoke billowing back into Scott's face. Inside the ICU, they found Doris stretched out on a sloping, high-tech bed, sedated. She had a tube down her throat to help her breathe. There was a shunt in her neck, a blood pressure cuff on her right arm. At every point she was connected to a drip or monitor, like a radio with its faceplate off, wiry guts spilling out. Staring down at her, Scott didn't recognize his own mother. They had pumped her full of so much fluid that her normally thin body was now a sausage, her face a giant moon, flushed and distressed. Hooked up to so many machines, she looked terminal. The power of the image made Scott feel small, inconsequential. He was a bug on a windshield, a speck of dirt on the bottom of a shoe.

His father rolled over to the side of the bed, took his wife's hand. He stroked her skin with his thumb.

"Hi, beauty," he said. "Hi, beauty. We're here."

Scott stood at the foot of the bed watching them. They had come so far together, been through so much, and this was how it was going to end. They were being pulled apart by their own bodies. Scott pictured them lying side by side in the ICU, connected to each other by machines. Her blood would pump through his veins, his medicines cycling through her body. Their vital signs would be displayed side by side, as if finally here, at the end of the line, they could truly become one, interchangeable, symbiotic.

Scott stood silently and watched his father commune with his mother. These two men, father and son, with no religion between them, were praying the only way they knew how, with grunts and curses.

If you take this woman, this wife, this mother, there will be hell to pay. Don't think there won't. We will track you down. We will make you pay.

The doctor came in, checked her chart.

"We're not pessimistic," he said. "We think we should have her off the machine and breathing on her own in a few days, but it's going to be tough. Is she a fighter?"

Scott looked at his father. Neither really knew how to answer that. She fought, yes, but only when cornered. Out of fear, not strength.

"She'll fight," said Scott's father. He said it with absolute conviction. He had survived six years of illness. He was a soldier who had lived through a dozen blood-soaked battles. He didn't fight all this way just to have his wife sicken and die in a weekend.

A week later Doris came off the respirator and went on oxygen. Ultimately, even that was phased out, leaving her to breathe the impure air of the normal world like the rest of us. And now here she is, sitting with a glass of wine and an oxygen line, waiting for her husband's doppelgänger to get back with the Chinese food. What Scott doesn't understand is that whether or not she tried to kill herself that day in New York is irrelevant. She has, after all, been committing suicide for most of her adult life, killing herself on the layaway plan, a little bit every day.

"Those were antibiotics," he tells his mother. "This is anti-anxiety medication. It's different."

She makes a face that tells him to stop kidding himself, that says, *doctors are our enemies, not our friends.* Scott is about to respond when he hears the sound of the key in the door. Roscoe comes back. They sit around the low coffee table, eating. They use paper towels for napkins. Scott can't remember the last time he sat at an upright table with his parents and ate with real napkins. His father's ashes sit in the center of the table, next to a container of Mongolian beef. Roscoe asks Scott about his work, and Scott rolls out the best stories. He has two beers with dinner. Outside the rain stops. The streets gleam under the city lights, and for a moment as they eat, everything feels strangely normal. Once again it is Doris and Scott and Joe sitting around the dinner table, though, of course, it is a different Joe, a strange hippie Joe, but there comes a point at the apex of emotional exhaustion where just sitting quietly around a meal can feel so deeply, reassuringly human. Because even in crisis you have to eat, even in the face of sickness and death.

And so that's what they do, scoop and chew and swallow, staring down at their plates, grateful for a moment's peace.

THAT NIGHT SCOTT has a dream that his father calls. In the dream, Scott is walking along a dark, winding asphalt road. It is a hot summer day and all around him are green fields. His phone rings. He answers. On the other end of the line his father says, *I just want you to know, I'm okay.* The sun is an orange fireball overhead. The connection is bad. His father's voice clips in and out, then disappears completely. As Scott is standing there, the phone rings again. A different sound now, more insistent. Rising up from slumber, Scott realizes his cell phone really is ringing. He fumbles around for the sound, unsure of where he is. He sits up, disoriented. It takes him a long time to recognize his mother's living room. He finds his phone. There on the LCD screen is Kate's picture. He pushes SEND.

"Kate?"

"Oh, shit. Did I wake you?"

He looks at the clock.

"It's two-thirty in the morning, Kate."

"Is it? I'm so sorry. Do you want me to go?"

He rubs his face with his hand, trying to focus.

"No. Just—what's going on?"

There is a long pause on the other end of the line. He is both hyperalert and still asleep. In his addled state, Scott can make out the box with his father's ashes on the coffee table. He has been sleeping three feet away, dreaming strange, ashy dreams. Waiting for her reply, he feels like an inmate on death row, that same panicked optimism. The phone has rung. Is it a pardon from the governor or the beginning of an execution?

"I just wanted to apologize," she says.

Finally, he thinks. His heart is a redwood tree grown a hundred feet tall. Their romance is every long shot that ever paid off, every team that ever came back from certain defeat to beat the spread, every crazy dream that became a reality.

Scott catches motion out of the side of his eye, looks over. Roscoe is standing in the doorway, naked.

"I heard talking," he says.

Scott covers the mouthpiece.

"I'm on the phone," he says.

Roscoe stands there, peering into the dark.

"I thought the phone rang," he says.

"It's for me," says Scott, worried he is now forever scarred by the sight of Joe's bushy gray pubic hair and naked member. "Go back to bed."

Roscoe stands there for another moment, befuddled, then turns and goes back into the hall. Scott uncovers the phone, heart racing.

"Sorry."

"That's cool. I just wanted to say, don't give up on me. I'm stuck at this party. For work. Boring. And now I'm totally drunk, but I'm still coming over. If that's okay?"

He runs a hand through his hair. She's speaking English, but her words don't make sense. He tries to clear his head.

"You're coming here?"

Her voice drops to a seductive purr.

"I'm not wearing any panties, baby, and I'm totally wet. I

want you to tie me up like last time. I masturbated today think-ing about your big hard cock."

It begins to dawn on him—the feeling rising up his gorge like vomit—that she has not, in fact, called him, but someone else. That she has drunk misdialed.

"Kate," he says, "it's Scott."

Silence.

"Who?" she says, finally, her drunken brain trying to com-prehend this turn.

"Scott. You called me."

"Oh, shit. Scott, I'm so sorry."

"Who did you think you were calling?"

"I . . . nobody. How are you? I've been thinking about you."

And, finally, in that moment, there is clarity. The fever breaks. The shirt does not fit. It looks ridiculous.

"Kate," he says, "you are a drunken slut of biblical propor-tions. Please burn in a fiery hell of herpes and incontinence."

Then he hangs up and turns off his phone in case she calls back. The apartment is quiet again. He gets up, goes to the window. Rain is falling gently in the dark, speckling the win-dows and glazing the streetlights. Scott presses his forehead against the cool glass and closes his eyes.

Sometimes you have to save yourself from what you want. Like how fucked up is that?

WHAT DO YOU believe is true, even though you can't prove it? Christians believe in the resurrection of Jesus Christ. They believe he was the son of God and that he died for our sins. This defines the world they live in. A world where salvation is possible, redemption. If you believe that God is everywhere and in everything, then your world becomes a glowing, magical place, where the things that happen, the way people act, are infused with a deep, rich meaning. A chair is not just a chair if you believe in God. A thunderstorm is not just a product of atmospheric forces. Likewise, if you know in your heart that there is no God, then everything that happens is symbolic of life's ultimate, random meaninglessness. A car crash, a giant wave that rises and swallows an island. It's all just noise. The problem is, there are moments in life when we lose our faith. Something happens to shake our belief. Questions arise. Suddenly the world stops making sense. Imagine believing in God, and then one day, you're not so sure. You stop seeing the magic in every living thing. The world takes on a cold, bluish tint.

What do you believe? What can you prove?

Doris Henry believed in marriage. This was her filter. She saw the world through the lens of partnership. For forty years she lived according to certain rules, scientific guidelines that defined her universe. Most of them were the same as everybody else's: Water is wet, an object in motion tends to stay in motion, etc. But there were other beliefs she had that made the world hers, uniquely. Namely, that she was one of a pair, that deep down she was never really alone. Couplehood became her navigation tool, the way she judged her relationship to things, her distance. Her husband, Joe, of course, was the closest measurable point. All other points were measured in relation to him. After Joe were her children, David and Scott, then came other family, friends. Picture a grid and every person in the world occupies a place on that grid, but to reach any point you have to pass through Joe. Now you see the way her world was structured. After forty years of marriage, Doris didn't live on the same planet as the rest of us. She lived on a small moon orbiting the planet, a snug asteroid defined and inhabited by two people.

She wakes to the sound of a phone ringing, struggles up from sleep, listening attentively. After seven years of caring for her dying husband, she associates the sound of a ringing telephone with bad news. She can't count how many times a hospital has called her in the middle of the night and said her husband wouldn't make it through to morning. His death was imminent. And yet he always lived. Always. Until, of course, he didn't. Until he died. But that came later, after years of false alarms, after surgeries and strokes, after a broken hip, after three bypasses, after liver surgery and heart surgery and who knows what else. There is no lonelier feeling in life than the one that comes over you once you hang up the phone, knowing in your marrow that at this very minute your husband is in pain, terrified, dying. Knowing that any minute now he will leave you finally and irrevocably alone.

She puts on her glasses. The ringing sound has stopped. It is two-thirty in the morning. Her heart is beating fast. In the old days she would have lit a cigarette, but now that isn't an option. When she first got it, she tried to sleep with her oxygen line, but one night she almost strangled herself, so now she slips it on only after she wakes up, feeling that reassuring hush of air, pure and delicious, floating up into her nostrils, flowing down into her lungs. The room is bathed in a flickering blue light, the TV still on. *CNN Headline News* is playing, the sound low.

On TV she sees images of Mecca, pilgrims in turbans crawling on hands and knees up cobblestone streets, supplicating themselves before the majesty of Allah. *There has to be a faster way to get there*, she thinks. Bearded men circle shrines, kneel and bow in tandem. Crowds ripple, cluster. Women ululate. This is the kind of world we live in now, one where what you believe in is the most important signifier of who you are. It is time to take sides. There is no room for the dispassionate, the cautious, the reserved. Now is the age of absolute truths. We have left the age of reason behind, with its calculated scientific method. Now is the time for absolute, unyielding dedication. The world has become polarized, and there is no longer a place for rationality. Rationality, the politicians and preachers tell you, will get you killed. While you're busy weighing the options, gathering data, the enemy is sneaking across your borders, working to exterminate your way of life. Never mind that your way of life is all about weighing options, making informed decisions. Never mind that by abandoning these scientific tools you are basically winning their battle for them. That is a rational thought, and rational thoughts will get you killed.

Then again, once your husband of forty years dies, there are few rational thoughts remaining. As far as Doris Henry is concerned, Earth has suddenly showed itself to be flat. Gravity is a lie. E no longer equals MC squared. For the last three months she has suffered from a kind of existential vertigo. Her sense of balance has been disrupted. All the visible and invisible signs she used to orient herself have disappeared. Now, when she stands, she has to place a hand against the wall for balance, and no, it's not because of how much she's drinking. The drinking is irrelevant. It's beside the point. This is about angles and motion. It's about disorientation. What was once solid land is now water, air.

On TV, Arab pilgrims are replaced by images of American tourists. She sees airports crowded with disgruntled fliers, queued up in long lines, arms outstretched like Jesus, as uniformed inspectors subject them to the most humiliating and invasive searches. There is no such thing as privacy anymore. It doesn't matter who you say you are. The question is, what can you prove? *Where are they all going?* Doris wonders. *What is the point of going anywhere anymore?* And yet she herself has a trip to take, a long, winding journey to her husband's final resting place. Maine, they will dump his ashes in Maine, and from then on this will be her point of reference, the place against which all things are measured. Wherever she goes, whoever she meets, the shape the world makes will always be a triangle, with her location as Point A, the things and people with whom she's interacting as Point B, and the great, rocky beaches of Maine as Point C. And this makes her wonder, *When your husband dies are you still married?* He's dead, sure, but the idea of him remains, the memory, and deep down there is always the suspicion that any minute now he's going to walk through that door, looking healthy, rested, his arms open, a smile on his face, saying, *I'm better now, beauty. You don't have to be alone anymore.*

Believing this makes her worry she's going crazy. It's not a sane thing to wait for your dead husband to return, not a rational thought, but then again, now is not the time for rational thought. Now is the time for faith. Jesus came back, didn't he?

These days conviction is the prevailing currency. The problem
is, Doris isn't convinced. She doesn't believe in anything anymore, even herself. She has lost faith.

From the other room she hears the sound of voices. She listens, but can't make out a word. It must be Scott, she thinks.
Could he be on the phone? Who would call at this hour? Her
heart is thundering in her chest. Anxiety. It is an ugly word.
There is something about the x and the y, the way it looks, the
long i sound, nasal, whining. It is onomatopoetic. And yet the
true feeling of anxiety, the oceanic magnitude, makes the word
seem pitiful, inadequate. This panicked, galloping fear should
have an entire dictionary dedicated to it, a bible. And now, of
course, is when it's worst, at three in the morning. That's the
hour at which your brain reaches its maximum speed, ideas ric-
ocheting around, growing in volume, magnitude. And all of it
amplified by one question: *What the hell am I supposed to do now?*

Doris Henry believes but cannot prove that her life is func-
tionally over. And yet she is still alive.

If you go back far enough, you will see that she has faced
abandonment before. As a child she was dumped one day on
an aunt's doorstep. Her mother, Ruth, had met a man and
they were getting married, but there was no room in their lives
for a nearsighted five-year-old girl. Her mother's fiancé didn't
want the stigma of Ruth's earlier relationship haunting him. He
wanted to start fresh, a new wife, a new family. So Doris was
raised by her aunt, one of six kids, but never truly one of them.
Always an outsider. In high school she started telling people she
was an only child. The family would all get together at holidays, her aunt's extended family, her mother's. Doris would
sit quietly at the kiddie table next to all the wanted children,
who were giggling, unencumbered. She would sit across from
her mother's two new girls, who were fresh faced and carefree,

watch her mother cut their food, fix the bows in their hair. In this way Doris came to understand the lie of family bonds. She saw the way that families can exist in a state of denial. The way they can ignore even the biggest elephant in the room. The only ones who didn't know that Ruth was Doris's real mother were her new sisters. And about this her mother made it very clear, the secret was to be kept from them at all costs. This is another way of being unwanted. To have the very fact of your existence denied. To be negated to your face, ignored. It is a powerful fuel for a young girl's insecurity. You are nobody's child, invisible, worse than an orphan, because even as you are isolated, you are surrounded by happy families.

Doris left home as soon as she could, quit high school, took a job. She lived alone in the city for a few years, going to work on the subway, fraternizing only peripherally with the people she met—always the quiet, doe-eyed girl in the corner. And then she met Joe, and for the first time in her life she felt she was part of something. Thinking about it now, that night, the memories are too painful. She is not a glass-half-full person. She can't focus on the positive, how they had forty great years together. Her husband is dead and that makes even the brightest memory ashen and cold.

Once he got sick, once his neediness surpassed hers, once he lost the ability to shelter her, cater to her, she threatened to walk. She's not proud of it, but there you go. You would think that after being cared for for so many years she would have turned around and returned the favor, stepped up and said, *now it's my turn*, but this was not the way she was wired. This was not the dynamic they had. Their relationship had worked so well for so long because each provided the element the other needed most. In her case, it was someone to take care of her. In his case, it was someone to love, someone to watch out for. She was the key and he was the lock. And he'd ruined everything by getting sick, because the lock doesn't open the key, and the key can't protect the lock. It's just not in their nature.

This is not to say she didn't try. In the beginning, when it was just his heart and there was a chance he could make a full recovery, she did everything she could. After the triple bypass surgery he stopped eating. A minor stroke, it turned out, had disrupted the taste centers of his brain, and nothing tasted the way it should. Doris spent the next three months running all over town, trying to find him something he could stomach. She went uptown for soup, downtown for brisket. She was the crazy lady in the cab rushing a box of noodles to Mt. Sinai. She called Scott in the middle of the night that fall and asked him where she could get pot, because she'd heard that marijuana stimulated the appetite. He said, *how the hell should I know?* She sounded disappointed, hung up, and called someone else. Three days later she smuggled a tray of pot brownies into the hospital. She thought she'd found the answer, but really she'd overlooked the most obvious obstacle, which was that brownies were food and, like everything else, Joe refused to eat them.

Slowly, his appetite returned. He left the hospital, came home to the apartment. For the next year he went through phases—the salami and fried egg sandwich phase, the liverwurst on white bread phase. For six months he ate only curry, and so every night the apartment stank of Punjabi spices. They stopped sleeping in the same bed. Joe would wander the apartment all night chewing ice. The electric thunder of the refrigerator's ice-maker would jar Doris from sleep. Joe was prone to episodes of moaning and sudden, sharp shouts of pain. His feet swelled. His circulation worsened. He would fall asleep in mid-conversation. He had terrible, humiliating bouts of diarrhea. For Doris, it was too much. Two years of constant crisis. This was not what she signed on for. How do you watch the person you love devolve into a set of symptoms? She had her own health to worry about, her sanity. So the next time he went into the hospital she insisted afterward that he go to a nursing home and stay there. She justified it in her mind by telling herself that this man, this introverted, grumbling skeleton, was not her husband. He was somebody else, a stranger, and what do you owe to a stranger? He had the same memories, sure, the same voice, but illness had changed him. The blood thinners made him loopy. The drugs he took for depression made him glassy. The painkillers made him distant, stumble-tongued. He would call her every morning at six from the nursing home, every night at eleven. He would call her seven times a day. He wanted cigarettes. He needed money. Could she bring him a sandwich? When was she coming to visit? *Tomorrow*, she'd say. Always tomorrow. Sometimes she'd take a taxi up to the nursing home just to smoke a cigarette with him standing outside under the awning, surrounded by old women in wheelchairs hoping to photosynthesize the January sun.

She loved him the way you love your own body, and she hated him the same way. The way you hate your body when it fails you, when your heart slows, becomes unreliable, when your hands start to tremble and your lungs stop working the way they used to. She pushed him away, but she never left. She never abandoned him completely. On some level, this made it worse, because pushing him away made her feel guilty, and the guilt made her anxious. It kept her from sleeping. As a result, her own health started to decline. She would lie awake all night imagining the worst. She would hit the bottle earlier and earlier until there was no difference between night and day. She used to say about his illness, *only one of us is going to survive this, and I'm not sure it's going to be me*. They had been married for forty years. Their fates were tied. There was no escape for one without the other. It was a riddle without an answer, and wrestling with it year in and year out drove her insane.

After a while this craziness became just another kind of normal.

In the doorway she sees a shape moving.

"Scott?" she says.

It isn't. It's Joe/Roscoe, naked.

"Can't sleep?" he says.

She stares at him. His belly is holding on to his rib cage like a rain-soaked hillside threatening to slide down onto his thighs.

"You're naked," she says.

He scratches his back.

"Nude. I'm a nudist. I heard the TV. Do you need anything?"

"No, thank you."

He comes over, sits on the edge of the bed. His chest hair is a tuft of gray.

"Your son seems like a good guy," he says. "A little uptight."

She keeps her eyes on the television. It's been forty years since she saw a man naked who wasn't her husband.

"I'd really feel more comfortable," she says, "if you put some clothes on, a robe."

He nods.

"My wife left me when Cindy was eleven. She ran off with this dry cleaner who had a rock band. It was tough, but we got by."

Doris picks up her wineglass, empty. She wonders if these are the kinds of things that are going to start happening to her now that she's a widow, strange naked men sitting on her bed in the middle of the night, confessing.

"Cindy's a champ," she says.

Joe/Roscoe nods.

"Your husband was a good man, it sounds like."

"Yes."

"The world is so sad sometimes, you know," he tells her. "But what always gets me through is my friend."

"Friends are good to have," she says, wondering if she should wake Scott up, raise her voice, cry for help. She doesn't know how these things work. Do people really rape sixty-three-year-old women? Is Roscoe dangerous or just lonely?

"My friend Jesus Christ," Roscoe says.

"Oh," she says, "him."

"Do you know Jesus?"

"No," she says. "I mean, not personally."

Roscoe runs a hand over his bald dome. The skin under his arm hangs like a chicken wing.

"I just think—you must be feeling very lost right now," he tells her. "When my wife left I ate nothing but donuts for two weeks. Cindy and me. We just ate donuts. And then Jesus came into my life. It was a Thursday morning. I hadn't left the house for ten days. I saw his face on a donut."

"Jelly or cream filled?" Doris wants to know.

If Roscoe hears the question he doesn't give any indication.

"He told me not to be so sad. My life wasn't over. It had only just begun. The world was a beautiful place and it needed me. I had a purpose, a function."

"You were young," she tells him. "I'm too old to start again."

"No. That's not true. We all have something to give. All of us. I know you're tired. I know nothing makes sense anymore, but I'm here to tell you that if you believe, if you give yourself to him, you will be reborn. Your life will be rich and meaningful."

"That sounds great," she says. "Is there, do you have a pamphlet or something?"

"Mom?"

She turns to look. Scott is standing in the doorway. From his expressions she can tell he has no idea what to make of this scene: Roscoe sitting naked on the edge of her bed. She can read the horror on his face.

"Sorry," he says. "I heard voices."

"Thank God," she says. "I mean, come in. Roscoe was just telling me about his friend Jesus."

Scott steps into the room, takes Roscoe's arm.

"Okay, chief. Time for bed."

Roscoe rises reluctantly.

"I just wanted to offer your mother some consolation," he says. "You too. I know how hard it can be to lose someone you love."

"Offer it walking," says Scott, applying force. He has never touched a naked man before. Roscoe's body is slack. His nakedness makes him feel closer, like at any minute parts of him could touch parts of Scott.

"Jesus understands our sins and forgives them," says Roscoe. "He feels our pain, because his pain was so much greater. He died so that we might live. All he asks is that we believe."

"What I believe?" says Scott, steering Roscoe toward the door. "You should put some pants on when you talk to people."

After they're gone, Doris lies in bed staring at the ceiling. She can feel the flow of oxygen on her face like a lover's breath. She thinks about crying, but she's never been much of a crier. The guilt is overwhelming sometimes, all those moments when she wished he would just die already. And then he did.

Last year, when she was on a respirator, she had the strangest dreams. She was on a hospital ship, cruising the Atlantic. It was a cruise ship filled with sinister Arab men. They were plotting some kind of attack, eyeing her warily. This is what sickness felt

like to her, a journey, a paranoid delusion. While her son and
husband sat by her bed, she was off in another world, floating,
at sea. How strangely the mind works. All these delusions and
metaphors.

Scott comes back, his hair askew.

"Cindy's dad, huh?" he says.

"I don't want to hear it."

He goes over to the window. She watches him, her thirty-
five-year-old son. Who ever thought she would be so old as to
have such a thing. A grown man for a son.

"Did somebody call before?" she says.

"It was nothing."

"Was it that girl?"

He shrugs.

"I hope you told her that reasonable people don't do things
like that, call people at two in the morning."

He sighs. *Manners are the least of her problems.* Looking at him
there, standing in the blue light of the television, Doris believes
Scott could be her husband, if she squinted. If she caught him
out of the corner of her eye. Joe as she'd first met him, before
the beard, back when you could still see his dimpled chin. It is
a prehistoric memory, excavated from the strata. But then this
is what sons do. They replace their fathers.

"I'm going to bed," he tells her. "I put a chair in front of
Roscoe's door so he can't get out."

"Isn't this fun?" Doris says. "Aren't we having a good time?"

He kisses her on the forehead and goes back to the sofa.

She lies there for a long time, watching the headlines cycle
on TV. The sky starts to lighten outside. She wonders if she will
ever feel anything like joy again.

WHEN DAVID HENRY hears stories of people whose faith drives them to do impossible things, he feels himself welling up with something like pride. Holy men who cross hot coals without getting burned. Sick people healed by prayer. Scientists refer to it as *mind over matter.* You've heard the stories. Ninety-eight-pound mothers lifting cars to rescue their trapped children. They tell them on TV, all the late-night real-estate hucksters urging viewers to visualize success in order to achieve it. They call it the *power of positive thinking.* David Henry watches the infomercials and docudramas in the dead of night when the rest of his family is asleep. He wants to believe that the human animal is capable of greatness, but deep down he is not so sure.

David's son Christopher is studying karate. On Tuesday afternoon David sits on a metal folding chair inside Chris's karate school, his *dojo* as Chris calls it, and watches his ten-year-old son prepare to break a wooden board with his fist. He is nervous. All the other kids in the group are so much bigger than Chris—though, of course, this is why they put Chris in the dojo in the first place, because he is small for his age, and the subject of bullying by bigger kids. David has taken the afternoon off work to watch. His brother and mother are arriving in a few hours and he won't be back to the office for ten days, though he will be reachable by phone and e-mail. He can still be paged, text-messaged, and IM'd. As always, work is his crutch, his escape. Sitting there, he is already inventing reasons to excuse himself from uncomfortable family moments, citing this or that sales memo that has to be revised, this or that crisis that must be addressed.

He sits in the second row with his eight-year-old daughter, Chloe. She has a single pigtail sticking out from the left side of her head, a sign that Tracey got distracted, probably by a phone call, while dressing her. *She's adorable*, David thinks, *and not just because she's my daughter.* Chloe has a way of talking that makes you think she's an absentminded professor trapped in the body of a little girl. There is a similar sensibility and style—that infuriatingly endearing mixture of arcane scientific knowledge and an inability to tie your shoes.

"Did you know a great-white shark bite is equal to twenty-five thousand pounds of pressure?" she says, kicking her little feet.

David loosens his tie. The class is going through its warm-up exercises, dozens of little fists punching the air, dozens of little mouths yelling, *Hai!*

"Yes," he says, even though he didn't. David doesn't like to be outsmarted, certainly not by an eight-year-old. "Did you know that most fruit flies live for only twenty-four hours?" he says.

"Duh."

He reaches out and rests his hand on the warm little crown of her head. The alarming thing about Chloe, the thing he hasn't come to terms with yet, is that she is already growing breasts. Eight years old, and her skinny little chest is already starting to sprout. *Is it a sign of the apocalypse*, he wonders, *that children are maturing so young? She's eight for Christ's sake.* Tracey blames the milk they drink, all the growth hormones. If only they'd bought organic, she says, her little girl would still have four more carefree years before facing the stares and taunts of other children, before anything like a sexual thought should have to come into her head.

"At least she hasn't gotten her period yet," David tells her.

"Yet," stresses Tracey, who hunts for red every time she washes her daughter's underwear. *This is the kind of world we live in*, thinks David, *where everything happens faster than it used to, where nothing follows a predictable course.*

Inside the dojo, Christopher sees his family and waves. Chloe waves back, using her whole arm. She loves her older brother the way some people worship gods. Seeing his son in his white karate uniform, David feels that irrational swell of love. That exuberant terror that comes from loving someone so completely and unconditionally you're certain they will be killed. It is a baseless fear of losing everything, and no less powerful for its ridiculousness. *What would I do?* David wonders. *How would I survive?* At the same time, the boy is such a pain in the ass that sometimes David thinks his head will explode. Unlike his sister, Chris is no brainiac. He's more physical, turning everything into a weapon or a game. The kind of kid who stays up past his bedtime playing hoops in his room with a trash can and a pair of rolled-up socks. He doesn't like math or science, isn't an eager reader. He likes to go out and get dirty, a quality David wishes he could appreciate more. Which is not to say David's not athletic himself. He loves a good game of catch, a long run, but you need to balance the physical with the mental, he thinks. That's how you get ahead in this world.

Right before the show starts, Tracey shows up with Sam, edges her way through the crowd of housewives to the seat David has saved for her. The baby is bundled up in her arms, as if for winter.

"Jesus, Trace," he says, pulling off the baby's hat, "it's eighty degrees out. This is L.A., not Anchorage."

Tracey collapses into the seat next to him, drops her over-sized shoulder bag on the floor. She loves being a mother, but after ten years gives the impression that she still hasn't quite gotten the hang of it.

"It was cloudy when we left," she says, shrugging out of her sweater. She is a gorgeous woman still, at thirty-seven, though there are dark sweat stains under the arms of her T-shirt. This is something David has always liked about her. She is a sweater, visceral, animal. Her breasts are big and have yet to drop fully, even after three kids. She rarely wears makeup and when she does it is artfully applied, as if by a freshman to a plastic head at some suburban beauty school. In bed she still bites him hard enough to draw blood.

"Did I miss anything?" she asks.

"No. They're just warming up."

The children jump around on mats in the center of the room. Their instructor, a pony-tailed stunt-man wannabe with a Steven Seagal voice, shouts encouragement. The whole thing has that imprecise amateur flavor of all family activities. As a parent you get used to sitting through bad theater, bad music, bad sports. You come to expect a certain level of chaos and inaccuracy. It is endearing to no one else. On the floor, Christopher sees his mother. He grabs the shirtfront of the girl in front of him, steps forward, and throws her over his hip. *Hai!*

Look what a big boy I am, he is saying.

"Hey!" shouts the woman to their immediate left. She comes half out of her seat, like she's about to sue someone, but when her daughter jumps up laughing, she is forced to settle back and wait for the next offense.

"They're just playing," David reassures her. The woman has her BlackBerry out and is checking her e-mail.

"Not so rough," she says absently. "I told them. My Sally has delicate skin."

Tracey leans over.

"Maybe this was a mistake," she says quietly to David, referring to the whole karate experience. She has never liked the idea of violence, and ever since he started taking karate, Christopher has been wandering the house punching things. They have dents in their Sheetrock and fist-shaped smudges on all the appliances. Tracey has, on several occasions, had to stop her son from demonstrating throw holds on his sister.

"It's for defending yourself only," she told him. "That was the point. Not to turn your body into a weapon."

Christopher liked this, the idea of his body as a lethal force. When his father came home that night, Chris jumped out from behind the coat rack, adopting one of his lethal karate stances.

"Ha!" he yelled.

"Ha, yourself," David said, throwing his jacket over the boy's head.

The instructor lines the kids up. He bows to them and they respond, their little heads almost touching the floor. They look like hand puppets next to the big man. He turns to the audience.

"Ladies and gentlemen, welcome. For the next half hour you will see a different side of your children. Discipline and honor, these are the facets we focus on here. We try to instill a sense of mindfulness and fair play. These are lessons I had to learn the hard way after many years of drinking and petty crime. But then, thanks to my sensei, I cleaned my act up, and now I do fight choreography for several fabulous Hollywood films."

Listening to him, David thinks they should have done more

research before enrolling Chris in this particular dojo. The younger kids, six, seven, eight, pair off and start sparring. They jump around on little legs, throwing their limbs about in exaggerated movements. It looks a lot like play-fighting, like the regular household spit-punching that goes on every day. *We're paying fifty bucks a week for this?* thinks David. But then the little kids sit down and it's time for the older ones to show their stuff. Chris walks out to the center of the floor. He turns and bows to his opponent, a hulking ten-year-old boy who looks like he was recruited from the Russian preteen weight-lifting team. David feels that familiar worry settle into his stomach. He wants to run out onto the mat and punch the kid in the face, protect his son at all costs.

Chris adopts a stance, elbows bent, knees. David can see the concentration on his face. He wishes he could lock his son up in the basement, keep him from harm for the rest of his life. Instead he is about to witness a juvenile reenactment of a Mike Tyson blowout. His hands are fists, the nails digging into the palms of his hands. He is a man who has taken out over two million dollars in combined insurance policies. The big kid lunges forward, and David rises involuntarily out of his seat, but just as the kid's arm thrusts forward, Chris steps aside and chops the bigger kid across the back.

"Point," yells the instructor, and David feels that bottom-of-the-ninth-inning thrill. What a warrior his son is, and by association, what a warrior his father must be. He looks over at Tracey, grinning, but she doesn't share his zeal. Her face is still tight with worry. He smiles at her to let her know everything is okay, puts his hand on her leg.

"There's almost no gravity on the moon," says Chloe. "If they were fighting on the moon, one of them could just fly right off."

David musses her hair. In two hours his mother and brother will descend on his house, bringing with them all kinds of emotional chaos, like a visit from the loony bin. But right now the five of them are a family, coherent, intact. Right now they are insulated, self-sustaining, robust. This will change the minute his mother arrives, dropping her casual cruelties, sitting with her liquor, watching the children play with pained skepticism on her face. *Don't they have anything interesting to say?* she will ask. *Which one is Sam?* David has made sure there is plenty of wine in the house. The kids have cleaned their rooms. They have prepared as if for a natural disaster, laying in water and batteries. The cars have plenty of gas, and for some reason, Tracey bought six cans of mixed nuts. David's cell phone vibrates in his pocket. He takes it out. The caller ID says J (for Joy). He slips his phone back into his pocket.

"Who was that?" his wife wants to know.

"Just checking the time," he tells her.

The match ends with Christopher easily besting the bigger, slower kid. His usual plodding deliberateness has been replaced by concise grace. He steps and turns, throwing crisp kicks and chops. No energy is wasted. David feels hustled, as if his son has been setting him up all this time, playing a role, the flat-footed, monosyllabic shlub. The other kids take their turn dancing around on the gray mats, boys and girls. Then the instructor herds his students into a circle. He pulls out a stack of wooden boards. As one, the parents lean forward in their seats. The boards look substantial, impervious, and the children's hands are so small, so fragile. Some mothers glance out through the plate-glass window to see if an ambulance is standing by. One isn't.

"Can I ask Christopher Henry to come up?" says the instructor. Chris jumps to his feet. Tracey reaches over and grabs David's hand.

"How can this work?" she says. "He's ten years old. He's basically punching a tree."

David doesn't respond. He watches his son step up to the instructor. Two big kids are holding the board between them.

"Okay, Chris," says the instructor. "Remember what we practiced. Close your eyes. See the board break."

Chris steps up to the board. He does a few choreographed arm maneuvers, then reaches out and touches the board with his outstretched fingers, his palm flat, thumb tight against his index finger knuckle.

Watching him, David thinks of his son praying, down on his knees every night before bed, hands clasped together before his face. David remembers the first time he saw Chris do it. He was stunned. Where had his son gotten it from? They weren't religious in his house. Nobody ever said grace. They said *bless you* if you sneezed, but they didn't mean it. And yet here was their son, down on his knees, praying. For what? To whom? David assumed it was the Christian God, but it could just as easily have been Allah, Vishnu, L. Ron Hubbard. What do you do in that situation? Had they taught him prayer in school? Taught him to believe in Jesus, to ask God for forgiveness, love? David and Tracey stood in the doorway looking at each other, their mouths agape. It was cute and disturbing at the same time. This was one of those moments when you wish your kids came with a manual. How do you question a ten-year-old's faith? When your kids believe in God and you don't, it makes you strangers. But then faith is the issue here, isn't it? A ten-year-old boy staring down a solid piece of wood. *The whole key*, David thinks as he watches his son prepare to do battle, *is believing you can do it*. He himself is not a man of significant faith, even in other people. He is always sort of surprised when things work out, when he closes a deal or the kids get good grades. To him, the world is a place of unanswered prayers and dumb luck. And yet there are heroes in the world, men who believe, who triumph over inestimable odds time and time again. There are soldiers who rely on their training to save them, snake handlers who've never been bitten. For these people failure is not an option. It doesn't even enter their minds. David wonders what it would be like to be so confident. He is a man with two wives, and yet he still can't believe he got one woman to marry him, can't believe he has produced four amazing children, despite the inarguable proof.

And then there is his mother, who doesn't even believe enough to do ordinary things: leave the house, stop drinking. She is the opposite of an achiever. She can't even work up the strength for failure.

Chris takes a step back, bows. The board hovers there in front of him. Tracey squeezes David's hand harder. David pictures himself carrying his son to the car, rushing him to the emergency room. He pictures the mangled fingers, the broken bones, then he puts these thoughts out of his mind. In that moment he is convinced that not only must Chris believe for this to work, for the board to break, but his father must believe as well. David believes that it is essential *he* see the board breaking in his mind, or else it won't. His son pulls back his arm, takes a deep breath. In the gallery everyone holds their breath. David visualizes his son punching, the board breaking. He wills it to happen. Then, in one sharp motion, Chris shoots his hand forward, shouting *Hai!*, and snaps the board in two. It breaks with a great, wooden crack. In the gallery everyone applauds. No one can believe it. David feels his heart surge and threaten to explode. Chris runs around the mat, a huge grin on his face. And then Chloe is off her chair and running over to her big brother. She throws her arms around him, and they jump up and down together, lost in filial bliss. And watching them, David finally understands the meaning of *family*. It comes to him like a great stone tablet handed down from above. Family is everyone you can't live without.

DAVID CALLS JOY from his car on the way home. He is alone. Chris wanted to ride with his dad in the Mercedes, but David said he had business calls to make, and so the three kids piled into the Land Rover with Tracey.

"Hey," he says. "It's me."

"Me who?" says Joy, though she knows exactly who he is.

"Me the Jolly Green Giant."

"Oh, that me."

Her voice is warm and thrilling. The sound of bacon frying in a pan. The sound of porn on TV.

"Sorry I missed your call," he says. "I was in a meeting."

"You missed one hell of an orgasm," she says. "I could have used your help."

David spends three days a week in New York, usually Thursday, Friday, and Saturday. Tracey thinks it's for business. That he is filling in as a New York sales rep until the company hires a replacement. Joy thinks he's in L.A. four days a week for the same reason. It is simpler, he has found, if all your lies match up. If they correspond. As a result he spends a lot of time on the phone managing relationships. With Tracey it is more about logistics, helping her figure out schedules and traffic routes: how to get the kids to the doctor and still get home in time for dinner. With

Joy, who is twenty-eight, there are other, more sensual duties required. They have been married almost a year now, have known each other only sixteen months. It is still the honeymoon phase, unlike with Tracey, whom he has known since 1991.

"Well," he says, "now I'm definitely sorry I missed your call."

"Sam wants to say hi," she says. "Say hi to Daddy, Sam."

She holds the phone to his son's ear and David can hear gentle babbling over the line. He has a hard time distinguishing the two babies in his mind, Sam from Sam. Both were born last summer. Both have brown hair and beaming brown eyes. Listening to his son Sam2 giggle, he feels like a criminal. *Am I crazy? How long can I really get away with this?*

"A-boo-boo-boo," he says into the phone. "A-da-da-da."

"Sexy," says Joy. "I like it when you baby-talk."

David believes but cannot prove that any minute now his life is going to fall apart. That everyone he loves will leave him. The feeling makes him desperate. It makes him miss people, even when they're in the same room with him.

He met Joy in October. He was on a business trip to New York and a client wanted to go clubbing, so David's New York associate hired one of those party services (a thing David had never heard of), where, for a fee, a few drab businessmen can be escorted to the hippest clubs by a beautiful woman, floating past the velvet rope like celebrities. All the arrangements are made in advance. Inside, they are taken to the best tables, where they order the most expensive drinks. In this way, money can make anyone feel like a star.

"An escort," his associate said.

"Like a hooker?" David wanted to know.

But she wasn't a hooker. She was a sweet, slightly off-kilter blonde from the Midwest. They met in Tribeca. Having grown up in New York, the city always had two identities to David.

There were the neighborhoods he frequented as a kid, and the places he knew only as an adult. Tribeca was one of the latter, a foreign grid of late-blooming hipness. He always felt out of place below Canal Street. He preferred the multi-angle spread of the West Village, the glaring confusion of Midtown.

There were three of them at the bar, David, his associate Monty, and the client, a mid-level purchasing executive at a large Midwestern hospital chain. Monty was a slightly cross-eyed but otherwise extremely handsome sales rep from Vermont. He had a fiancée who taught nursery school and could, apparently, "suck the change out of a parking meter," a skill David suggested could come in handy if they ever found themselves broke and living in her car. The client, Douglas, was a little man with a big belly and a penchant for brown. The three sat drinking rye shots and beer and talking sports, the international language of business. The client showed them pictures of his kids, three fat babies, their hair plastered down. They lived in a suburb in Oklahoma. He said he was excited to see New York, the nightlife.

"It's funny," he said. "You spend nine months trying to get out of a pussy, and the rest of your life trying to get back in."

David chuckled along with Monty. He had never been comfortable with this variation of business talk, the way men invariably spiraled down into conversations about tits and ass.

"David here has a great wife and two kids," Monty said.

"Fucking terrific," said the client. "But tonight we're all single. Am I right, or am I right?"

David started to say something, but Monty threw him a look, meaning, *This is an important sale for us. Don't fuck it up.* So David nodded and threw back his rye.

"Single as they come," he said.

"Which means," said the client, "the wedding rings come off."

He lifted his chubby left hand and tugged at the thin gold band until it yielded, slipping it onto his keychain and putting it in his pocket.

"Now you," he said.

David nodded. He thought about something his wife once said: *There is nothing more pathetic than a married man hitting on chicks.* And yet the cold, hard reality was that he was in the running for a major promotion at work, head of West Coast sales, and he needed this sale to firm up his chances. He hadn't taken off his ring since the day he got married. It had itched him for weeks after he first put it on, his finger feeling swollen, sweaty, but he had doggedly resisted the urge to pull it off, and then, over time, he had gotten used to it, stopped noticing it, even as he played with it absently, turning it on his finger whenever he talked. What would it feel like to be without it, to be naked again?

The client watched him expectantly.

"No attachments," said David, and slipped his ring off. He took out his wallet, slipped his ring inside. This was the moment Joy walked in, twenty-six and gorgeous. Every head in the place turned, men and women. She had that kind of energy, those kinds of pheromones, like phosphorescent lichen lighting up an undersea cave.

"Gentlemen," she said. "I believe I'm your date for the night. I hope you had plenty of caffeine this afternoon. We've got a lot of ground to cover."

It was pathetic really, the way they fell all over themselves to get her a stool, to tell her their names and ask where she was from. They were three men, the youngest in his mid-thirties, and she was the promise of a new beginning. A woman who still remembered what it was like to be a girl, to be the lustful center of a high-school boy's infatuation. She greeted them each with a warm smile and a kiss on the cheek, and the smell of her, her intoxicating nearness, made them giddy.

"I'm Joy," she said, and if ever there had been a more perfect name, David had never heard it. "And before we start I just want to make one thing clear. There is no way that I am going home with any of you tonight. I am here to make sure you have a fabulous time, that you get into the most exclusive clubs. I will even help you meet the girl of your dreams, but I will not *be* the girl of your dreams. Are we clear?"

They nodded. The bartender came over and she ordered a club soda, pulled out her itinerary.

"Okay. It's seven o'clock. We'll hit Feral first, get a drink. It's an after-work spot in SoHo, very hip, then we'll head down to Rivington and hit a couple of speakeasies. After that it's time to get serious. I hope you boys brought your dancing shoes."

David sipped his beer. The whole thing felt ridiculous. In his mind, you either were hip or you weren't, and no amount of money—especially if the whole hedonistic adventure was being billed as a business expense—was going to change that. For a moment he wished he were at home, curled up on the sofa while Tracey put the kids to bed. He missed the sound of their little voices, the smell of dinner in the air, that late-night calm after the little ones were asleep, after Tracey was in bed, when the house was dormant, like a deep breath before a sigh. He missed the comfort, the security. He didn't like being on his own, the threat of all that empty time.

"Before we go," he said, "I just need to make a phone call."

He left them at the bar and went outside to call Tracey. It was almost Halloween, and this year she had decided she was going to make costumes for the kids.

"How's it going?" he asked.

"I'm up to my ears in felt," she said.

"It's not too late to buy," he said. "I can pick up a Spider-Man costume on the way home tomorrow."

"No," she said. "I started this. I'm going to finish it. What are you up to?"

"Drinks with the client," he told her. "I promised him a fun night in New York."

"Well, don't have too much fun. Not without me."

"Don't worry," he said. "I'm sure I'll hate every minute of it."

As he said this, Joy came out of the bar and took a pack of cigarettes from her purse.

"I gotta go," he told his wife. "I'll call you tomorrow."

He hung up. Joy lit her cigarette.

"Girlfriend?" she said.

"My brother," he told her, lying without thinking. "Another broken heart. I swear, he's got the worst taste in women."

She inhaled, chewed off some of her lipstick, then blew smoke from her nose.

"Taste," she says, "is in the eye of the beholder."

Monty and the client came out of the bar, arm in arm. They were laughing about something. Joy dropped her cigarette, ground it out with her heel.

"Okay," she said. "Ready for round one?"

A town car was waiting at the curb. They climbed inside and set out for the first hot spot. Everywhere they went, David was amazed at the way they just slipped right in, past doormen and security, the velvet rope coming up the minute they arrived. It turned out everybody knew Joy, all the bouncers from the outer boroughs, all the party planners with the tight blond ponytails and baseball caps. She carried with her an expanding bubble of coolness. It was a holographic projection. If you were with her, no matter how poorly dressed you were, how hang-dog your face, you were *somebody*. Of course, David realized there was money involved. That it wasn't just her atmosphere that got them in, but by nine o'clock he was convinced that she could have whisked him into a presidential inaugural after-party with nothing but a smile. Two hours later they were in a retro basement disco in Queens. Monty and the client were on the dance floor, ties off, shirts unbuttoned, getting down with two thick-hipped women of questionable beauty who worked in advertising. David sat in a corner booth, sipping a vodka cranberry and checking his watch. He felt like a sponge, a cloud, an alien sent down from another planet to research the strange mating rituals of humans. But then he had always been detached; of a thing, but also somehow outside it. Even at his most Zen, his most immersed, there was some part of his brain that remained absent, disengaged. Joy came off the dance floor and sat down next to him.

"Not much of a dancer, are you?" she said.

"I prefer traditional folk dances," he told her. "The polka, the tarantella, and that Russian thing where you squat and kick your legs out."

She ordered a drink from the waitress. He watched her. She seemed so cool and self-assured, and yet just under the surface he could see the part of her that still couldn't believe she was a grown-up, that she could stay out as late as she wanted. Right there behind her glowing, perfect skin was that awkward adolescent whose body had grown up overnight and suddenly seemed foreign, clumsy. The lanky kid with braces who suddenly realizes she's got breasts.

"So how does a person get into this line of work?" he said. "What do you do?"

She brushed the hair from her face. To be heard she had to put her face near his and yell. He could smell her perfume, her sweat.

"I like to go out," she said, "have fun. I never thought it was something I could make money doing, but then my friend saw this ad in the *Voice.*"

Her drink arrived. She raised her glass.

"To the tarantella," she said and smiled, and in that moment he knew he would do whatever it took to make this woman love him.

They talked for an hour, sharing stories, background information. David told her about being a sales rep for a major pharmaceutical company, the bottomless expense accounts and private skyboxes at sports arenas.

"I could go to Saks right now," he said, "and buy you a mink coat, tell my boss you were a senator's daughter, and no one would question it."

"I need a new stereo," she told him.

"Give me your address," he said. "I'll have one shipped."

She took a cocktail napkin, wrote down an address in Brooklyn. Watching her, he felt a thrill he had forgotten existed. To meet someone new, make a connection, to have her write in her own hand an address or phone number, penning the digits in the personal, cursive scrawl she has practiced since childhood, with its sloppy *B*'s and heart-shaped *O*'s. It seemed, at that moment, like the most tremendous intimacy. The address, the street name, all embodied an actual place, an apartment with a doorbell, a bathroom—sink covered with makeup kits and moisturizers, shower with loofah sponge hanging, curtain still beaded with the dew of this morning's shower. The address was a place and the place had a bed and the act of writing it down was an invitation. It was a promise: *You will come over. We will drink wine from water glasses and undress to music. You will see the dresser I keep my underwear in, will piss in my toilet and brush your teeth using my paste and your finger. You will taste my darkest places on the base of your tongue.* The address might as well have been written on a condom wrapper. Phone numbers were suggestive, certainly, but not definite. A phone number could be fudged, the promise of sex undelivered. Six digits instead of seven, messages left but unreturned. An address was the greatest intimacy. It was a flash of nipple, a tongue in your ear. David felt himself harden as Joy wrote the address down and handed the napkin over.

"I have a lot of books," she said. "So maybe bookshelf speakers."

"I'll make a note of it," he said, and slipped the napkin into his jacket pocket. Yes, he'd had a few drinks, but he felt clear. He felt that crisp, winter clarity—the focus of a crystalline day after it's snowed, where the sky is so blue and your breath forms clouds in front of you. A hunter's clarity, crouched in a forest, bowstring pulled taut, your prey grazing innocently on a patch of grass that juts up from the frozen earth. These are the moments in life when you realize that everything happens for a reason. Moments of prognostication, when you can feel the thing happening before it does. Looking at Joy, seeing the slight flush in her cheeks, the arch of her eyebrows, the telltale signs of her interest, he could see before it happened the first touch—hands across a restaurant table—could picture the first kiss, a stolen hit-and-run in the back of a taxicab, before she leapt out and ran off into the night, a kiss he would feel rather than taste, a heady collision that would leave him tracing his lips with his fingertip as the cab rocketed uptown. He could already hear her voice on the phone, could half remember her murmured endearments as if she had already spoken them. Seeing her turn her head to the dance floor, the impossible grace of her long neck, the thrilling foreignness of her thick blonde hair, he knew before he knew it that this woman would be his.

DORIS AND SCOTT show up at five, descending from the main airport concourse to the baggage-claim area in an elevator. Scott is pushing a wheelchair, Doris seated before him in a black turtleneck, her clunky red purse clutched firmly to her lap. David watches them emerge from the elevator, and is seized by a sudden panic. They haven't seen him yet, and for a moment he has the urge to hide, to duck down behind a stack of oversized bags and let them wander past. But he doesn't, because he's a grown-up. Hiding is something Scott would do. It is the act of a single man, a man with no responsibilities other than to himself. David is a father, and thus reliable, steady. A man who *does the right thing.* And besides, Christopher is next to him, holding his hand, and how would it look to his son if David bolted from his own family, took off in a desperate crouch, weaving serpentine, racing for the parking lot? He looks down, sees his son still flushed from his victory at the dojo, lost in some private daydream. If he were being honest, David would admit that he brought the boy as a kind of human shield, a conversation piece that will keep the focus of this family reunion off the box of ashes that Scott and Doris are hauling around in their carry-on, ashes that have now crossed state lines, ashes that represent the final remains of his recently deceased father. Having Christopher here will keep things light, he hopes. In this way, the boy is an offering, a sacrifice.

He steps forward, waving.

"Well, well," he says. "How was the flight?"

He leans down and kisses his mother on one fuzzy cheek. He and Scott eye each other for a moment before hugging. There is still, in those initial moments, the memory of childhood, a memory that makes the hug feel artificial, the way you feel when you're a kid and a grown-up offers to shake your hand. Children hit the people they love. They hold hands. They don't shake them. He feels Scott's body against his, at once familiar and foreign.

"Have you been working out?" he asks when they separate.

"I started running," Scott tells him, and the phrase itself is symbolic on so many levels.

"Christopher," says David, "say hi to your grandmother."

Christopher steps forward awkwardly. He has seen Doris only a few times in his life. She pats him on the head.

"Nice to see you, ma'am," he says. *Ma'am?* thinks David. *Where did he get "ma'am"?* First the praying, now the down-home politeness. Christopher might as well be a preacher's son, for all the recognition David feels in these moments.

Scott scoops the boy up, hugs him like a life preserver.

"I broke a board," Christopher tells him excitedly. "I broke it with my fist."

"Wow," says Scott, "really?"

Christopher squirms and struggles, dropping to the ground. He reenacts the pivotal moment.

"*Hai,*" he yells, thrusting his arm forward. David can see the confusion on his mother's face. She is not comfortable around children. They are too reckless, too loud. There is always the danger that they will break you somehow, with their rough-housing and crazy, pell-mell running.

"He's so big," she says.

David nods, though to him his son is tiny, a runt. They have talked about steroids, he and Tracey, about growth hormones, but she says *have faith. He'll grow.* They head over to the conveyor and stand waiting for their luggage. The Land Rover is parked in short-term parking. Tracey, Chloe, and Sam are at home making last-minute preparations, Doris-proofing the house.

"Did you bring the..." he asks Scott in a quiet voice. *Ashes,* he means *ashes.*

"They're in your mother's suitcase," Scott says.

"You checked them? Dad's ashes?"

"Apparently you have to," says Scott. "They don't want them in the passenger compartment, like maybe you would use them as a weapon or something. It's beyond me, but you can't argue with these people—airport security—they'll just take you to some fluorescent room and stick their hand up your ass."

"How was the flight, Mom?" David asks. His son is fascinated by Doris's wheelchair. He's hanging off it, his butt inches above the floor, kicking his legs.

"I had to use the oxygen," she says, the chair jerking from Christopher's weight. "Does he have to do that?"

"Chris," says David, "can you go look for Grandma's luggage?"

"Black," she says, "with a red scarf around the handle."

Chris runs to the mouth of the conveyor, watches as the bags are disgorged.

"I got you a room at the Bel-Air," David tells her. "They have beautiful grounds."

"As long as there's someone there who can bring me a bottle of wine," she says. "I need a drink."

David and Scott exchange a look. The look embodies in seconds the following conversation:

David: She looks terrible. Has she been like this the
whole time?

Scott: You have no idea.

David: Should we say something? The last thing I want is
to confront her. It's easier to just let it go, muscle
through the next week. I mean, it's not like she's going
to change.

Scott: So, what? We just continue to look the other way,
continue to open the bottles, to flush the cigarette butts,
and say nothing, do nothing?

David: I'll say something if you do. If you go first.

Scott: It's exhausting. The whole thing. I'm exhausted.

David: We're in this together now, though, right? You're
not going to ditch me.

Scott: You mean the way you ditched me years ago to
deal with them all by myself, to fly around the country,
to spend nights in the emergency room, to help him off
the toilet, help him wipe his ass?

David: Don't lecture me about emergency rooms. I've
been just as involved as you. Maybe not recently, but I
have a family, responsibilities.

Scott: If you say that word again I'm going to punch you.
I have responsibilities, too. I wish we could just go back
to being kids. I wish we could have our parents back. I
wish, I wish, I wish.

David: Don't get emotional. I hate when you get emotional.

Scott: God forbid you should be uncomfortable or emotional after your dad died. God forbid you should fall

apart a little. Show some kind of grief. Lose control. For
fuck sake, go to pieces.

David: Do you really want to do this now? Here? Because
if we're judging, I've got some things I could say about
how you live your life.

Scott: (staring, reconsidering)—

David: (staring, backing down)—

"That one's mine," says Doris, pointing. Christopher grabs the
suitcase, tries to muscle it from the conveyor, but it's too heavy.
David goes over to help him.

They ride home from the Burbank airport in the silver Land
Rover, climbing Coldwater Canyon, turning onto Mulholland
Drive. It is a low-smog day and from the hills they can see
the swimming pools of the valley stretching out below them.
There is a box in Doris's luggage filled with ashes. It is traveling at thirty-one miles per hour, just like the car. It remains
at a resting temperature of seventy-two degrees, having been
super-cooled earlier by the luggage compartment of the 737.
How strange it is to imagine your body traveling without you
after death, the physical remains of what you once were now
reduced to a smaller, more portable size. David can sense the
ashes with them in the car, can feel their import, their weight.
He drives carefully on the windy roads, not wanting to imagine
the contents shifting like the inside of an hourglass.

They pull into the driveway of David's home, a large four-
bedroom in Beverly Hills. It is the house of a successful man, a
vice president. A house with a green lawn watered and mowed
by Mexicans. A house with hedges and a swimming pool.
He helps carry their bags inside, Christopher running ahead,
yelling *we're here. We're here.*

Tracey comes out to greet them, smiling, laughter in her

voice. She is wearing jeans and a knit top. Her hair is up, face fresh and welcoming. She greets Scott and Doris warmly, offers them something to drink. Seeing her, feeling her expansive, welcoming energy, David thinks, *I can do this. We can, together. Thank God I'm not alone. I have my family to protect me from my family.* Watching Tracey move between him and his mother and brother, like an offensive lineman throwing blocks for a running back, David loves his wife more than anything. She will save him. The kids swarm around, lit up by the novelty, wanting to show off, to be noticed, appreciated. He can see discomfort on his mother's face. It's too much for her. She likes quiet, calm. She wants a glass of wine, a comfortable chair. The crazy thing is, he remembers her being fun when he was a kid, playful. He remembers her as a woman who wasn't afraid to get down on the floor and get dirty, a mother who liked to prompt her kids' imagination, a woman who had *fun.* How did she turn into this frightened, joyless shell? But, of course, he knows how. Two decades of booze, a decade of sickness and struggle, all leading to this moment: isolation, widowhood. His mother has become the kind of person who feels alone even when she's surrounded by others, because her filter is gone. She doesn't live in this world, remember. She lives on the moon, on an asteroid orbiting high above Earth, and now that her husband is dead, she is alone up there, spinning around on a cold, lifeless rock, stuck on the dark side of the planet.

They settle into the living room. Scott and Doris sit on the sofa. David and Tracey are on chairs, like it's an interview, like Scott and Doris have applied for some domestic position— butler, maid. Tracey has Sam on her lap and he's fumbling with her breast, trying to free it from her shirt. The older kids have been dispatched to the yard to give the grown-ups a chance to talk. Promises have been made to get them to go. Scott is on the hook for a ball game and to read some books and see Chloe's dollhouse and whatever else the kids can think of.

"So," says Tracey, after the final decibel of kiddie chaos recedes.

Nobody speaks.

"How was the flight?" she continues.

Doris shrugs.

"It's only two hours. I thought it would be longer."

"No," says David, "just two."

"Which surprised me, really," says Doris, "because I thought, two hours, I can't understand why you don't come up more."

Ah, thinks David, *a trap*.

Tracey, the offensive lineman, steps forward, intercepting the rush.

"We would love to," she says, "but with the new baby... Three kids are so much harder than two."

Doris sips her wine. Her eyes tell the story, that look of wounded judgment.

Scott takes over, moving to block the next blitz, shifting focus.

"How's business?" he asks David.

David sits back. He is wearing his standard uniform, khakis and a button-down shirt. His hair is trimmed every week. He shaves religiously each morning, admiring the smooth planes of his face in the mirror.

"Sales are up," he says. "We made a huge foray into China last year. It's such an untapped market. I mean, they're still using powdered monkey butts to treat their headaches, for God's sake."

"Well," says Scott, "powdered monkey butts..." But he loses the joke and spends a moment chewing his tongue, trying to get it back. They wait for him to recover, but he doesn't.

"The company asked me to help open the Beijing office," says David. "It's a great opportunity, but I couldn't do that to the kids. Going to New York every week is hard enough."

"I know," says Tracey. "We hate having him gone so much."

The kids run through the living room, circle the couch twice, then tear back out into the yard. Doris watches them, squinting.

"Does the girl...," she says.

"Chloe," says Scott.

"Does Chloe have breasts? How old is she?"

Tracey and David exchange a look.

"She's developing a little early," Tracey admits. "But it's perfectly normal. The doctor says kids are doing that more and more these days."

"Normal? She's what, six?"

"She's eight, Mom," says David. "I can't believe you don't know that."

Doris raises her eyebrows, her mouth set and aloof. She can dish out guilt, but she steadfastly refuses to acknowledge it when it's lobbed back at her.

"Your father just died," she says. "You're lucky I can still tie my shoes."

Touché. She knows the best defense is a good offense. David wants to tell her to go fuck herself, but he doesn't.

"How's the apartment?" Tracey asks Doris, a rookie mistake she recognizes instantly. Doris, the defensive tackle, pivots easily around the block, rushes the QB. Never ask the woman to express an opinion. Given the opportunity, she will always complain.

"It's like Nazis," she says, "that building. It's run by Nazis."

"Well," says Tracey, "I'm sure they're not actual Nazis."

"There's never anyone in the halls," says Doris. "It's like something out of Kafka."

"Ask her about Joe," says Scott mischievously, a glint in his eye.

"Who's Joe?" David wants to know. He says it cautiously, knowing he's being set up.

"He's nobody," says Doris.

"Joe is her roommate."

"Her roommate," parrots David. He hates not having all the information beforehand, having to plod his way around in the dark. Ignorance is the fastest way to lose a sale.

"He's Cindy's father," says Doris.

"And a nudist, apparently," says Scott. "Not to mention a close personal friend of Jesus Christ."

Doris makes a face.

"He's harmless, and he runs errands."

"Are you making this up?" David wants to know. A nudist Christian with the same name as his father, it seems like a joke. *Two dead fathers walk into a bar....*

"I swear," says Scott. "I've seen him with my own eyes. All of him. Believe me, I wish I hadn't."

"Okay," says Doris, "so he's a little weird, but what choice do I have? I don't see any of you up there taking care of me."

"We have lives, Mom," says David. "Responsibilities."

"And what am I—a stranger?"

"Doris," says Tracey, reacquiring her target, moving in for the block, "we've talked about you moving down to L.A., about finding you a place."

"I can't breathe this air. You know that. It's brown."

"Well, we can't move to Portland now, can we?" says David, using his senior-vice-president voice, his most patronizing tone. "I have a career and the kids are in school."

He glances at Scott, who shakes his head.

"Don't look at me. I have a life, too, a job, friends."

"It's nice to know I'm such a burden to my children," says Doris.

David sees red. He refuses to be manipulated, blackmailed in his own house. He starts to speak. Tracey sees his anger rising, reaches over, touches his arm. They've talked about this, about not letting Doris get to him, her emotional bullying.

"You're not a burden," she says. "We love having you, it's just you can't expect us to drop everything. You have a place to live, people who take care of you. You seem like you're doing fine."

"Well, I'm not," she says.

They sit in silence for a moment. David stares out into the yard, watches his kids play. He would give all the money he has to be out there with them right now, pitching the Wiffle ball, running the bases. He takes a deep breath. It's a question of time management. They'll eat in half an hour. He'll drive Doris to her hotel. Then there are only nine more days to get through. You just have to put your head down and muscle through. He is a man with two wives, for God's sake. If he can navigate that, he can navigate this, nine days with his mother.

Scott's cell phone rings. They watch as he pulls it from his pocket.

"Excuse me," he says, and goes into the kitchen. There is another quiet moment, then Tracey speaks up.

"You'll like the hotel," she tells Doris. "It's beautiful."

"Trying to get rid of me already?" Doris says.

Tracey smiles.

"Not at all. Like I said, we love having you. We'd ask you to stay, but I know you can't do the stairs."

With this she stands, hoisting the baby onto her hip.

"Excuse me. I have to check on dinner."

David throws her a pleading look, but her back is to him. His heart rate increases, sweat beads forming on his brow. His defender is abandoning him, giving up, leaving him exposed. She walks off the field without looking back, and then he is alone in the living room with his mother, like the whole front four of the Chicago Bears bearing down.

"You look good," he says.

She smiles to show him she knows he's kidding.

"I'm lonely," she says.

He doesn't want to do this, to have her open up to him. It's easier to joust, to have her play her role—the kvetching mother—and have him play his—the all-suffering, responsible son.

"I'm sure you are," he says. "But you have people up there taking care of you."

"Strangers," she says. "Everyone keeps asking me, *where's your family?* I say, *what family?*"

He watches the kids play on the swings in the backyard.

"Remember when we were little," he says. "A thousand years ago. You and Dad—how you kept all those beer cans for us to make a robot out of? And we spent like a week gluing them all together, made this crazy robot, and then the cleaning lady threw it out?"

Even as he tells this story, he sees how fucked up it is. He and Scott were like that damn cat, playing with the refuse of his parents' addictions, fashioning toys out of wine bottles, cigarette wrappers. But now that he's told it, he is forced to embrace the story in an effort to find common ground. He is trying to wrench his mother out of the present and into the past, a better time. Trying to relate to her as a parent, an equal. *Isn't it fun to have kids? Aren't we both grown-ups now, deserving of respect?* He can see from her face that it isn't working. The obstacle between them is too big, her descent too deep.

"Your kids got so big," she says. It is an accusation, like he has done it on purpose, hidden them away, fed them steroids, urging them to greater and greater heights.

"They're amazing," says David, responding to the statement, not her tone. "Christopher just got his green belt in karate, and Chloe is—we're thinking of skipping third grade. She's reading at such an advanced level."

"And she's got tits."

David doesn't know what to say to this. Doris sips her wine.

"I just wish someone would tell me what to do," she says. "Where to go."

"Well, what do you *want* to do, Mom?"

"I don't know. I'm just so tired."

Maybe if you stopped sedating yourself, he thinks.

"It's still really soon," he says. "It's only been a few months..."

Since Dad died. David can't bring himself to say the words out loud.

"You ask a question, you get a symphony," says Doris, smiling her most self-pitying smile: the brave warrior struggling against overwhelming odds. *How can you not feel sorry for me, rush to my rescue?*

"No," says David, "it's fine. I like symphonies. I just think you need to go easy on yourself. Rest up. Make sure you eat. You're exhausted, underweight. A few big meals, a good night's sleep, you'll feel a lot better."

"Hmm," she says, and he can tell she doesn't believe in such a thing, recovery. She has no proof such a thing exists. In her mind, once you fall, you don't get up again.

Tracey comes back from the kitchen with Scott. David looks at them the way a castaway eyes his rescue helicopter.

"Do you want to start the grill?" Tracey asks him. He can

see from her face that she feels bad for abandoning him. This is
her out. She is like a wrestler reaching into the ring for the tag.
My turn.

He jumps to his feet.

"Consider it done," he says, and goes out into the backyard.
It is a thing of beauty, his backyard, a plush green expanse,
surrounded by eucalyptus trees. There is a tasteful black fence
around the pool, the water a deep, satisfying blue. The color of
a glacier, a summery Italian sky. The whole thing, the house,
the yard, is a symbol of arrival, a magazine spread for achieve-
ment. *I made this happen*, he thinks, and the thought is soothing,
reassuring. *All of it. Look where I came from, the apathy, the impulse
to fail. Look what I've accomplished.* The yard is his pep talk, his
halftime locker-room speech. Standing in his yard, looking at
his pool, his kids, he feels like a hero, a survivor who has tri-
umphed in the face of overwhelming odds. Mind over matter.
The kids are still on the swings, kicking their toes toward the
sky. He opens the lid of the grill, turns on the gas. The burn-
ers light with a satisfying *woomf*, blue flame leaping. He runs
the steel brush over the grill, even though the Mexican woman
who cleans scrubs it every other day. But this is part of the rit-
ual. You prep the grill, clean it, heat the metal, then apply the
meat, the vegetables, inhaling the malty aroma, enjoying the
percussive sizzle.

Scott comes out of the house.

"Hey," he says. "I'm not gonna stay."

"What?"

"I've got, like, a splitting headache. I need to lie down."

"Just go up to our room, close the door. The kids won't
bother you."

Scott looks at him. The look embodies in seconds the following conversation:

Scott: Don't do this. You and I both know that I'm leaving because I've spent the last three days with her,
listening to all the complaints. If I don't go now, I'm
gonna split someone's head open, probably my own.

David: Just a little longer. I can't do it by myself. I'm not
ready.

Scott: Buddy, there's not enough money in the world to
keep me here. I'm twenty minutes away from a beer and
a swimming pool, and a crowd of beautiful women in
bikinis.

David closes the lid of the grill.

"The kids will be disappointed," he says. *Don't leave me.*

"I'll be back tomorrow." *Don't make a scene. Let me slip out
quietly and one day I'll return the favor.*

"Do you need me to drive you?" *Can I escape, too?*

"That's okay. I called a cab." *Nice try, but you've gotta stay to
cover my tracks.*

Tracey comes out with a platter of meat.

"Scott's going," says David, sounding wounded.

Tracey looks at Scott sympathetically, nods.

"I understand completely," she says.

"I'll be back tomorrow to play with the kids," Scott tells her.

"Great," she says. "They'd love that."

A taxi pulls into the driveway, honking. The three of them
head back into the house.

"What's happening?" says Doris.

"I'm heading to my hotel," says Scott. "I've got a splitting
headache and I need to lie down."

Doris looks at him. She knows she is being abandoned,
scraped off on her other son, like a game of hot potato.

"I guess I'll see you back there," she says.

"Actually," says Scott, "I'm not staying at the same place. Too expensive."

This catches Doris off guard.

"That's ridiculous," she says. "I'll pay."

He feels the trap closing but won't succumb.

"That's okay. I like staying someplace a little more downscale. It's more my speed."

David and Tracey watch this exchange the way you watch the Nature Channel, wondering if the lion is going to catch the gazelle.

"Who's going to watch out for me?" Doris wants to know.

"I'm sure the staff at the hotel will be more than happy to get you anything you need," Tracey offers.

Scott gives her an appreciative look. The taxi honks again. He leans down, kisses his mother's cheek.

"I'll see you tomorrow," he says, heading to the hall for his luggage. They watch him go, a sailboat floating off into the sunset, leaving behind all the woes of the world.

★ ★ ★

They eat in the dining room. After everyone is served, Christopher bows his head.

"God bless Mommy and Daddy. God bless Chloe and Sam. God bless Grandma and Uncle Scott. Amen."

Doris looks at the boy like he's insane.

"What the fuck was that?" she says.

David shakes his head at her. *Language.*

"Christopher likes to say grace before we eat," says Tracey. "We respect his right to do it."

Doris shakes her head. In her mind, religion is the sign of a weak mind, the crutch of the lowbrow and the average. As far as she's concerned, whatever promise her grandson once showed, he is now destined to end up in a trailer park drinking beer from a can and giving all his money to fish-eyed televangelists on TV.

Tracey begins a long monologue about the kids, how they're doing in school, what they dressed up as for Halloween. She tells Doris that she and the kids will follow Doris and her sons to New York on Friday after the kids get out of school.

"Don't put yourself to too much trouble," Doris says. She is now clearly drunk. A stranger might not be able to tell, but David can. He notes the telltale slowness, the subtle lack of focus. In his mother, true drunkenness looks just like sleep, the way his kids can't keep their eyes open after ten o'clock at night. The way they fall asleep in mid-sentence. Another glass of wine and his mother will pass out right where she's sitting.

"Don't be silly," says Tracey. "It's Joe's memorial. Of course we want to be there."

David nods. The whole thing is very tricky. New York, after all, is home to the other wife, Joy. For weeks he considered the logistics, before deciding that the only way he could go to New York for the memorial and have Tracey and the kids come would be to tell Joy that he couldn't make his regular weekly visit, that he was staying in L.A. In other words, to lie. But then, of course, one lie leads naturally to another. The key is not to run into Joy or any of her friends, to slip into town and operate under the radar, as they say, which is why he's booked them rooms at the Waldorf, well above Joy's usual urban circle. He will be in New York for three days, and his plan is not to go below Fourteenth Street, except for the memorial. All he has to do is steer clear of their usual downtown terrain and he should be fine.

After dinner David suggests that Christopher show his

grandmother some of his karate moves. Chris runs upstairs to put on his uniform. David goes into the garage to see if he can find a board. He is still flushed with pride in the boy, wants to show his mother that no matter what she thinks, the impossible is sometimes possible. Miracles do happen, if you believe, if you banish doubt from your mind. Look at him and Joy. If you'd asked him in the beginning, he would have said there was no way he could maintain two families on two coasts without either discovering the truth, but it has been almost a year now, and they have all settled into a comfortable routine. *So don't tell me there's no magic in the world. I have proof.*

He comes back into the dining room carrying a piece of three-quarter-inch plywood. Christopher is already there, showing his grandmother some of his moves, arms sweeping smoothly, legs kicking. He grunts under his breath as he hits each pose, brow furrowed with concentration. He is as adorable as any child has ever been, so true and pure of heart. His sister claps after each routine, licking ice cream from her spoon.

When Chris is finished with his floor exercise, David stands with the board.

"Wait till you see this," he says. He holds the board up in front of his stomach. Christopher approaches, touches the wood with his fingertips. He studies it, familiarizing himself with the grain, even leans forward and smells it, inhaling the pulpy aroma, the musty odors of the garage.

"He can't break that," says Doris. "Are you crazy?"

"We don't say *can't* in this house," David tells her, still energized from this afternoon's lesson in the power of positive thinking. "We believe in visualizing things."

He holds the board tight, looking down at the top of his son's head, that sandy brown spiral. How many nights has he breathed in the boy's smell, listened to his gentle snoring? And now his son is becoming a man, capable, competent. It is a testament to good parenting, he thinks. A sign of their success.

"Well," says Doris, "I'm visualizing a lot of weeping and carrying on."

David reaches out and touches his son's head.

"Don't listen to her," he says. "You can do this."

Christopher steps back from the board. He measures the distance with his arm. David steadies the board. Everyone's eyes are on him. He glances at his wife, his daughter. They are hypnotized, nervous. Everyone wants this trick to work. They want to demonstrate the magic of which their family is capable, to share it. Even the baby is watching, food splattered across his pudgy face.

Do it, thinks David. *Do it. Show her that in this house we can accomplish anything we set our minds to.*

Christopher closes his eyes, takes a deep breath.

"For God's sake," says Doris. "He's just a kid."

Christopher opens his eyes. He looks up at his dad, and in that moment David sees doubt. *Just a kid.* The words hang in the air, dismissive, reductive.

"Don't listen to her," says David. "You can do it. Just like this afternoon."

Christopher nods, readies himself. Watching him, David is filled suddenly with doubt. This afternoon was a fluke, he thinks, an anomaly. It was someone else's son breaking that board, a tough kid from a confident family, a well-balanced kid who doesn't have the gene of collapse lurking in his blood.

Christopher pulls his hand back, strikes. There is a sickening *whack*. The board shivers in David's hand but doesn't break. Christopher cries out in pain, clutching his fist to his stomach. The sound of impact lingers in David's mind, the meaty smack of failure. There is no magic in the world. He sees this now.

There is only disappointment, raised hopes, and the predictable descent of ruin.

He drops the board, kneels, pulling his son to him.

"Let me see it," he says, trying to pry the wounded hand loose. Christopher is reluctant to let go. He knows that only the pressure of his fingers is keeping the hand together.

"I told you," says Doris. "Why doesn't anyone ever listen to me?"

"This is all your fault," shouts David, glaring at her.

"My fault?" she says. "How is it my fault?"

"You have to believe, don't you understand? You have to believe for it to work."

His mother looks at him pityingly.

"Listen to yourself, what you're saying. He's a little boy. It's a piece of wood. The whole thing was crazy right from the start."

He glares at her with pure hatred. She is the problem, the kryptonite. He has seen the magic with his own eyes, has seen dreams come true—all the miracles, his children born and raised, his career blossoming, his beautiful wives. But now his mother has come and spoiled everything, just like she always does, with her doubt and her undermining, godless critique. Christopher isn't crying, though it's clear he's in pain. He is being brave for his father. Tracey comes over and kneels next to them.

"Let Mommy see, sweetie," she says, gently prying his wounded hand loose. She examines it. The knuckles are red. She reaches out and touches them gently, one by one.

"Does that hurt?" she wants to know.

He shakes his head, though it's clear it does. Tracey looks at David.

"I'm sure he's fine," she says, "but why don't you run him over to the emergency room just to be sure?"

David nods. In a sick way he is glad. It will give him a chance to escape.

"You can drop your mother at the hotel on the way," she continues. He nods. Her point is clear: That's enough for one day, enough awkward silences, enough negativity.

"Come on, Mom," he says. "I'll take you to the hotel."

Doris gets shakily to her feet. They help her to the car. She will be asleep before they arrive, her head thrown back, snoring quietly. It has been a long day, a long trip, a long life. In the backseat, Christopher will sing quietly to himself, clutching his throbbing hand, his voice like a distant seagull, while up front David watches the road like a good father, a good driver, checking his mirrors every time he changes lanes.

STEPHEN HAWKING HAS a theory. He calls it the Thermo-dynamic Arrow of Time. According to Hawking, time moves in an irrevocably straight line. It doesn't look around. It never slows down. It just keeps going in one irreversible direction. But which direction? To quote Elmer Fudd, which way does it go? Which way does it go?

Backward, says Hawking. Time moves backward.

Think about this. Imagine that instead of moving from past to future, time is moving from future to past. For this to be the direction of time, we must imagine that the universe was at its most *disordered* in the beginning. Picture it, the chaos before the big bang, the scattershot universe drawing a deep, frazzled breath before giving birth to itself. Given this theory, disor-der should naturally *decrease* with time. It's like a jigsaw puzzle. Open the box, shake out the pieces. There is only one arrange-ment in which they make a complete picture. (A complete picture being the end.) On the other hand, there are a very large number of arrangements in which the pieces don't make a picture at all. (Disorder being the beginning.) Thus the order of the universe increases with every piece added, and therefore time moves from chaos to order.

However, says Hawking, all scientific evidence points instead to the conclusion that disorder actually *increases* with time, so then why should our perception of time be what it is? He suggests that it's because people are like computers. Our brains function in a way that requires us to see and remember things in an order in which entropy decreases. We can't handle watching broken cups gathering themselves together and jumping back up onto the table.

If you believe that the universe was at its most disordered at the beginning, then you must see that it gets more orderly as time goes forward. However, if based on the laws of physics (of which ignorance is no excuse, but similarly no crime) disorder *increases* with energy production, then actually the universe is becoming *less orderly* as time goes and, therefore, we must theoretically be moving backward toward the beginning. Why, then, do we see time as moving contrarily?

Because we have an absolute aversion to remembering our futures.

Scott Henry sits in a strip club on Sunset Boulevard. The place is filled not with seedy trucker types, but young Hollywood hipsters, men and women. Strip clubs are the new nightclubs, the kitsch capital of ironic escape. Scott sits at a table in the back, by himself. He has had a few more drinks than when we last saw him. Everything around him is watery, fluid. The egg of sorrow has cracked, you see, and everything is coated with a broken yellow glaze.

It is nine P.M. He has checked into the Standard Hotel, stowed his bags in his blocky, concrete room, thrown open the curtains and stepped out onto the balcony. Below him lay the neon blue Astroturf of the pool area, and beyond that the dense southern sprawl of Los Angeles. A silver beanbag chair slumped near the railing at his feet. He stood for a second breathing in the warm air of freedom. Scott loves Los Angeles, the blatant lie of it. *We can be young and rich and beautiful forever.* L.A. is all about the suspension of disbelief. From impossible movie pitches to houses stilted up on fault-ridden hills, the whole city is based on an idea that anything you dream up can come true.

But his room was small and concrete and sitting in it he found himself with far too much time to think. So he called a cab and came here, to a strip club, where for a hundred dollars a half-naked woman will tell you any lie you want to hear.

It doesn't have to *be* true.

It just has to sound true.

Recently Scott has been reading about the German mathematician Kurt Gödel, who suggested that a mathematical proposition could be true even if there was no possible way of proving it. *What do you believe is true even though you cannot prove it?* Gödel called it his First Incompleteness Theorem. It made other mathematicians uneasy, this idea that there are no absolutes. What is math, after all, if not a kind of rigidly structured religion, a promise of order and rationality in an otherwise crazy universe? In 1940, Gödel left Germany and emigrated to America. He found himself at Princeton University, teaching alongside Albert Einstein. Einstein, of course, had coined the Theory of Relativity, which stated simply that there is no such thing as absolute time. He suggested that whether an observer deems two events to be happening "at the same time" depends on his state of motion. In other words, there is no universal *now.* The flow of time depends on motion and gravity. The division of events into *past* and *future* is relative.

Gödel used to walk home with Einstein every day after school (picture two old grandfathers strolling down tree-lined streets dressed in fraying tweed). He said, *Your theory of relativity is interesting, but personally I don't believe that time exists at all.* Einstein was intrigued. *Tell me more*, he said. So Gödel showed him an epic equation, pages and pages of letters and numbers. He painted a picture of a universe that was not expanding, but rotating. An observer of this universe would see all the galaxies slowly spinning around him. This spinning, the equation showed, mixed up space and time, made them interchangeable. By completing a sufficiently long round-trip in a rocket ship, a resident of Gödel's universe could travel back to any point in his own past. The equation it took to prove this would look like a wall of gibberish to you and me, but Gödel saw it as a code, a code that proved once and for all that *time itself does not exist*. A past that can be revisited has not really passed. Time, like God, is either everywhere or nowhere. If it disappears in one possible universe, it is undermined in every possible universe including our own.

This is the beauty of theoretical physics. Past a certain point science becomes a question of faith. It is a question of creating equations that "prove" your theory, while at the same time understanding that such proof can only ever be theoretical.

Now, in what you call the present, Scott sits in Hollywood, California, and the strippers who wander the floor with their boxy little purses are buxom, oversized. They are impossible blondes and bottle redheads—part-time porn stars. Before Kate it never would have occurred to him to come to a strip club, but tonight it was all he could think about. He is like a criminal returning to the scene of the crime. He gives the strippers money and they laugh at his jokes, tell him he's sexy, tell him he's hysterical. A fucking riot.

He sits in the dark funk of the club, enjoying his anonymity, enjoying the fact that none of these people are related to him. His definition of the word *family* goes as follows:

Family [pham-i-lee] *n*. **1**) a cage or similar restraining device often used in the practice of torture: *e.g.*, Senator

John McCain spent seven years in a Vietnamese *family*, eating bugs, while all feelings of self-worth were beaten out of him by his *parents* (see *parents*). **2)** a highly debilitating congenital disease, slow acting, but almost always paralyzing. Symptoms include but are not limited to: mood swings; irritability; an inability to form close bonds; neediness; increased emotional stupidity; unexpected spikes of intense anger; shortness of breath; feelings of worthlessness; feelings of moral superiority; fear of intimacy; fear of abandonment; increased promiscuity and/or frigidity; an unnameable, unstoppable yearning; an unnameable, unstoppable dread; unexpected periods of intense desire followed by unpredictable decreases in caring; a simultaneous desire for and hatred of small children, puppies, and seals; illogical feelings of self-pity and resentment; and a deep-seated desire to be held.

Right now he is talking to Candy, a busty brunette. She sits on his lap, dressed in pink hot pants and a tiny black bra.

"So what do you do?" she asks him. *Are you in the movie business? Can you help me?*

"I listen to other people's phone calls," he tells her.

"Like a voyeur?"

"You know how you call your bank and they say *this call may be monitored for quality assurance.* That's me."

She squirms a little in his lap. She smells like waffles. It is the universal stripper scent, the artificial odor of sweet breakfast items and tropical fruits.

"I'm an actress," she says. "Of course. Who isn't?"

"You're beautiful," he tells her.

"You're sweet. I like you. But who isn't beautiful in this town?"

He has his hand on her hip, and the warmth of it, the strength of the bone, the soft, yielding flesh, makes him want to cry. She's right, of course. Beauty is the currency of this place. It's like living in a golden city. You feel rich, and yet how much can gold really be worth when your sidewalk is made of the stuff, your toilet?

"Do you want a dance?" Candy asks him in a sultry, baby-doll voice.

"Yes, please," he says.

She stands, takes off her top. Her breasts are impossibly round. She starts to move to the music, brushing against him, her hands on the arms of his chair. Her hair falls in his face. He is a warm sunny field on a hot summer day. He is a Long Island beach in August, waves lapping gently at the shore. She moves her face beside his. He feels the electric charge of her skin. She kisses his cheek. It feels so real, like love. The hum of her breath on his face is intimate, the way her hands move against his chest. She presses her tits against his face and for a moment he is lost in the deep well of her chest, breathing her in, her warmth, the real human smell of her, his mouth an inch from her heart. (It occurs to him that the space between a stripper's breasts is probably the most germ-ridden inch on the face of the Earth.) Then she turns and sits on his lap, grinding herself against him, undulating her hips. He gets hard from the friction, the sight of the smooth plane of her back, the tattoo above her ass—a crucifix— the way her thighs are pressing down against his legs. He has lost his faith in people. Nobody is who they say. Nobody tells the truth. He hears it on the phone every day, the way people act on hold—honest, human—and the artifice that comes over them when the operator comes on the line. Fake, plastic. Nobody says anything real. Nobody wants to be vulnerable. He is so tired of being disappointed, so tired of wishing for things that don't hap-

pen. What's the point of living if you're afraid to hope? He is
exhausted by his own emotions, his own needs. Nothing lasts.
Women leave. Fathers die. And how do you plan a life when you
can't count on anything? It's like living in a city where every day
the landscape changes. Each morning you wake to find yourself
in a strange house on a strange street in a strange town. Every
night the streets shift while you sleep, avenues turning to alleys,
rivers turning to mountains. How can they expect you to keep
a job when the office keeps moving? When your home isn't
where you left it? Not to mention that every day the people you
see are different. They act like they know you, sure, but it is just
an act. Familiar faces, but inside who knows?

This is it, he thinks. *The bottom. The lowest point.* He has no
idea how far he still has to fall. He thinks, *We spend so much time
looking for love, but none of it matters. The truth is, we're all alone.*
He is embarrassed by these thoughts, the clichéd pathos they
represent, and yet they're not thoughts. They're nodules in his
chest, brittle calcium deposits forming on the inside of his rib
cage. They are tumors, changing the architecture of his body.
The stripper turns and places her left breast against his lips. The
nipple is hard, fat. It is a sexual gesture but also strangely maternal. She touches his hair. The beat of the music is in his chest,
the tribal rhythm of drum and bass. He wants to throw his arms
around this woman, to take her to his hotel and lose himself
in the lie of her. He's sure if he offered her enough money she
would go. He thinks of it, going to the ATM, emptying his
account for her. Right now it feels so important to make a connection, to feel the truth of another body pressed against his.
Is that so wrong? He has always thought men who go to strip
clubs to be deviants, pathetic, and yet there is something honest
about getting what you want, something safe about reducing
the interactions of men and women to a question of money.

Here he doesn't have to wonder if Candy likes him or not. Here it is understood: Money buys you time. It buys you a conversation, a touch. It buys you a blowjob in a private booth. As long as you have money at a strip club, there is love for you, redemption.

The songs shifts. Candy stands, refastens her top. He hands her two twenties.

"Thanks, lover," she says.

His cell phone vibrates in his pocket. He takes it out, looks at the caller ID. It's his brother. He checks the time, eleven-thirty.

"Hello?" he says, plunging his left index finger into his ear, straining to hear.

"It's me," his brother says. "We've got a problem."

"What?"

"A problem. We've got a problem."

Scott looks up at Candy, but she's already looking around the room, searching for her next customer.

"What's going on?" he says.

"The hotel just called me," says David. "They're throwing her out."

"What do you mean? She's sixty-three. Who throws a sixty-three-year-old woman out of a hotel?"

"They caught her smoking with her oxygen machine. She could have blown up the hotel. The fucking Hotel Bel-Air."

Scott closes his eyes. Smoking with her oxygen machine. *There are cleaner ways to kill yourself*, he thinks, *but this one has a certain inventive charm.* He starts laughing, and for a minute can't stop. *Fucking perfect*, he thinks. *Death by explosion.* Of course, you take a lot of other people with you, too, but then that's always been his mother's approach. *If I'm cold, everybody's cold. If I'm dying in a fire, everybody's dying in a fire.*

"She's in the lobby with her stuff," says David. "Apparently some security goon is looming over her, making sure she behaves."

"So go get her," Scott says. "What do you want from me?"

"I can't," says David. "Tracey's sick. Something she ate at lunch, she thinks. She's throwing up. Can you hear?"

Scott opens his eyes. A stripper with an impossibly flat stomach stops in front of him, slips her hand into her G-string, and gives him a look that would melt a glacier. Behind her there is a black woman onstage with an ass like a pair of hams. Through the cell phone, Scott's precision hearing can identify exactly what Tracey ate for lunch today from the way she's heaving; a Niçoise salad and two glasses of Chardonnay.

"I'm busy," he says.

"Doing what?" his brother wants to know.

Scott pauses. The black woman jumps up, grabs the pole, and slides down with her legs jutting out at a forty-five-degree angle.

"It would take too long to explain," he says.

His brother makes an exasperated sound. This is how it always is with them, the tug of war. *You go. No*, you *go.* They might as well play Rock-Paper-Scissors for who gets to take care of their mother.

"She's sitting in the lobby," David says. "It's past her bedtime."

"Let her rot."

"Yeah," says David, "clearly *that's* not an option."

Scott stands, grabs his jacket. He is furious, volcanic.

"What's the address?"

"Just grab a cab. They'll know the Hotel Bel-Air. I called and they can take her at the Standard. That's where you're staying, right? I don't think we can trust her on her own."

Scott takes a deep breath through his nose, lets it out.

"So I get her."

"The stairs. We'd take her, but..."

"Yeah, whatever. You owe me so big."

"Don't be like that. I do a lot."

Scott can hear the anger in his brother's voice. *Don't push me. I know I'm pussying out, but don't call me on it.* Scott wants to reach through the phone line and strangle him, wants to take a cab to his brother's house and climb into bed with the kids. *If you're going to act like my daddy*, he thinks, *I should at least be able to act like your child.* He exits the strip club, leaving behind the myth of beauty, the myth of availability, the myth of freedom through sex. He stands on Sunset Boulevard and looks for a cab. Muscle cars troll slowly down the four-lane blacktop. One of the bouncers approaches him.

"You need a cab?"

Scott nods. The guy is six foot four, with shoulders like a highway overpass.

"What about a limo, travel in style?"

Scott looks over. There are three black stretches parked in the lot, the drivers sitting on folding stools reading the paper.

"A limo," he says.

The bouncer has a ponytail and a twenty-five-inch neck.

"Fifty bucks, they'll take you anywhere you want to go."

Scott nods. His heart is a red-hot bullet, a fist.

"Sounds good," he says. "Let's do it."

The bouncer gestures, and one of the drivers stands, folding the paper and putting it under his arm. Scott walks over. The driver opens the back door. Scott slips inside. He feels giddy, out of control. The seats are leather. There is a bar, a TV, a moon roof. The car smells like air freshener. Scott can only imagine how many high-school sweethearts have had sex back here, the tinted interior partition rolled up, how many strippers have tumbled from the club clutching rich men with cowboy hats, and then fallen into this very backseat, how many drunken bachelorette parties have raged in the elongated rear of this limo, the dark cavity packed with smart, young professional women all standing on the seat and flashing their tits to the passing city streets.

The driver climbs into the front seat.

"Where to?" he says.

Scott stretches out his legs. He is buzzed, feels reckless, and so far off the map that even the word *map* sounds made up. There are no words for this feeling. It is a Red Bull overdose. A crystal meth bender with a bottle of Nyquil thrown in.

"Two stops," he says. "The Hotel Bel-Air and then we're going to the Standard back here on Sunset."

The driver puts the car in gear, pulls out into traffic. He says his name is Lou.

"This fucking town," he says. "Everybody thinks they're such hot shit, like all those people who believe in past lives, how they're always Cleopatra or Teddy Roosevelt or some such shit."

"Well, I'm nobody," says Scott.

"Me too. Nobody. I been nobody my whole life, and you know what? It suits me just fine. We can't all be rocket scientists, you know? Can't all be Brad Pitt. Who wants to be famous, anyway? Sounds awful, people taking pictures of you all the time. I mean, don't get me wrong. I'm sure the pussy is incredible. World class. Believe me, I drive enough of those fuckers in my car to know. Women melt for that shit, celebrity. Get a celebrity in my car, the whole thing smells like cunt for a week. Rich guys get laid, too, and pretty well, but nothing beats a famous face. Even these reality-show assholes get pussy like you wouldn't believe."

Scott sits in the back wondering what it would be like to be rich, insulated. This is what money does—it pads the world around you, dulling the edges. Getting rich, having rich friends, surrounding yourself with comfort, is like baby-proofing your house. You put plastic in the electrical outlets, a lock on the toilet. You are creating the illusion of security.

In front, Lou goes on and on. He flattens his vowels and grunts as he changes lanes. The limo moves down the Strip, past the House of Blues, the Viper Room, Sunset Boulevard changing from commercial real estate to residential, the street widening. The shops become estates. The median turns green, leafy.

Scott dozes for a minute, exhausted. He dreams of faraway beaches, of single-family houses, dinner on the table at six, apple pie on the windowsill.

"Hey, buddy," says Lou. "We're here."

Scott wakes, disoriented. They are in the secluded parking lot of the Hotel Bel-Air. A footbridge leads across a stream to the entrance of the building. A valet steps up, opens the door. Scott steps out.

"Good evening, sir. Checking in?"

"No. I'm here to pick someone up," he says. "My mother."

"Very good, sir. Just go to the lobby. Someone will help you there."

Scott nods, turns to the driver.

"I'll be right back."

He crosses the footbridge. There is a pond below, swans floating under soft outdoor lights. The grounds must cover several acres, with footpaths leading off into the woods. The hotel itself is pink, sprawling, ornate. Scott walks into the lobby. A bellman approaches.

"Can I help you, sir?"

Scott looks around. His mother is sitting in a puffy chair, luggage at her feet, looking sleepy, disoriented.

"Never mind," he says. "I see her."

He walks over. A hotel manager in a designer suit moves to intercept him.

"Hey Mom," says Scott. "How's *your* night going? 'Cause I gotta tell you, I'm having a blast."

She blinks up at him, trying to place the face. She looks spooked, like a baby squirrel, eyes wide. The manager joins them.

"Are you here for Mrs. Henry?" he asks politely. He probably majored in polite at U of M.

Scott nods.

"Can you give me a sense," he asks the manager, "of what the problem is?"

His mother, having focused finally, having come to terms with who he is and what he represents, looks up at Scott with immense gratitude, hope. Finally, after all these months, someone has come to protect her, save her. Here is her son, her knight in shining armor.

"Mrs. Henry was smoking in her room," says the manager. "A nonsmoking room, but apparently she's on oxygen as well, and, well, we just can't have that. The risk to our guests. This is an historic building."

He actually says *an* historic building. Scott wants to pull the pencil-thin mustache from his face hair by hair.

"I'm sure it is," says Scott. He turns to Doris. "Is it true, Mom? Were you smoking?"

His mother looks up at him.

"It's the fucking Spanish Inquisition," she says. "I tried to tell them, I don't smoke. I can't. Look at me."

"Mom," says Scott.

"The oxygen was off," she said. "I had the window open."

Scott turns to the manager.

"I'm really sorry. I'll get her out of your hair."

He helps his mother to her feet. It's clear she doesn't want to go.

"It's the middle of the night," she says. "Throwing an old lady out of a hotel. It's criminal."

"Come on," says Scott. "Save it for the judge."

He holds her arm, helps her walk. She can't weigh more than ninety pounds soaking wet. Her hair is like straw. The bellman follows them to the door, carrying her luggage. They exit the building, cross the footbridge. Lou is standing by the limo. He sees them, opens the back door.

"What's this?" Doris wants to know. She is panting, out of breath.

"Nothing but the best for my mother," says Scott, helping her inside. The bellman loads the bags into the trunk. Scott and his mother sit side by side in the palatial expanse of the back-seat.

"A limo," she says, exhaling through pursed lips.

"What do you think," says Scott, "should we go to Vegas, hit a few casinos?"

"Do you smell waffles?" his mother asks.

"It's the air freshener," says Scott, picturing Candy's over-sized breasts, the way she ground her ass against him.

"No," says Doris, sniffing, "it's coming from you." *Sniff, sniff.* "Have you been eating waffles?"

Lou climbs in, starts the car.

"The Standard, you said?"

"Please," says Scott.

They drive in silence for a minute.

"Where's your brother?" asks Doris. "I thought he would come."

"Tracey's sick, apparently. Something she ate."

"It wouldn't surprise me, the way she cooks."

"At lunch, they're saying. At a restaurant."

"Well, I still don't see why they couldn't come and pick me up. You saw the size of that house. You're telling me there's not a room I could sleep in?"

"There are stairs," says Scott. "All the bedrooms are on the second floor."

"So I sleep on the sofa. They don't want me, is what it is."

"*I* don't want you. Who would want you? All you do is complain."

She pouts, looking picked on.

"I do not."

"Listen, Ma," says Scott. "Please. It's been a long day. Let's just get to the hotel and check you in and we'll talk about it tomorrow."

She pouts for another minute. Up front Lou puts on the radio, golden oldies. The night is beginning to feel like a Billy Wilder movie. Soon there'll be a dead monkey and a man in a suit floating facedown in the pool.

"Is it nice, this hotel?" asks Doris. "It's where you're staying, right?"

"It's fine. It's—I think it's a little young for you, but..."

"What are you saying, I'm old?"

"Yes, Mom, that's what I'm saying. You're old."

She looks out the window, satisfied. Doris doesn't trust a conversation where somebody is not picking a fight with somebody else.

"Your father and I came to L.A. sometimes when he had business," she says. "We always stayed at the Beverly Hills Hotel. I liked to sit by the pool and have a salad or go shopping. He would come back from a meeting in his suit and knit tie—

remember those knit ties?—and we would have a drink and there were palm trees and it all seemed so beautiful."

Scott sighs, watches the trees go by outside the window.

"I'm trying to picture the future for me," says Doris, "but I just can't see it."

They reach the hotel. It's midnight on a Tuesday night and the place is packed, cars lined up in the driveway. Scott steers his mother through a crowd of twenty-year-old models in hip-hugging jeans, past scruffy young men in velvet suit jackets and trucker's caps. He feels every eye in the place turn to them, a thirty-five-year-old man with his shambling, out-of-breath mother. Looking up, he realizes he forgot to warn his mother about the half-naked woman in the display case behind the front desk, the bored, sometimes sleeping model/actress lying behind glass in her underwear, reading a book or checking her e-mail. Scott saw her there earlier and stood dumbstruck. *Beautiful women are so plentiful in this town*, he thought, *they are literally being used for decoration, like a table, a lamp.*

"Is that a mannequin?" his mother wants to know.

Scott rushes through the check-in process. The lobby is filled with the stutter beats of tomorrow's techno. Waiting for the clerk to run his mother's credit card, Scott glances nonchalantly around the lobby. His eyes linger on the faces of women he thinks he could love, like a baby bird looking to imprint.

The bellman takes the bags upstairs. Scott helps his mother to her room, sets up her oxygen machine, unraveling the long plastic line, plugging the squat, boxy device into the wall. Then he kneels and starts going through her bags.

"What are you doing?" his mother wants to know.

"Looking for cigarettes."

He digs through the main compartment, through sweaters and underwear, before finally finding a pack jammed down into the side pocket of her suitcase. He puts it in his pocket, takes her lighter, too, just in case.

"You're mean," his mother says.

"I'll see you in the morning," he tells her, and closes the door behind him. He is exhausted. He doesn't know how he will survive the next week. Physically it seems impossible. He pads down the hall to his room. Inside he brushes his teeth, washes his face. He is practically asleep on his feet, but looking at the bed, he feels too wound up to lie down, so he steps out onto the balcony. The patio below is empty now, cleared of partiers so that the guests can sleep. There is only the faraway sound of traffic, the low whistle of the wind. Below him, the pool is lit from within, a dappling green glow, and beyond that, the lights of L.A. glitter hazy and mysterious.

"You don't have a cigarette, do you?" says a woman's voice from the next balcony.

Scott turns. A young blonde is reclining in her beanbag chair, a glass of wine in one hand.

"As a matter of fact," says Scott, digging in his pocket. He leans over the rail, hands her his mother's cigarettes.

"Keep the pack," he tells her.

"You're a fucking lifesaver," says the girl. He takes out his mother's lighter, leans out. The woman bends over the rail of her balcony, cupping his hand with hers. She is twenty-one at the oldest, wearing jeans and a skimpy camisole. Her body is like a song. The flame dances against the tip of her cigarette. She inhales, exhales smoke.

"I'm Kelly," she says.

"Scott."

"Nice to meet you, Scott."

"Likewise."

They stand for a moment in the quiet. Music from the lobby

is a subtext of the dark. Scott risks a tiny smile. He doesn't want to read too much into it, but maybe this girl is his reward, the last-minute field goal that wins the game, snatching victory from the jaws of defeat. Scott takes a deep breath, lets it out.

"Long day?" Kelly asks.

"You have no idea," he says.

Kelly holds the cigarette between her thumb and middle finger, like a joint.

"So," says Scott. "Are you—"

A young, shirtless man comes out of Kelly's room onto the balcony. He is in boxer shorts. His stomach muscles are so well defined, it looks like you could grate cheese on them.

"John," says Kelly, "this is Scott. Scott, my boyfriend John."

John nods at Scott.

"Hey, what's up?" he says, then to Kelly: "Babe, I'm turning in. I gotta be at Fox by nine in the morning."

She kisses him.

"Okay, baby," she says, taking his hand. "Let's go to bed."

"Nice meeting you," she tells Scott, heading inside.

"You too."

Their sliding door closes, followed by the curtains. Scott stands on the balcony, alone again. He thinks the two worst words in the English language are *my boyfriend*. He hears them all the time from women he meets. I'm here with *my boyfriend*. *My boyfriend* got me the tickets. I'm going to Italy with *my boyfriend*. At least with a husband you know. The ring is a dead giveaway. But the girl with a boyfriend is like a submarine, stealthy. She is a game of Russian roulette. You never know if there's a bullet in the chamber. He pictures his mother in her room, pajamas on, Larry King on the TV. It's been fifteen minutes, but the minibar is probably open already, a glass of wine by the bed. He pictures her sitting there in the dark, lonely, afraid.

He thinks of her, but all he can see is himself, old and abandoned, a stubble-faced old man in a dirty undershirt talking to his plants.

He takes off his clothes, sits naked on the edge of the bed. The far wall is all mirrors and he studies his reflection in the glass. He is losing weight, that much is clear. Maybe five pounds in the last two weeks. It keeps slipping his mind to eat. His body is hungry for something other than food: connection, meaning. Now would be the time to start doing sit-ups, take advantage of his heartbreak and whip his body into shape. But the thought of it is exhausting.

From the next room the sound of John and Kelly having sex floats through the wall. It is subtle at first, a low hum of excited breathing, a vague physical shifting. Then Scott hears the sound of the bed moving, the steady *thump thump* of the headboard against the wall. Words begin to penetrate. Kelly's voice. *Oh, baby. Oh, yes. Don't stop.*

Scott lies back, closes his eyes. His erection feels like betrayal.

Fucking perfect, he thinks for the last time today, darkness descending, the world catching up with him, smothering him, dragging him down into sleep.

DORIS WAKES IN the middle of the night, the words *born again* on her lips. The TV is on at the foot of the bed, and there is a televangelist onscreen preaching to the near-empty room.

"...when you renounce your sins," he is saying, "when you bathe in the water of righteousness."

She sits up dizzy, unsure of where she is. Her breathing is shallow, panicked. Deep inside her lungs there is only blackness, the tissue singed, crackly, like the outside of a marshmallow cooked too long over a campfire. She reaches reflexively for her oxygen line, slips it on over her ears, placing the plastic nubs under her nose. *Some kind of hotel room*, she thinks, looking around. She catches sight of herself in the mirror wall, and for a minute believes she is not alone. That she is sharing the room with some old lady. But then she realizes the old lady is her. That this is what her life has come to, displacement, disorientation. *I'm a refugee*, she thinks, *a wandering gypsy*. She puts on her glasses, reaches for the water glass that sits beside the bed. It is filled with red wine, like some kind of Jesus miracle, as if the televangelist has reached through the screen and performed an act of transmutation. Sipping it, there is that familiar taste, the oak-dark swallow of purple tannins.

She gets up, goes to the bathroom to pee. Coming back she

trips over her suitcase, goes down hard. She lies on the floor dazed. *Please God*, she thinks, *don't let anything be broken.* She moves slowly, one limb at a time, but it is just her pride that is hurt. She sits up, one hand on her suitcase. Inside she can feel a hard, boxy shape. For the life of her, she can't figure out what it is, so she opens the suitcase, and the minute she sees the wooden box she knows. *His ashes. These are his ashes.* The recognition takes her breath away. Forty years and this is what's left, a box of sand. Gristle.

Born again. The words come back to her, the ones she woke up with. It's not hard to understand why so many people have surrendered to the idea. A second chance. The opportunity to renounce your past and start over. To her God has always been a bully, a thinly veiled threat. God is the bogeyman whose name is thrown around to subdue and intimidate. His *wrath*, his *vengeance*. She caresses the box that holds her husband's ashes. They met at a restaurant. She was there on a date with another boy. *What was his name?* They were sitting in a booth at a restaurant in Little Italy and Joe came over to the table.

"Excuse me, miss," he said. "You have a phone call."

Puzzled, she slid from the booth and followed him back into the kitchen, but just inside the door he turned and smiled at her. He was tall and handsome with a dimpled chin. His eyes were sparkling and blue.

"I lied," he said. "There's no phone call. I just wanted to meet you."

It was hot in the kitchen, a stifling August night made worse by the humidity of boiling water, and she swooned, literally. She had never swooned before in her life, but there is no other word for what happened in that moment. He reached out a hand to steady her.

"Careful there," he said. "So, could I get your phone number?"

She gave it to him. Of course she gave it to him, then went back to the table, back to the date. It was the most mysterious and romantic thing that had ever happened to her. The rest of the night was a dull blur in comparison. Joe called the next day. They met for coffee. He told her the story, how he'd been out to dinner with some friends after a show, how he'd seen her sitting there with her date and she was so beautiful. How he turned to his friends and said, *watch this.* They sat at a café in the West Village and he told Doris about his life. He came from Ohio, a tight-lipped Protestant family. He'd been in the army. Now he worked in advertising, inventing log lines for dishwashers.

"But who cares about me?" he said. "You're the doll."

The waiter came by the table. He ordered a beer. She asked for an ice cream sundae.

"With chocolate and nuts and whip cream," she said.

The ice cream came and she ate it like it was her last meal. She was as skinny as a pencil. He had two beers, watched her go.

"I like a girl who's not afraid to pack it away," he said.

She was a girl who'd been raised by her aunt, a girl who'd spent two decades living a lie, unwanted, unrecognized. Half the time she felt invisible. And now this man was watching her eat ice cream on the corner of Bleecker Street and Bank, and the way he looked at her, she felt seen, maybe for the first time. Like he was looking through her skin into her meaty brown organs. Like he had X-ray eyes and he could see everything, every secret, every insecurity. She felt like bolting from the restaurant, dashing out into traffic. It was 1961. *Nineteen sixty-one.* Thinking of it now, she can't believe those numbers ever went together. New York was a different city then, lower, wider, a brick labyrinth. Even her memories of it are in black-and-white. It's amazing how the past recedes. You can't hold on to a second of it. In 1961, Joe Henry sat in a café on the corner of Bleecker and Bank and lit a cigarette. He sat back, crossed his legs, and laughed smoke. He was the man she would marry eight months later on an April afternoon at City Hall. His teeth were white and straight and he smiled at her the whole time she ate. Truly in his life he had never seen anything more beautiful.

In the hotel she rises unsteadily to her feet. She is almost sixty-five years old now. If she were a comic book, she'd be vintage. If she were a car, she'd be classic. If she were a song, she'd be a golden oldie. Her hair is frizzy. Her bones are kindling. She sits on the edge of her bed holding the box of ashes in her lap. She is afraid of it, but she can't put it down. It is her own death, but she needs to be near it. She is too old to cry, she thinks, all dried up. Instead there is just numbness. More than anything at this moment she wants a cigarette.

So stupid, she thinks. *To be thrown out of a hotel. How humiliating.* And for what? One lousy smoke? It's fascist, that's what it is. Absurd. But what do people expect? She's not strong enough to take care of herself, not strong enough to resist the temptation. The cigarettes will kill her, sure, but what's the point in sticking around?

There she was in the plush interior of her room at the Hotel Bel-Air, a hotel ten times classier than this dump, with tasteful floral curtains and a puffy leather sofa, and all she wanted before bed was a cigarette. Just a drag, two puffs, and then she could turn in for the night. Is that so much to ask, something to steady the nerves? She took the pack from its hiding place, looked around for a place to smoke. She could have gone outside, she supposed, but it was a long walk to the elevator and then across the lobby and out onto the patio, and she was tired, having traveled all day. All she was going to have was one puff, maybe two, so she stepped into the bathroom, but there was a sign on the sink that clearly read *no smoking*, and a smoke detector on the ceiling, so she went back into the bedroom and opened the window. Maybe if she kind of half leaned out to exhale, she could just smoke in her room like a civilized person. This whole crusade against smokers was ridiculous, anyway. It was a charade, a witch hunt. She didn't live to be this old just to be persecuted by a bunch of humorless zealots.

She put her thumb and forefinger into the pack, rooted out a cigarette. Her mouth watered a little at the dark scent of tobacco that rose from the foil interior. She put the cigarette between her lips. How many times had she done this in the last fifty years? Thousands? Literally hundreds of thousands? An average of thirty cigarettes a day for over fifty years, that's an easy half million cigarettes. *Half a million.* It is the single defining gesture of her life, to place a cigarette between her lips, to light it. She has done this on five of the seven continents of the world, has done it at sea level, at thirty-five thousand feet, on an airplane, in a desert. She has smoked a cigarette in the capital of every major European country. Cigarettes are her landmarks. They are the second hand on the clock of her life. Out of the thousand-odd pictures that have been taken of her in the last fifty years, only seven show her without a cigarette, either in her mouth or between her fingers. Only seven.

She flicked the lighter, cheap, disposable, and a blue flame sprung up, licked the tip of her smoke. With the first puff she knew she had done the right thing, as nicotine was absorbed by the soft tissue of her lungs, as chemicals in her brain were triggered, releasing a flood of relaxing endorphins. Sure, there was tightness, a certain sense of suffocation, but it was manageable. *Can you blame me*, she thinks, *for wanting a moment of peace, serenity?* This is what cigarettes were for her, a respite. A moment out of time, where everything felt balanced. She exhaled a cloud of smoke, placed the cigarette to her lips. How many times during Joe's illness had she taken refuge in a cloud of blue-tinged smoke, camouflaged by it, hiding behind a literal smokescreen from all the pain, all the humorless projections of disaster? In the end what was left that resembled her old sweet love? In the end what remained of the vibrant, intelligent man who'd smiled at her while she ate ice cream? He was a shell, a tenth-generation Xerox, degraded, smudged, illegible.

Above her head the smoke alarm started wailing. The volume of it, the sudden shriek, almost gave her a heart attack, and for a few moments she had no idea what was happening. It felt like the end of the world, the dire sonic beeping of the apocalypse. Then it hit her, what it was, and she threw the cigarette out the window, started waving at the air. If she could stop the sound, if she could silence it quickly, maybe no one would notice. Never mind it was just before eleven and the hotel was as silent as a tomb. Never mind that the piercing shriek of the alarm could probably be heard in the basement, she was convinced that if she could silence it fast, she could escape detection. What she didn't count on was the fact that in a control room somewhere a light had gone on that corresponded to her room. What she didn't count on was that at the first cry of the alarm an automated call went out to the dispatch center of the local fire department, and that as she waved frantically at the ceiling with a folded magazine, fire engines were already on their way.

When they arrived, when seven burly firemen in heavy, all-weather gear, carrying oxygen tanks and axes, burst into her room, they found it empty. They were accompanied by the hotel manager, a fastidious man in a designer suit, who rung his hands and fretted. He told them to *be careful, please.* The drapes were delicate. The furniture was antique. The firemen checked the bathroom, looked under the bed, but there was no sign of Doris Henry, the guest who had checked into Room 314 this evening, accompanied by her eldest son. It was the hotel manager who noticed the thin plastic line leading from the boxy oxygen machine as it threaded across the brown Berber carpet and into the closet. It was the hotel manager who stepped forward, calling *Mrs. Henry? Mrs. Henry?* and opened the door to the closet, only to find Doris Henry crouched down behind the ironing board, wide eyed, terrified, her oxygen line looped over her ears and under her nose. She had forgotten she was wearing it, had lit a cigarette an inch from the flow of pure, flammable air. Dumb luck was all that had kept her from going up in flames. Dumb luck and the strong, dispersing wind from the air-conditioner. Gazing up at the gang of hulking firemen, Doris Henry was convinced that they were the gatekeepers of hell sent to bring her down. As they reached in to help her up, as the paramedics stepped forward to check her vitals, she told herself that these men had come to kidnap her, to take her hostage. She was certain her sons had called the authorities and had her committed, that her life from here on out would be lived in institutions. Doris Henry had left the confines of rational thought. She was born again into a world of confusion and paranoia. All the recognizable markers had been removed, and she was, for the first time in years, at sea, truly unmoored. And everything that came after threatened to be unrecognizable.

Born again. What a beautiful sentiment. Who doesn't want a second chance? And all we have to do to get there is renounce the past and beg forgiveness.

TWO DAYS LATER they are back at the airport, Doris and Scott and David, the last remaining members of the original Henry family. Scott is wearing sunglasses indoors. He is listening to music on his iPod and speaking only in monosyllables. David is similarly subdued, checking his e-mail on his Black-Berry. Doris can tell that he feels naked without his wife and children to protect him. The last time the three of them were alone together was in New York, for Joe's sixtieth birthday.

As they're sitting in the boarding area waiting for their plane—surrounded by fat people, men with mustaches, screaming bratty children—a company of soldiers disembarks from a neighboring gate. They are veterans returning from the Gulf, men and women in uniforms, some in wheelchairs, all of them missing an arm or a leg or both. All the bustle of the airport dies down. Doris watches them go, her heart in her throat. This is what she feels like, a veteran of some foreign war, missing some vital part of herself, learning to live off-balance, reaching out to people only to find her hand isn't there, her arm. In the waiting area a man stands and starts to clap. Soon everyone is standing, applauding. *What are they clapping for?* Doris wonders. It seems depraved. *We send our sons and daughters to fight and they get blown to hell and we applaud, as if to say, good show.* It's sick.

You survive things in this world that you have no business sur-
viving and people clap you on the back and say *well done*, like
there's some kind of future, like you are moving on to bigger
and better things instead of just looking for a dark hole to curl
up in. What happens after the ovation stops? Where will these
people go? And if the war continues and our children keep getting blown to hell, then we will one day live in a society where
an entire generation is missing something. We will be a nation
of paraplegics. And who will take care of me then?

On the plane she drinks scotch from little bottles. Scott has
won the coin toss and is sitting in the back of the plane, while
David sits next to her in first class, pretending to sleep. She
wonders where he came from, this officious, corporate man-
child of hers. He is nothing like her, nothing like his father.
He was such an angry boy, always smashing things, always hitting other kids and running away. Where did it come from,
that rage? And then, as quickly as it had arisen, some time
around college it disappeared. He bottled up his anger, trans-
forming into this tight-lipped withholder, always in control,
and so smug. The way he talks to her, like she's a child, worse
than a child, a retard, someone incapable of understanding the
simplest points. Does he think she's deaf? She can hear the disdain in his voice when he calls (which is rarely), the guarded
affect, like she's a ticking bomb and he will only get so close.
You give birth to a child, you nurse it and raise it only to have
it turn on you once you are no longer needed. To turn, not
with hatred or venom, but ambivalence; how did she end up
in this place again? Sixty years later and here she is being ignored by someone she loves, someone she needs. When she
looks at David all she sees is a wall, towering, impenetrable,
and in a high parapet, a solitary guard looking down with insulated disdain.

Fuck him, she thinks. This is her approach. The best defense is a good offense. Do unto others before they do unto you. She sips her scotch and adjusts the oxygen line under her nose. Every twenty minutes a flight attendant comes by to check it, make sure the tank is still full. She tries not to think about New York, the chaos of it, the import, all the relatives she will have to face at the memorial, their hangdog faces, their hollow, sympathetic words. She didn't want to do this. It was the kids' idea. Every day is a memorial service to her, and besides, she doesn't want to share her husband with anyone, even in death. She and Joe always kept a level of distance between themselves and their families. Even their kids were kept at arm's length once they left home. They were two people of singular focus. But once he got sick the cocoon fell apart. Joe's family stepped in and tried to wrestle him away from her. They swooped in with their constant visits, their calculated kindness. Once he was in the nursing home and out of the house, he became exposed, an easy target. This is how she feels. Like her poor, sick husband became the pawn in some kind of demented family power struggle. And now, in death, she knows they will try to claim him fully, to steal his memory, turn him into something he wasn't. They will deny her her proper place, her proper respect.

Scott comes up from the back.

"Just checking in," he says. "Everything okay?"

She raises her eyebrows.

"You'd think your brother hadn't had a good night's sleep in twenty years," she says, looking at David, his body curled and pivoting away from her, eyeshades on, earplugs in, his head turned to the window.

Scott shrugs, eyeing the collection of tiny bottles lined up on his mother's tray table. He is easier to place. He has his father's romanticism and his mother's cynicism. A little lost maybe. A little unfocused. Less judgmental certainly, and yet this son, too, is lining up against her. She can feel it. He's stopped looking her in the eye, a sure sign that some dark conspiracy is brewing. They will make their play in New York, whatever it is. She can feel them aligning against her, ganging up. Now that their father is gone, they will cut her loose, leave her to fend for herself. They will put her in a home and throw away the key. The thought of it makes her lungs constrict. It is a terrible thing to find yourself slowly suffocating to death, to get winded simply by sitting up in the morning. A flight of stairs, forget it. She may as well be stuck at the bottom of a mountain. Time is not her ally. She knows that. Her lungs may as well be a fuse, slowly burning. She is right on that edge. A bad cold is all it would take to push her over, bronchitis, pneumonia. There is so much panic at the thought of it. She remembers waking up on the respirator, the invasive pressure of the tube down her throat, her hands strapped down so she couldn't pluck it loose. She remembers the transition to the oxygen mask, and then the startled panic when they tried to remove it, the way she felt like she couldn't get enough air in the open room, no matter how hard she tried. This is what it feels like to drown on dry land. You suck and you suck, but nothing comes. Her body has become her enemy. This is what old age is, the betrayal of the physical. She knows now that, as designs go, the human animal is deeply flawed. We are like tins of meat, set to expire on a certain date, our bodies spoiling, our brains breaking down.

It is proof of the non-existence of God.

She saw it in the nursing home whenever she went to visit Joe. The men died young, the women went crazy. She remembers hallways filled with drooling old ladies in their wheelchairs, the clock slowly ticking away the hours, maddeningly perky music playing over the loudspeakers. She remembers the forced jocularity of nurses, the removal of human dignity as you succumb to an infantilizing institutional existence, the return to baby food, diapers changed every hour. A nursing home is like kindergarten, except the joy of youth has been replaced by the creaky surrender of old age. If these are her options, she will take suffocation. Except she is scared, and the fear keeps her up at night. She doesn't want to die. She's not ready, and yet what is she living for?

She thinks of the memorial service, all the distant cousins come to pay their respects. *They* will be there, of course. Her *cousins*. Her mother's other daughters. They will cluck their tongues and say *how awful*. All these years and they still don't know the truth. *That would shut them up*, she thinks. To know that she is really their sister. What a scandal. Doris is the only one left who knows the real story. Think of their faces, their scandalized confusion, disbelief turning to horror. *I am one of you*. The pilot comes on to announce that they are beginning their final descent into the New York area, and for the first time in months, Doris finds herself looking forward to something. There will be chaos, anarchy. Let them all try to take her husband away from her. She will rise from the ashes and smite them all, because she has the truth on her side.

She still has the power to surprise.

FEBRUARY IN NEW YORK. The temperature drops. Arctic Canadian air sinks down through the Hudson Valley, sweeping across the river from New Jersey. Picture the glacial emptiness of Eleventh Avenue, as wide and foreboding as the tundra, steam rising from the moist, hungry mouth of the Holland Tunnel. Walking the streets, your cheeks freeze from the wind-chill. Snow falls in the dark of the night, white, angelic, and, as if by magic, turns black by morning. In fifth-floor walk-ups and elevator buildings across town, radiators clang and rattle, keeping people awake. The subways are like ovens, cooking commuters alive in their heavy coats. When the temperature drops below freezing, the normally kinetic city speeds up even more. Surfaces harden, shrink. The city becomes brittle and everything in it turns to a smooth, frictionless pinball shooting through slick corridors, racing against time and weather. Riding into Manhattan in the back of a cab, David feels the smug satisfaction of a Californian. He feels the moral superiority that comes with a healthy tan. He doesn't miss New York at all, doesn't miss the competition for cabs, the crowding, the daily brawl for space, respect. He doesn't miss the zero-degree winters, the humid summers. Once you leave New York, you discover that life doesn't have to be a fight. Such a thought would never occur to you otherwise, but standing in a green field or a small town, it is a revelation, not unlike a religious epiphany. There *is* such a thing as privacy. When he first went West, he was stunned by the wide-open spaces, vast stretches of land where a human being could actually hear himself think. Not that L.A. doesn't have its problems, the traffic, the smog, but unlike New York, in Los Angeles you are not jammed into a sea of sweating, cursing bodies every time you leave the house. There is distance, privacy, respect. You sit safely inside your car, moving in measured intervals. It's not like New York, where three times a day you are surrounded, fleeced and cursed.

They take the BQE to the Fifty-ninth Street Bridge. The New York skyline rises up to meet them, and despite his smug veneer, David feels a swell of something like excitement rise up in his chest. The city has that kind of energy, like it or not. A sense of activity, possibility. There is also a different kind of stirring, this one more localized in the region below his belt. He has had some of the best sex of his life in New York, and most of it recently. Crossing the East River, his body responds to the signals his eyes are sending, the erect corporate towers rising before him, all that rock-hard concrete. It has nothing to do with his mind. The fact is, he has conditioned his body over the last year, week in, week out, to sense when Joy is near. His body knows that a five-hour plane ride is the first step to a night of extreme passion. It knows that descending from the bridge onto pitted city streets is a precursor to a certain animal release. New York is where he lets it all go—his heartbreak, his fear, his need for control—and though consciously he knows that this time is different, his body wants what it wants. He is like a rat that has been trained to salivate every time a red light goes on. And yet when you're living a lie, it is important to establish boundaries, rules. There is no place for spontaneity. This is the key to success. When you're trying to live two different lives, every move must be planned down to the smallest detail. Which is why this time he cannot see her, cannot let her know he's here. The risk is too great. The chance for discovery. When you're building a house of cards, you don't open a window.

But the problem is, he *needs* her, his second wife, needs her silliness and her youth, her physicality. Now more than ever. His father is dead, and he is on a journey from hell, and deep in his bones he feels that if he could just spend an hour with Joy, listen to her giggle, watch her shave her legs, flirt, he could get through this. He wants more than anything to be restored, reborn, and this is her specialty. She is a magician, a hypnotist, an alchemist. Partly it is her disconnection from the rest of his life. She is his secret, shared with nobody. He is not himself with her. He is a better him, a weightless him. With Joy he has no past. With her there is no chaos. Needy alcoholic mother? She doesn't exist. Dead father? Around Joy he never has to talk about it, never has to think about it. America is the land of reinvention, after all. It is a country of second chances, of makeovers, and Joy is his new beginning.

To this end, he has invented stories. As far as she's concerned, David is an only child whose parents both died when he was in college. He is an orphan who rose above the tragedies of his life to become a successful businessman, the embodiment of the American Dream, a noble human being, an achiever. This is the nature of his secret life. *Everybody should have one*, he thinks. *An escape, a place they can go to be someone different. Life is a cage, a set of railroad tracks, and before you know it—as you make choices, job, family—you find yourself locked in, unable to deviate from the course you're on. Having a secret frees you. Give a man a key and his prison becomes his home.* It sounds insane, he realizes, but it is his second wife who makes him appreciate his first. His secret life in New York allows him to enjoy his normal life in Los Angeles, truly appreciate it. When you are not tied to one woman, the women in your life become easier to love, easier to tolerate and forgive, their idiosyncrasies and habits.

For example, Joy pees with the door open. The first time she did this, David was shocked. Tracey wouldn't even brush her teeth in front of him, but sitting on Joy's bed watching her pad into the bathroom, pull down her panties, listening to her tinkle even as she continued to talk in that excited ramble of hers, he felt both the excitement of the new (mixed with a certain level of arousal) and also a deeper appreciation for Tracey, a love of the old. Someone once told him, *when you are given a choice between two things, choose both.* And this is what he's done. He has decided to have it all: a smart, modest grown woman and an impulsive, passionate young one. In this way, his life has become an English lit essay test: *Compare and Contrast.* And the two women couldn't be more different. Where Tracey is tall with brown hair, Joy is a tiny blonde. Where Tracey is a control enthusiast, Joy is delightfully unorganized, chronically late. Alone either trait might be infuriating, but combined they balance each other out. Being married to two women has made David more tolerant, he likes to tell himself. More patient. And personal hygiene is not the only difference. Tracey has always been cautious with money. She had her first savings account when she was five. Joy, on the other hand, has wads of cash crammed into every pocket. At the end of a spin cycle, her washing machine is filled with wet bills and loose change.

Tracey is physically reserved, shying away from public displays of affection. Joy has been known to throw herself at David on crowded streets, jumping into his arms and wrapping her legs around his waist. She can put on lipstick with her cleavage like Molly Ringwald in *The Breakfast Club*, has shoved her hand down David's pants on a crowded street, grabbing his dick. The differences don't stop there. Take motherhood. Where her children are concerned, Tracey is a woman with a plan. She was researching schools when Christopher was still a newborn, had David saving for college before Chris was five. By contrast, Joy can't think more than an hour ahead. In her mind, *tomorrow* is a strange word in a South Pacific language that, loosely translated, means *later on today*. She likes to strap Sam to her body and go, take a trip, have an adventure. She believes that things will work out. It has taken David a few months, but he is beginning to come around to her point of view.

You have to have faith.

The taxi pulls up in front of the Waldorf-Astoria. Around them, Park Avenue slumbers under blackened snow, dreaming of April tulips. The doorman comes out to get their bags. Scott helps Doris out of the cab. She is shaky, fumbling. She stands on the corner trying to catch her breath. It is seven o'clock at night. Her tiny, hungry breaths form shrunken white clouds in front of her face. David got them a corporate rate for three rooms. He could have expensed it—the company doesn't care—but he believes in paying what you owe.

"The Waldorf-Astoria, Mom," he says. "Didn't you always want to stay here?"

She shrugs, lips puckered, exhaling. Watching her struggle for air, David feels that combined human wavering, a simultaneous desire to rescue her from illness and push her down a flight of stairs. He spent so many years watching his father die, watching that agonizing slow-motion erosion, that the idea of investing another five (ten?) years observing his mother's slow decline is enough to make him want to shove her in front of a truck.

Doris says she's tired from the trip and wants to lie down, so they help her to her room. Then, as if by unspoken agreement,

David and Scott head down to the bar. They get a table, order a couple of drinks. David can't remember the last time he
was alone with his brother. He has been a married man for so
long, always surrounded by a blur of children's bodies. Ten years
maybe. God. He studies his brother's face. They are getting
older, the both of them. Their faces have broadened. Wrinkles
have appeared. How does it happen? In his mind David is still
ten years old. His children might as well be his peers. It's crazy
how you can be a grown-up for so long and still feel like an im-
postor. Even though his father has been reduced to ash, David
still doesn't believe it is possible to die. Actually die. You reach
the end of your life and then what? Nothing. Silence. Space.
The idea of it is too terrifying to contemplate.

"Everything okay?" asks Scott, who seems pale, a little
jumpy.

"You're kidding, right?"

The waitress comes with their drinks. David is having beer.
Scott ordered tequila. He raises his glass.

"To Pop," he says. They clink glasses.

"Still listening to other people's phone calls?" asks David after a moment's silence.

Scott sips his drink.

"They offered me a promotion—floor supervisor—I turned
it down. I like my voices to be anonymous. I don't want to have
to deal with real people, personalities, office politics—Frank's a
pedophile, Sarah's on heroin—I don't want to know the people
I work with that well. They make you supervisor and you never
have a moment's peace again."

David studies his brother like he's a strange form of undersea
life, some kind of bulbous, translucent cephalopod.

"Is that what matters to you most," he says, "peace?"

"What most people don't understand," Scott says, "is that

peace and quiet are not the same thing. Everybody always treats them like they are, *peace and quiet*, but peace is a state of mind, and quiet is...not always helpful. We grew up in New York City. Too much silence makes me crazy."

David smiles.

"Try living at my house for ten days and see if you still think quiet is overrated."

Scott chews an ice cube, brow furrowed. He has never been good at small talk. He takes things too seriously. You can see it on his face. He doesn't understand that David was making a joke, trying to lighten the mood.

"Sure," says Scott, "too much is too much, but I'm starting to think that life is about seeing yourself in other people. All the voices I hear, people's problems. They're all me, you know. The housewife who's not sure if baby aspirin is safe for her baby, the mechanic who calls poison control because he accidentally drank a bottle of motor oil."

"How do you accidentally drink a bottle of motor oil?"

"I hear these people, their problems, and I—I want to believe that we're all in it together, you know? Life. Society. We've set up these governments, these countries, a whole architecture of social systems and rules, all to try to create some kind of harmony. Democracy, right? A system of checks and balances. We're supposed to protect each other. This is what I do. It matters. I am the man on the phone who makes sure everything is being handled correctly, that you are getting the help you need. I listen to your calls. I make sure you're not being lied to, misled. I am there to assure quality, to give you peace of mind. And I like that. Say what you want. Career advancement, blah, blah, blah. I like my job. The world needs people like me. I talked to this guy, this limo driver, who said, *We can't all be Brad Pitt. Some of us have to clean the toilets.*"

David mulls the yeasty aftertaste of his beer. His brother doesn't sound exactly sane right now. To David's ears he is like one of those late-night radio hosts, high on Benzedrine, ranting about secret governments.

"And what about girls?" he says. "Mom says you found another lunatic."

Scott sits back, sighs.

"They find me. I'm beginning to think I've been implanted with some kind of homing device, like an ear tag you see on a big cat on the Nature Channel, and these women are just honing in. How else do you explain it?"

"Well, for one thing, you like crazy girls."

"Absolutely. Absolutely." He sips his drink. "Do you want to know why?"

David thinks about it. Part of him doesn't want to hear another word. Once you know someone else's problems, you become responsible somehow for helping them solve them, and the last thing David needs right now is more problems. He signals to the waitress for another beer. He remembers when they were kids, the girl Scott had his first crush on, Sally Embrecht. How Scott, moon-eyed, puppy-dog smitten, stole his mother's jewelry and gave it to Sally. How he wrote her love letters, and how Sally's dad called the principal, who called Doris, who sat Scott down and said, *What the fuck are you doing?* This is Scott's M.O. In his world there's no such thing as halfway.

"Tell me," says David.

"The crazy ones are easy to read," says Scott. "They fall hard and fast. They flirt. Everything about them is oversized, like those books you get with large print. When they're sad they're *really* sad. When they're happy they're manic. Sure, they can turn on a dime, but there's never any mystery to it. I mean, other than the underlying—that seductive funk of unavailability. It makes the fucking hair stand up on the back of my neck just talking about it. With the crazy ones you never have to wonder—do they like me? Not in the beginning. That comes later."

The waitress brings two more drinks.

"God bless you," says Scott. He sits back, rubs his eyes. Looking at him, David thinks, *Our lives are set, our fates. There is nothing that can happen to knock us off the paths we're on.* What David doesn't realize is that these things are not always your choice—which direction you take, what happens to you along the way. But then this has always been his problem. He is way too invested in his own sense of control.

"Well," he says, "maybe you should find a nice girl for a change. Somebody boring."

But the look on Scott's face says he's not sure they exist.

"How's Tracey?" Scott says. "The marriage. Three kids."

David purses his lips. *Typical,* he thinks, *I say boring and he thinks of Tracey.* He should say something, but he doesn't. This is how it is in their family. Their relationships are all based on things they won't say out loud.

"Great," he says. "I mean, it's chaos, don't get me wrong, but that works for us."

"Don't you ever get tired of it, the same thing day in day out?"

David laughs.

"Believe me," he says, "if you only knew. My life is full of adventure."

Scott's expression says *yeah, right.* Somewhere along the way, they got so awkward around each other. Brothers, but with the body language of strangers. David can't put his finger on when that happened. They used to be close. Growing up, in high school, they told each other everything. Now you could measure the distance between them in light-years. This is what happens when people grow apart. Life happens to them and before you know it, you're no longer speaking the same language. All your points of reference disappear. It's like someone from Omaha talking to someone from Budapest, trying to give directions like they still live in the same town. *Make a left at the post office, go ten blocks, turn right at the French restaurant.* And you expect to end up in the same place? It's madness. And yet deep down who knows you better—the real you—than your brother? Even in disguise, even after all these years, fundamentally aren't you the same people?

"So," says Scott, two drinks in him, feeling better, "what are we gonna do?"

"About what?"

"About her."

They sit in silence for a minute.

"She'll never agree to go into a home," says David.

"I know, but she almost blew up her hotel."

David runs a hand over the back of his neck. There is a headache starting there, threatening to climb into his brain.

"What does she want?"

"Who cares what she wants?" says Scott. "She's drinking herself to death, smoking with emphysema. It's crazy-person behavior, so why does everyone keep asking her what she wants? She's a danger to herself, that much is clear. And after the hotel thing, I'd have to say others, too. We should just dump her in a home and throw away the key."

David thinks about this. He wonders why life is increasingly filled with impossible choices.

"Maybe she'll just...," he starts, but doesn't finish.

"What?"

Die, thinks David. *Maybe she'll just die.*

They finish their drinks. It's eight-thirty. Scott says he's going to try to catch a movie. He asks David if he wants to come.

"No. I think I'll take a walk, clear my head."

The two brothers part ways on the sidewalk, their breath commingling in clouds. There is an awkward pat on the shoulder, a stiff good-bye, and then they are walking off in two different directions. This is the story of their lives. They're like magnets of repellent polarities that can get only so close before some kind of invisible field pushes them apart. Scott heads downtown. David walks northwest, toward the park, his hands jammed down into his pockets, scarf fluffed beneath his chin. Everything around him is brake lights, yellow taxis. An arid wind blows across the park, sucking moisture from his face. His lips chap. He takes out his cell phone, calls home.

"I wanted to say hi to the kids," he says. "Are they around?"

The sound of Tracey chewing crosses the miles—celery maybe, a carrot. She's on a health-food kick these days, trying to rescue her figure.

"Yes, we're having a mutiny about dinner. I'm not sure we're really in control here, you and me. I think the kids are making all the rules. The trick is not to let them see you sweat."

David crosses Madison Avenue. He feels the cold settle in the base of his spine. It makes him jittery, nervous.

"It's like five degrees here," he says.

"Is there snow? I miss snow."

He switches the phone to his other hand. His right thumb feels frozen.

"There's snow, but it's that black snow. The gutters are slushy lakes."

"I miss that."

"Give me a break. You hate the cold."

"I know, but don't you ever miss something you hate? I tell

you what I miss really. I miss the act of hating it. Hating things makes us who we are. Like now I hate traffic. I hate smog. I hate all the actress wannabes who screw up my coffee order at Starbucks. My hates are L.A. hates. I used to have New York hates. It's funny the way things change."

"Can I talk to Christopher?" asks David. At Sixty-first Street he turns left, heading for Fifth Avenue. The cold is in his legs, his toes. He can't feel his nose. Tracey puts the phone down, goes to get her son. David waits, the sound of his own breath heavy in his ears. He crosses Fifth Avenue, and there it is: the park. Buses pass him, heading downtown. A man in six coats pushing a shopping cart rattles past. David always feels weird talking to his children on the phone. It feels so grown up, and they're these little people. With kids you should talk into tin cans tied together with string. You should pass crumpled notes from hand to hand while the teacher is talking. He hears the sound of running feet, of Christopher and Chloe fighting over who gets to talk first.

"Daddy, Daddy, hi." It is Chloe, breathless.

"Hey, baby."

"I ate a clam."

"That's great."

"Clams are shellfish. Jews can't eat shellfish."

"They're not supposed to, but it's not like they're allergic."

"Like Becky Two Teeth last year. How she ate a mussel and her whole face swolled up. She had to go to the emergency room."

"Did you go to school today, pumpkin?"

"Duh."

He hates it when she does that, treats him like he's stupid. It's a quality she inherited from her grandmother.

"How did you do?" he asks.

"I learned how airplanes fly. Do you know how airplanes fly?"

He has no idea.

"Tell me," he says.

"There's lift and drag and the shape of the wing. That's why they have to go so fast, so they don't fall out of the sky."

"Right. Sure."

David walks south along the park. It is a dark void, an urban abscess. Overhead, the trees are bare, strung with white Christmas lights. This is the catch-22 of New York. Just when you decide you can't stand it for another second, something magical happens. He wishes his kids could be here with him now, seeing it, snow, winter. He pictures their excitement, the discovery of new things.

"Let me talk to your brother," he says.

"Okay, Daddy. Bye, Daddy."

He hears her give the phone to Christopher.

"He wants to talk to you," she says formally. His heart swells, threatens to burst. They are such tiny ambassadors to the human race.

"Where are you?" his son wants to know. He, too, is chewing something.

"I'm in New York. What are you eating?"

"Raisins."

"Since when do we eat raisins before dinner?"

"Mommy said no more cookies, but fruit is okay. Is raisins a fruit?"

"They're grapes," says David. He has reached the base of the park. Horse-drawn carriages idle in the cold, the horses restless, inured to the chill, waiting for passengers who won't come. Not on a night like this. The air around David is filled with the earthy stink of horseshit. To his right, the Plaza Hotel shines like a diamond. He should go in, drink something warm, and yet, before him, Fifth Avenue stretches out its moneyed arm, beckoning. He crosses Fifty-ninth Street, heading south.

"How can they be grapes?" says Christopher. "They're raisins."

"They used to be grapes. That's what happens. Somebody picks the grapes and dries them out and they turn into raisins."

"Who?" his son asks, and David can hear the skepticism in his voice, like maybe his father is trying to fool him, embarrass him in front of the class if the subject ever comes up. How he will stand up and announce in a strong, confident voice that raisins used to be grapes and all the other kids will laugh.

"I don't know," says David. "Farmers."

Christopher chews.

"Did you say your prayers yet?" David asks him.

"Before bed. You're supposed to say them right before you go to sleep. Don't you know anything?"

David is at Fifty-fifth Street now, moving fast. The walk is warming him up. He is sweating under the arms, even as the cold air burns his lungs.

"Who taught you to do that?" he wants to know. "To pray?"

"Nobody taught me. I just do it."

"Did you see it on TV, though? One of your friends?"

"Jesus is God's son. He died and now he lives in the sky with Grandpa and Blossom."

Blossom is the corgi they had when Christopher was five. She was hit by a car, had to be put to sleep.

"Who told you about Jesus? Do they teach you that at school?"

In the kitchen, Christopher is lying on the floor, his feet propped up against the wall. He is knocking the back of his head softly against the floor because it feels good. There is a bag of raisins on his stomach. Tracey comes in.

Christopher says, "Jesus...no, that was Peter. He was an apostle. That means he was Jesus's friend...uh-huh...No, you go to confession and say you're sorry and God forgives you...I don't know...the Holy Ghost..."

"Who are you talking to?" Tracey asks.

Christopher covers the mouthpiece.

"Dad." Then into the phone: "But you have to really be sorry. You can't just pretend, because God knows."

David crosses Forty-eighth Street. He shouldn't be doing this, heading south. He has promised himself he won't go below Forty-second Street, but his legs seem to have a mind of their own.

"Does it make you feel better?" he wants to know. "When you pray?"

David takes a raisin out of the bag, tries to balance it on his nose.

"God likes it when you talk to him," he says. "I think he gets lonely."

David feels like there's a hole in his heart the size of a ham. His father has been dead for three months. He weighed ninety-one pounds in the end, died mumbling, fists clenched.

"It's nice of you," says David, "to want to keep God company."

"Did you know that people in India worship cows?" says Christopher. "They don't eat them with ketchup like everybody else."

"Some people," says David, "think cows are holy."

"I think they taste good."

David reaches Forty-second Street and stops. *This is it*, he thinks, *the point of no return*. He feels like he is negotiating something here. He wants to understand his son's faith, because deep down he envies it. As a rational man from a liberal East Coast city, David doesn't know how to believe in a higher being. In his mind, it is something that yokels do, alcoholics and lunatics. He has that Ivy League prejudice, the same as his mother. There are book smarts and common sense, and then there is the self-righteous zealotry of the undereducated. Picture the Taliban in their cutting robes, roaming the countryside smashing record players and stoning women. Picture David Koresh with his baker's dozen teenage brides holed up in a fortified compound, firing automatic weapons and speaking in tongues. Religion is the surrender of reason to hope—at least this is how he's always seen it. But what a lonely world it is when one day you wake up and realize that the list of things you don't believe in is greater than the list of things you do.

David is a corporate vice president. He reads the *New York Times*. He listens to NPR. He knows that we are living in a time of spiritual hardening, where those who believe are waging war against those who don't. It is a war that David feels has snuck up on him before he has had time to choose sides. This makes it a dangerous time to start thinking about God. Now whatever questions he might have, whatever yearning for a more spiritual life, are politically polarizing. *Whatever happened to the privacy of a man's beliefs*, wonders David, *where an otherwise rational person could maintain a quiet faith in what's holy? When did religion become an arms race? If you don't believe*, they tell you, *you will be left behind. You will be destroyed by the might of what's holy, Insha'allah.* These are the stakes you face these days, salvation or annihilation. All or nothing. They are symptoms of grief. That wounded impulse to lash out, strike back. And yet when did grief become the prevailing motivator in this world? From suicide bombers to terror victims, earthquake casualties to abortionists, when did death become the global obsession?

He thinks this, and yet isn't David Henry also overcome by

grief? His father is dead and he is hurrying downtown, shivering with cold, and what is going through his mind if not the sum total of life's deepest question—*Why are we here? What is the point of living if everyone has to die?*—all of it building to an irresistible impulse to pray.

Traffic roars around him, exhaust clouds rising up like jet trails. The cold is an animal, teeth clamped down on his face. David steps into the street. Tracey gets back on the phone and they talk about logistics. The memorial is in two days. She and the kids will fly out tomorrow. David will meet them at the airport.

"Are you okay?" she wants to know. "You sound weird."

"I'm fine. Just a little tired."

"What was all the stuff with Chris about Jesus?"

"I don't know. We never talk to him about it. I just—I wanted to know what he thinks."

"Should we be worried?"

David crosses Thirty-seventh Street, has to run the last few feet to avoid being hit by a truck. He is worried about so many things, there doesn't seem to be room for anything else. His head feels like a beehive sometimes and, though she means well, Tracey can be like a stick, stirring him up. She's a worrier, a planner, trying to map out every possible contingency. They have an earthquake kit and a flash-flood kit and a drought kit. Her backup plans have backup plans. They live with the possibility of disaster looming over them at every turn. Joy, on the other hand, is fearless. To her the threat of disaster is what makes life fun. For David, a man with two million dollars in insurance, there is a desire to let it all go for once, to free himself of fear, to stop expecting the worst.

"I'm sure he'll be fine," says David. "I know we have this big-city prejudice, but plenty of bright, successful, well-balanced people believe in God. It's not a sign of inbreeding."

"I know. And it's fine, whatever he wants. I just—I don't know where he gets it from, if somebody's teaching him this stuff. Do ten-year-olds join cults? I don't want him to end up at some airport handing out daisies."

He tells her not to worry, says good night. He puts his phone away. His left hand is an ice cube. He keeps walking. That's the great thing about New York, the thing David still loves, how you walk everywhere. How it's not unreasonable to go a hundred blocks if the feeling is in you. He hits Twenty-third Street, passes the Flatiron Building, hits Eighteenth, crosses Fourteenth. He is in dangerous territory now. She could be anywhere, Joy, her friends. He heads west, winding through brick town houses into the heart of the Village. He remembers every time he had to visit his dad in the hospital, tubes running out of him, shunt in his neck. He remembers seeing his father sprawled out in bed, skeletal, unconscious, his bedclothes thrown back, and the sight of his father's shriveled penis, his sad, white pubic hair, was like a physical blow. *I sprang out of that miserable thing*, he thought, *that sad, flaccid organ.* How many times did David have to help his father up off the toilet? How many times did he have to drop everything and race to the emergency room? It was exhausting, demoralizing. In the end they took Joe's dignity, his humanity, and left behind this pissing, shitting human shell. David's children have more control over their bodies, their lives, more self-determination.

He reaches Bank Street, takes it to Bleecker. What would he think if he knew that his parents had their first date on this corner, in the bakery that used to be a bird store, that used to be an Italian restaurant, that used to be a butcher shop, that was once a café? This is the way life is in big cities. We are always passing ghosts without realizing. Everything connects, intersects. There are echoes in life, rhymes. On this very spot where David now

stands waiting for the light to change, his mother sat at an outdoor table eating ice cream. His father smiled his pirate smile
and touched her hand, the moment electric, expansive. It was
the beginning of everything and it happened right here where
he is standing. How many tears would he shed if he could see
them there now, the tears freezing to his face like icicles of
grief? David crosses Abington Square Park. He is a block away
now. He can almost taste her, his secret wife, can smell the
baby-down of his son's head, his secret love child. He feels like
an appliance that's been left in the on position for too long, a
blender or Cuisinart, gears grinding. His skull feels fractured.
There is that deep bone ache, that nausea, that powerful sensation of wrongness. Where does it come from? What does it
mean?

He stands across from their apartment building on Jane
Street, shivering in a doorway. When he and Joy were looking
for an apartment, David chose this place because it was around
the corner from the apartment he grew up in. He didn't tell
her that, of course. There was something about starting a new
life, a secret life, so close to his childhood home that was irresistible. This way he could keep the truth and the lie together,
side by side. This way he could remember who he was, even
as he pretended to be someone different. Across the street, Joy's
building glows like a pair of headlights racing toward him in the
dark. The doorman is bundled up in the lobby reading a magazine. David searches the facade for their window, sixth floor,
second from the right. The light is on. He is so close to this
other life, all he has to do is cross the street. He could disappear if he wanted, switch tracks. He could tell Joy he is done
with L.A., start a new life here in New York. He could change
his phone number, buy new clothes, never look back. No one
would ever know. You think it's the hardest thing in the world,

to change your life, but really it's as easy as falling downhill. All you have to do is let go.

He takes out his phone, dials her number. He sees her appear in the window, cross the room. She picks up the phone. His heart is in his throat.

"Hello?" says Joy, answering.

He doesn't speak.

"David?" she says, reading his name on her caller ID. The sound of her voice makes him want to cry.

"Am I waking you?" he asks.

"No," she says. "I just got back from the supermarket. Sam has a little fever. He's been really cranky all day. How's L.A.? It's so cold here I was thinking maybe we should get on a plane, come see you."

"I'm in San Diego actually, for a conference. It's pretty boring."

His nose is running, great liquid rivers of snot rolling frigidly toward his mouth.

"I miss you," she says. "It sucks you couldn't come."

"I know," he says. "I'm sorry."

He can see her in the window. She's wearing a camisole and a pair of his pajama pants. She is small breasted, hard bodied. She does Pilates four times a week. Her muscles are clean, defined. When she sits on top of him, her body bearing down, she arches her back and he can count her ribs, trace them with his fingers.

"Are you okay?" she asks him. "You sound weird."

When she says this he has an overwhelming moment of déjà vu, forgets which wife he is talking to. There is a moment of panic, but then he remembers that both of his babies are named Sam, so if he feels lost, he can always just ask *how's Sam* and he will be safe.

"I'm fine. How's Sam?"

"He's my little monkey, but he's got a cold. Who knew babies could make so much phlegm? I chased him around all day with a Kleenex. Sexy, huh?"

David watches her sway absently in the window. He could cross the street, say hi to the doorman, ride up in the elevator. She would hear his key in the door. He can picture the look on her face when she sees him, the surprise and delight. How she would take him in her arms and for two hours there would be no death, no family drama. There would just be them, man and woman, husband and wife.

"Can I ask you something?" he says.

"Sure, baby. Whatever you want."

"Do you believe in God?"

Beat.

"Why?"

"No, it's nothing, I just—we've been married a year and I realized I don't know."

She thinks about this.

"I grew up Catholic. We went to church every Sunday. My parents were really devout. Did you know there's actually no Easter Bunny in the Bible? It's just Jesus on the cross, the Resurrection. The whole thing was too male for me. All that smiting."

"I've never read the Bible," he says. "Do you believe in God?"

He watches her breathe on the windowpane, write something in the mist, his name.

"I believe in coincidence," she says, "accidents. I believe in luck. You should see me in Vegas. I get these streaks, hot, cold. It's funny. I never really think about it anymore. New York isn't really about God, you know? It's not that organized.

In the Midwest you can see how the idea of God could take hold so strongly. Everything is slower, more deliberate. You live in New York and you start to see how complex the world is, how many moving parts, how many players, and it just doesn't feel like all this could be controlled, manipulated by one all-powerful deity. New York City, it feels like too much for even God to handle."

David's teeth are chattering now. He has stuck his cell phone into the interstice between his hat and scarf, tied tight, and his hands are jammed down into his pockets. He remembers the flight in from California, looking down at the great grids of Midwestern states. It seems to him the farther you get from the ocean, the more religious people become. It is impressive really, the unflappable belief of the landlocked. Why is it the biggest religions were all born in arid desert lands? Judaism, Christianity, Islam. The god of the desert is a god of ultimatums, all or nothing. Gods born in lush countries are more laid back—Vishnu, Buddha—they're lovers, not smiters. *And while we're at it*, he thinks, *why are the most religious people always the ones who've had it worst, inner-city kids, warring tribes, the poverty stricken? Why are piety and wealth such opposites? Why are the fortunate, those with a true sense of accomplishment, usually the least devout?*

Like me.

He bundles himself against the cold. There is a part of him that thinks he will never be warm again, like you could run a blowtorch over his body and he would just melt like a block of ice. Nearby a siren begins its deploring cry. He stands silently, waiting for it to pass, the sound overwhelmingly urgent, like a baby in need.

"Sweetie," says Joy. "Where are you?"

There is a jolt in his spine as he realizes that she can hear the siren, too, both through the window and over the phone.

"I told you," he says. "I'm in San Diego."

She comes over to the window, peers out. He shrinks into the doorway, his haste loosening the phone from its precarious cradle. It clatters to the street. He crouches, fumbles for it, trying to keep his body in shadow.

"Are you here?" she asks excitedly, peering out. "Did you come to New York to surprise me?"

"I wish," he says, shrinking back into a doorway that smells like piss. "I've been in a windowless conference room all day listening to men in suits drone on about pain relievers."

She sighs.

"Why can't you just live here full time?" she wants to know. "I think I'm officially getting tired of missing you."

"I know. Just a few more months." He says this, though he knows it's not true. A few more months until what? Until he leaves his family? Until he gives up everything sane and grounded? He was an idiot to come here, to call. It's worse than drunk dialing, this late-night, grief-stricken booty call, all his weakness bubbling to the surface, his need. What happened to being a man with rules? What happened to sticking to the plan? He watches the window, and the second she turns away, he is running. He darts out of the doorway and heads up the block to Hudson Street. His frozen legs feel like they might just shatter, feet fracturing against the pavement. He pumps his arms, his legs. The air in his lungs is like a knife, but once he starts running it's hard to stop.

"What are you doing?" she says.

"I'm late for this dinner," he pants. "I'm trying to catch a cab."

He hears her cluck.

"I didn't know they had cabs in San Diego. I always thought you could just catch a ride on the back of a dolphin."

He runs south on Hudson past the park, past the White Horse Tavern, where two days from now his family will assemble to mourn their absent father. He runs toward Canal Street, away from the New York he knows. There used to be two towers you could see from this spot. He watched them being built when he was a kid, saw them rise like magic into the sky, but now they're gone. It's like his life. His father is dead, and without him the world seems so unfamiliar. His landmarks are missing. He has become disoriented. It seems impossible to know if he's going in the right direction.

"I'll call you tomorrow," he says, gasping.

"I love you," she tells him, and it makes him close his eyes. Everything is too bright, too powerful. New York was a terrible place to come. All the memories. Everything is so extreme here, exaggerated. New York is all Scott's crazy ladies wrapped up into one giant landscape.

"I love you, too," he says, and buries the phone in his pocket. He is wearing the wrong shoes for this, his body stuffed inside a heavy black overcoat. He runs south, passing women in parkas walking dogs in seven-hundred-dollar sweaters. He crosses against the light, racing cars. His sleeves make a *whisk whisk* sound as he pumps his arm, wool scraping wool on the torso of his jacket. He runs as if someone is chasing him, like he ran back in sixth grade when Pete Amandallo threatened to scrape his face off on the sidewalk and pursued him for thirteen blocks shouting dirty words and spitting. His breathing is ragged, lungs burning. Things have gotten out of control. He wishes he could consolidate his life, somehow meld his two worlds together, force his two wives into each other until they became one. He wishes he could calm down. He's always been so steady, so sure of himself. What happened? How did everything get so fucked up? And yet there is something beautiful about breaking down, letting go. *I'm a mess*, he thinks. He has fought so hard for so long to be in control, and yet the thought is a relief. *I'm a fucking mess.* He runs toward SoHo, jumping potholes, a thirty-seven-year-old man in flight. Maybe he should ditch everything, move to another city, change his name. He can't think of any other way out. How could he ever choose? There's no way to navigate this, to go back to a simpler time, one wife, one family. He has passed the point of no return.

He runs faster, arms pumping, fingertips reaching for the future. His face feels like a sheet of ice, eyes watering, nose running.

It's a test, he thinks. The idea comes from nowhere, just pops into his head. What kind of test? he wonders. *A test from who, for what purpose?*

A test of faith.

He hears the words in his head. *A test of faith.* The idea of it seeps through his body like warm water. He doesn't know what it means, not exactly, but there is something liberating about the words, contextual. He is like Job, like Jonah and the whale, like Noah on his ark for forty days and forty nights, wondering if he'll ever see the sun again. It's a test, all of it. His mother, his two families, his father's death. He remembers his son's karate, tiny fists flying forward, splitting the board. *When you apologize to God*, he said, *you can't pretend. You have to mean it.*

David grimaces. He feels both heavy and light at the same time, elated and exhausted. He is literally gasping for air, head low, knees bent, his impractical shoes pounding the pavement.

I'm sorry, he thinks. *I'm so sorry.* He apologizes to his father, to his mother. He apologizes to Tracey for betraying her, apologizes to Joy for lying. *I'm sorry. I'm sorry. I'm sorry.* He mouths the words, grunts them. He apologizes to Scott for always feeling superior, apologizes to his children for being such a terrible person. He apologizes to everyone for everything. He thinks, *If there is a God, then please, please help me. Please believe that I have never been so sorry in all my life.*

Please God. Please. Help me.

This is when the cab hits him.

HE WAKES IN a puddle. People are standing over him. Everything is cockeyed, skewed.

"Don't move," says a man, kneeling beside him. "You've been hit by a car. An ambulance is on the way."

Behind the man's head a traffic light turns from red to green.

"I'm okay," says David, sitting up. And he is. Miraculously. Not even a scratch. He gets to his feet. How long has he been unconscious? It can only have been a few minutes, but somehow he feels rested, rejuvenated, like he has slept for weeks.

"Are you fucking crazy?" says the cabdriver. "This is what I want to know. Are you a fucking nutjob running out into traffic?"

David straightens. He sees the taxi's windshield is cracked from the impact of his body. The smell of burning rubber hangs in the air from when the driver slammed on the brakes, and yet David doesn't feel a thing. He takes a deep breath, exhales. There is no pain.

"I'm sorry," he says. "Really. It's my fault."

"You heard him," says the driver. "He admitted it."

David steps up onto the curb. He feels elated, redeemed.

"Maybe you should wait for the ambulance," says the man who was kneeling beside him. He is tall, well dressed. His wife or girlfriend stands on the curb, a look of concern on her face.

"No," says David. "I'm fine. Really."

He walks away, leaving the scene of the accident. His hat is gone and the cold air musses his hair. He has no idea what happened, can't really remember the moments before the accident. All he knows is he feels alive, deeply, truly alive.

It was a test, he thinks. *It's all a test.*

The words taste strange in his mouth. They seem familiar, like there's an important thought in there trying to get out, but he can't remember what it is. What kind of test? Then it hits him. The feeling starts low in his belly, spreads through him. He knows what this is all about, his life, his problems, the taxi.

God.

The idea of it is so simple. He smiles, embarrassed. Can it really be that simple? He stops walking, stands on the corner catching his breath. He touches his chest, his arms. He has been struck by a car and emerged without a scratch. It feels like a miracle. This is how it happens. You hit bottom and then there is a light at the end of the tunnel that shows you the way. He wants the light to be real. He wants the way to be righteous. He is so tired of remorse, so tired of doubt.

I believe, he thinks.

He wants to shout it, actually has to cover his mouth with his hands to stop himself. The words rise up inside him. He pictures his son in his animal-print pajamas, praying on his knees. What is that line, *And the children will lead us?*

He wants to hug everyone he sees. He is man who has built a life on keeping secrets, and now he has the biggest secret of all, and he wants to yell it in the streets. God, fate, luck, Mother Earth, the Universe, whatever you want to call it, he believes now. He believes there is some higher power. There has to be.

All of this can't be random. The things that happen happen for
a reason. They must. He feels giddy, shy. God is like a celebrity
he's run into on the street. There is that same blush of familiar-
ity. In recognition there is fear and awe. There is power and joy.
He feels embarrassed. What does he really know about God?
Nothing. Just a few TV clichés and hackneyed catchphrases.
David feels delinquent. He should buy the Bible or the Torah
or the Koran or something. He should familiarize himself with
the Lord's work. You don't want to get on your knees and talk
to God and say something stupid, like seeing Paul Newman and
saying, "I loved you in *On the Waterfront*." David should know
about the Garden of Eden and stuff. Where was Jesus born
again? Bethlehem, right? And what about Mohammad? He was
a prophet or something. The whole thing feels overwhelming
right now. Belief is one thing, but he needs to do his research.
The feeling is in him. He knows he believes. Now he just has
to figure out in what.

But he doesn't let that dampen his spirit. He can feel the
faith inside him, even if he doesn't know its exact name. *Words
just get in the way, anyway*, he tells himself. People pass him on
the street. He tries to look them in the eye, but this is New
York and people don't do that. *We're all sinners*, he thinks. *Where
have I heard that before?* He doesn't know, but the idea of it
makes him feel better, to know that everyone out there is just as
fucked up as he is, that the world is full of people all puking and
shitting and making a mess of their lives. He is standing on the
corner of Hudson and West Houston. It is exactly midnight,
marking the thirteenth of February. His father's memorial service is in thirty-six hours.

David smiles at everyone who passes him, his feet moving
again, heading back uptown. He has been saved, reborn. The
realization is like a lightning strike. *I have been thinking about the*

world all wrong, he thinks. *It is not a matter of order. It is a question of love. To have two wives, two families, it's not a crime. It's a blessing. What's wrong with wanting to make people happy, with trying to provide for them?* He is a man with two wives, four children, a mother, and a brother. He loves them all. How can this be wrong?

The future is a freight train bearing down.

PART TWO

BARRIERS

AND CONSIDER THIS: If the center of this story is the punch that broke Scott Henry's nose, then all other events revolve around it. If the blow is a stone dropped into the center of the timeline, then it sends ripples into both the future and the past. It is an event with gravity, and as you move farther away from it in either direction, that gravity lessens. So, too, does the event become less clear, a series of words, of images, of sounds.

If you think of this story as a composite of three stories all moving from different directions at the same speed toward a single destination, then you understand that we are on a collision course. Each line on its own, like a chemical, is inert, but throw them together and you have combustion. If you believe that at every moment in life we are faced with choices, and each choice we make presents us with an infinite number of possible choices, then you know there's no way the future could be predetermined. But if, like Gödel, you believe that there is no such thing as time, then you realize that every choice you make in your life, you make at exactly the same moment. Therefore, we know a thing will happen because it is happening as we speak.

But this is not the way time *feels.* And in the end isn't that what really matters? What difference does it make if time moves backward if we perceive it as moving forward? Who is to say that our experience of time is not accurate? Where one person sees time as moving quickly, it moves quickly. For the person who sees it move slowly, it moves slowly.

And what about this: If time has a beginning, mustn't it also have an end? And if this is so, does it mean that time itself is taking a journey? But what is the goal or end of that journey? Is it simply a date, time, and place, a set of coordinates that will signal the end, or is it the accomplishment of some goal, the realization of a dream?

If time does indeed move in an arrow shooting in one of two directions (backward or forward), then we must wonder about the beginning of the universe. If in the beginning there was complete chaos, it only makes sense that at the end there would be complete order, and if at the beginning there was complete order, then the end would be complete chaos.

People would like to feel that the universe is moving away from anarchy into order, because then we would know that life improves with time. We could relax, knowing that our lives will become more meaningful, more comprehendible, with each passing year. We think this, because we believe that at the end of any story we will know the whole tale. Think of every story you've ever heard. At the beginning you have no idea what to expect. In the beginning there are an infinite number of possible stories you may be about to hear, but the more you learn, the narrower the scope, until in the end you see that there was really only one finite story being told all along. In this way, we have been trained to believe that every story we encounter will have a beginning, middle, and end.

As a result most of us secretly believe we will see the big picture of our lives when we are older. Our lives are stories, too, are they not? But what if time moves in the other direction? What if at our birth things are at their most ordered, their simplest, and at our death our lives are at their most disorganized and complicated? What if when we die nothing makes sense? What if only when we are born is the universe truly under-standable?

Doesn't this make storytelling inherently unlike life?

SCOTT HENRY IS still awake when the sun comes up. He doesn't mean to be. He had every intention of going to bed early last night, curling up in his hotel room and sleeping the night away. God knows he needs the rest. But one thing led to another and now look at him, staggering out of an after-hours club in the Meatpacking District at seven o'clock in the morning, squinting at the sudden glare. For a moment he doesn't know what to make of it. He feels like a convict caught in a prison-tower spotlight. His hands go up reflexively to protect his face. He considers running. He can't, for the life of him, figure out where the hours went. Seven A.M. How is that possible? He remembers checking his watch at two and then... what?

It started innocently enough. He had a drink with David and then walked to the subway. It was what, eight, nine P.M.? He had every intention of heading uptown to see a movie, but inside the station he found himself walking to the downtown platform, climbing onto a southbound 6 train. His head was full of so many thoughts. Being back in New York did that to him, sent his mind racing in every direction. The city is one big *what if?* for him. The streets are filled with paths not taken, smoky contrails of what might have been. Where you and I see a map of Manhattan, he sees a grid of memories, sectioned into streets and avenues. Being here brings it all back. He used to think of memory as a kind of library with books you could take off the shelf, but now he sees it as a motion picture, a movie you mount on a projector, flicking on the lamp, engaging the gears.

As he rides downtown, Scott watches old footage in his head, memories of Sally Embrecht, the first girl he ever loved, the girl to whom he gave his mother's jewelry. It was at Grace Church School on Tenth Street in the Village. He was twelve. She was like this tiny swallow, this beautiful young bird. He had never been in love before. The feeling came over him like some terrible avian flu. There was fever and congestion. There were aches and pains. How many times has he sat in a subway car on the East Side thinking these same thoughts, passing Forty-second Street, passing Twenty-eighth? She was a mousy thing, dark-haired, bug-eyed, but she made his heart tack like a Geiger counter. What was this crazy new sensation? More. He needed more. He couldn't stop thinking about her curtain-straight brown hair, her twiggy little legs. She was better than a fly ball, better than waffles, better than a Hundred Thousand Dollar Bar. To show her how much he cared, he left notes in her desk, followed her around the school yard at recess. He stole things from people he loved and gave them away.

Do you see how much I love you? Do you see why I'm worthy?

Across from him on the subway, a man with a handlebar mustache reads the *New York Post*. KNICKS CHOKE AGAIN is the back-page headline. Overhead, the loudspeaker screeches, a computerized voice announcing their arrival at Fourteenth Street. Scott closes his eyes and dreams of Sally Embrecht. He has had these memories before, of course. He has them every time he comes back to the city. It makes him wonder how many times in his life he will revisit the same places. How many minutes will be filled by the same internal visions? Imagine now, if you can, that though Scott is remembering Sally while riding the 6 train downtown, he is also recalling her as he sits in the third row of his tenth-grade science class. He is remembering her as he steps out of Ray's Pizza on Sixth Avenue and Eleventh Street, eating a paper-thin slice; the year is 1992. Imagine him passing over those memories as he sits at his father's memorial service the day after tomorrow, everyone drinking solemnly, chatting in whispers. You see what we are doing, jumping around in time. It is all happening at once, right before your eyes like a giant wheel turning.

Stop the wheel. Look at Scott. He is lying in his bed ten days ago, holding Kate in his arms. Even as he is caught in her twisted web, he is lost in nostalgia for that first perfect love, that innocent adoration of youth. All he wants is something pure. He will remember Sally when he is a paunchy, beslippered man in a broken rocking chair wishing he could take a decent shit. Some things you never forget. Stupid, isn't it? She was just a little girl. It was just a fleeting desire, a hummingbird of romance, tiny, unborn, and yet it lives in his mind like a hermit in a forest, building a shack, writing a manifesto of loss.

He gets off the subway at Astor Place, walks west. It's not too late to see a movie. He could head over to the Quad or down to the Angelika, but he doesn't. Instead he crosses Broadway, takes Eighth Street all the way to Sixth Avenue, passing head shops and record stores, T-shirt emporiums and cheap shoe outlets. He is a man on a mission.

The night is the temperature of the chill you get when someone walks over your grave. His coat is thin and he has no gloves, no scarf. There are only his memories to keep him warm. He takes Waverly to Eleventh Street. He is heading for his childhood home. It is like a beacon calling to him. He crosses West Fourth, passes the Bleecker Playground, where he used to play when he was a kid. An hour from now his brother, David, will stand on this very spot, waiting for his common sense to kick in, drawn downtown by the pull of his secret life. How strange that both brothers will come to the same spot on the same night. Perhaps they are more alike than they realize. Scott crosses Hudson, past what used to be an A&P. The memories are so thick now, they are like a veil hanging between him and the world. He remembers being eleven and standing on this very corner waiting for the light to change, and then, just as the cars started coming, yellow cabs gunning in at speed, he took off, racing across four lanes of traffic. It was a challenge, a dare.

And yes, yes . . . there used to be a concrete boat in the playground and a tower that, if you stacked two garbage cans, could be climbed. Standing there, fifteen feet above the sandbox, you could take in the neighborhood, cast your eyes like a king over the broad expanse of Hudson Street, staring down at Abingdon Square Park, and the turnaround where Hudson hits Bleecker. You could stand on the lip of the tower looking down at all the other kids frozen in awe, pimpled across the concrete boat with its central, cabin-like interior, its thin moat of sand, and defining outer wall—back in the days before rubber mats and ergonomic climbing structures, back when a kid could still, in the course of ordinary, everyday playing, crack his skull on a wall or tumble from a rusty metal jungle gym to the hard concrete below. Before lawsuits and wheelchair ramps, before local news exposés and consumer protection reports. You could, hovering fifteen feet above the sandbox, live in the thrill of that moment before the jump, fear and elation coursing through your veins. It was for many kids the first time in their lives they ever took a risk, and that feeling—the electric threat of it—would live on in their minds well into old age. Every time they hovered on the verge of something dangerous, they would remember this moment. It was inherent in every thrill, just as your first kiss is embedded in every kiss that follows. Scott remembers standing on top of that concrete tower looking down. David was knees-down in the sand, staring up, mouth agape. He was two years older than Scott, but he never would have dared to climb the tower, never would have risked injury or death just to have a *feeling*. Scott remembers standing there, his palms still raw from where he'd pulled himself up on the concrete. His mother was at home. His father was at work. They had no idea that their youngest son was about to jump into a filthy sandbox, to leap and hang weightless over a maze of sharpened concrete. If they'd known they would have run screaming. Imagine all the things that can go wrong—the limbs broken, the fractured skull—and yet isn't this the very heart of childhood? Those moments where you stand outside the realm of good sense, ready to do the unthinkable on a dare?

It was a cool November day. Below him the traffic lights changed from green to red. He took a deep breath and jumped.

At Greenwich Street he turns right, walks one block to Bank. Halfway down the street he can see the house, the brownstone he grew up in. It is a worn brick building, concrete stoop out front leading up to a weathered wooden door. Why does he come here? What brings him back? He is like a pigeon returning to the roost, a golden retriever walking a hundred miles to find the family it has lost. Every time he returns to New York he comes here, stands on the sidewalk staring up at the windows that used to be his. It is reassuring somehow, this revival, this return. The ghosts are all around him. They played stoop ball on this stoop. It snowed eighteen inches and he went outside and his foot came up without his boot. Why does he remember these things? What point is there in memory? Everything recedes. This is the nature of time. Now Sally Embrecht's face is just a blur. She is a shape, a shadow on his brain. He remembers the feeling but not her face. What is the point of all this memory if the memories fade? How ridiculous to find something so important that you would hold on to it, cherish it, only to have the memory crumble in your hands. How maddening.

This time, however, Scott has come for a reason. It is time to unbury a secret, to make things right. He stares up at the brownstone, three stories tall with a basement level. A duplex, with one apartment upstairs and one down. He crosses the street, stands staring up at the darkened windows of his childhood home. They played baseball in his bedroom, busted lightbulbs with fly balls, slid feetfirst into bases that weren't there. He can close his eyes and picture every detail, the way the doorknob felt in his hand, the sound of his father's knees cracking every night as he climbed the stairs, having cleaned up the kitchen, turned off the lights. It seems ridiculous, but the sound made him feel safe, the percussive cartilage pop of each knee on each stair. He remembers stifling August nights, the windows thrown open, all the city sounds pouring in, the ebb and flow of traffic mixed with the angry cries of grown men and women going insane in the heat. He had his first erection in that room, his first orgasm. Scott stands on his old front stoop remembering how in third grade he stopped on this very step and wet his pants after running home from school. His mother couldn't answer the door fast enough. How delicious it felt, the warm wet spreading across his lap, running down his leg. He feels dizzy with the memory. He hasn't eaten since breakfast, has flown three thousand miles today. His mother is asleep in her hotel room, a bottle of wine by the bed. His brother is who knows where. (Thirty-fourth Street and Fifth Avenue and closing in fast.) His father is a bag of ashes in his mother's luggage. He rubs his hands together for warmth, jams them into his pockets.

It's been twenty years since Scott was last inside, but he can still picture the upstairs apartment as if it were yesterday. What he's looking for is not inside, though. It's in the tiny backyard.

He goes around the corner to Bethune. There is a gate there, and through it he can see the back of his childhood home. This is where the Frisbees used to disappear, the footballs and tennis balls. Boys playing on the pitted macadam, stoop ball and stick ball. Foul a ball off and it disappears over a roof or through a window and you have to run like hell. He stamps his feet, trying to stay warm.

The Halloween parade used to go right by here, back in the '70s. It started at Westbeth and took Bethune to Bleecker. Every year they would stand on the corner and watch it go, his mother, his father, his brother. He remembers the huge papier-mâché heads, the giant puppets operated by five men at a time. It was an amazing conglomeration of artists, drug addicts, and sexual deviants. This was back when freaks were rumored to put razor blades in apples, the city hovering somewhere between beneficence and cruelty.

His friend Matthew Gruber would come and watch the parade sometimes. Matthew's parents were divorced and his father lived in a town house on West Thirteenth Street. He was the author of the novels *Great White* and *Killer Bees*, which had both been made into B movies. Matthew and Scott were at that age, twelve, thirteen, when puberty is just starting, a rush of wakefulness as the engine of maturity turns over. Matthew's father had a girlfriend, what Scott now recognizes as a trophy girl, beautiful and buxom and given to sunbathing topless on Matthew's father's patio. Scott remembers her breasts in the sunlight, the gentle brown slope of her hair. It is his first true sexual memory. Matthew lusted for this woman, who was not his mother but who shared his father's bed. What a strange twist on the Oedipal myth. What an unsettling thing to suddenly recognize your father as a sexual being, and see yourself in his shadow, stalking the same unsuspecting woman. One day after school Matthew showed Scott the walkie-talkie he kept in his room. Its mate was taped in the on position to the underside of Matthew's father's bed, where it would broadcast, loud and clear, the sounds of his father's fornication.

Now when he thinks back on those memories, Scott pictures Matthew lying there at night, the odd, urgent, ghostly sounds emanating from the plastic box in his hand. This was what haunted Matthew, not ghosts or goblins, or city freaks, but the specter of his parents' divorce, the mixed feelings of love and hate he had, and how he was now forced to separate them, to have specific feelings for each parent, as opposed to the commonality of feeling most of us have. He was haunted by his own impending maturity, by his own future relationships and their inevitable failure, by the likelihood of following in his father's footsteps. He was haunted by urges he didn't understand, urges that made him bug his father's bedroom, that made him crouch at the top of the stairs spying on his father's naked girlfriend splayed out in the sun. And at night he was haunted by her cries, cries he probably didn't really understand, sounds of passion and pain, a woman, not his mother, grunting, yelling, speaking in tongues, begging for some kind of mercy.

How does it happen? One day you feel like the world is in your control. You stand on the lip of a tower, a giant, the master of all you see, and then somehow it all gets lost. Somehow you end up a grown man sitting on a frozen stoop wishing it would snow. Wishing that the sky would open up and everything would turn white. *Erase it all and start again.*

This is what Scott thinks as he stands and rubs the feeling back into his legs.

He puts his hands on the gate, the cold metal sticking to his skin. He can see the tree from here, a New York City oak that has fought its way through asphalt and concrete to stand tall, branches sheltering the yard from heat and sun and the prying eyes of neighbors. It's icy now, bare, covered with patchy snow. Scott stands at the fence, traces the crossbar down to the lower right quadrant, guided by memory. Even as he does it, he knows that what he's hoping for is impossible. Twenty years have passed, and sure enough, the spot where he and David cut the fasteners between the chain link and the crossbar has been repaired. But all it would take is a pair of wire cutters and he'd be in.

A police car cruises past. Scott sees it from the corner of his eye, straightens. His heart is beating fast. Is he crazy? Breaking and entering? And yet the fear is good. The quickened pulse and bright adrenaline sheen across his field of vision. For the first time in weeks he feels alive.

Tomorrow there is brunch with Cousin Florence and Cousin Alice. And the next day is the memorial, the public good-bye. He has to come back here before then, find the spot and dig. The idea is in his head like a rosary he can't stop worrying. He has come three thousand miles to lay his father to rest, and he can't do it without the thing he stole and buried.

Not for the first time, Scott thinks of his father standing on the side of the road in North Carolina. In the vision, Joe is a young man, younger than Scott is now. The image comes from a story his father once told him about his army days. Joe volunteered for the infantry, left home, and was trained to drive tanks for the Korean War. But they weren't using tanks in Korea, so he stayed at a base in North Carolina. And one day he got a pass for a little R&R. He took a bus to Memphis. *What did he do there?* Scott wonders. *Did he go with buddies? Was there drinking, fighting, women? Did he eat three square meals a day and sleep until noon?* The details are fuzzy. All Scott knows is that when the weekend was over, his father went to the bus station. He stood in line waiting to buy a ticket back to base, but somewhere along the way, shuffling forward, kicking his duffel bag along the linoleum floor, he made a very different choice. Was it hot out, muggy, the heat prickling against his skin, sweat running down his back? Scott doesn't know the details. What he does know is that when his father reached the front of the line, he bought a ticket for someplace else. He had decided to go AWOL. Scott pictures his dad stepping up to the window. Was there fear in his eyes? Did his voice shake? It is no small thing to run out on the U.S. Army. What was going through his head?

"Round-trip or one way?" the ticket lady asked him.

"One way," he said. "I'm not coming back."

His dad took his ticket (to New York or Boston or maybe even California, he never specified) and walked to the bay that held his bus. Did he feel like a ten-year-old boy standing on the lip of a concrete tower staring down at the street? Was there that same giddy, reckless hope? Joe took his seat on the bus, sweat pooling in the small of his back. He was a big man with a crew cut and a tattoo on his left shoulder. It would be years before he met Doris, before he sat on a New York street corner drinking beer and watching her eat ice cream. He couldn't see it from where he sat now, but he would be happy one day. He would not be shipped off to war, would not die in some Asian jungle. He would not be arrested for desertion, would not spend the rest of his life in a prison cell. None of this was clear to him, though, sitting in a window seat, watching the depot recede as the bus pulled away. The future is the only true mystery we have. All he knew was that he was breaking the rules. All he knew was that he was risking everything to save his own life, to be free.

Scott pictures his dad sitting rigid, watching the Southern landscape pass. How long did he sit there? An hour? One stop, maybe two? And then he did something strange. He got to his feet and walked to the front of the bus. He tapped the driver on the shoulder and said, "Drop me up here, will you?" And when the bus stopped he climbed down into the torpid August heat. He stood in a cloud of dust and exhaust watching the bus pull away, taking with it his freedom, his escape. Somewhere in the last five miles he had decided to go back, to face his responsibility. Scott pictures his father standing on the side of the road, waiting for another bus to come, one that would take him back to Memphis, take him back to camp. He imagines his father steeling himself then with a cigarette, pulling the pack of Lucky Strikes from his pocket, setting one between his lips. The sun was like a hammer pounding a nail. What went through Joe's head at that moment? What had made him change his mind? Scott wishes he had asked. He wishes he could call his dad right now and find out. There are so many things he wants to know. So many questions that will never be answered. So many moments his father lived that Scott will never understand. Where do those memories go when you die? All the things you lived through, all the private moments that no one else shares, do they just disappear? If a thing happens to you alone and you never tell a soul, does it really happen? If, after you're dead, there is no one left to remember it, do those actions cease to exist?

Scott's father told him this story when Scott was ten. He showed Scott his dog tags. They were tarnished metallic wafers on a ratty chain. The only piece of jewelry a real man wears, designed to be torn from his neck after he dies. Scott held them in his hand. They were an object of musty import, a symbol of bravery and adventure and something darker. Death. He studied the faded words embossed on the tags, the acronyms, his father's name, religion (atheist), and blood type (O positive). They were evidence of a greater service, a magic amulet given to the journeyman at the start of an adventure. Scott studied the dog tags and vowed they would be his.

Two days later he snuck into his parents' room when his dad was making dinner. He found the dog tags in his father's sock drawer, slipped them into his pocket. He knew he would be the most obvious suspect once the tags were discovered missing. He guessed that his person would be searched, his room. So he put the dog tags in an old coffee can and buried them in the yard.

Now, crouched on a cold New York street, he pictures his dad standing on the side of a North Carolina road. He had so much life ahead, so many triumphs, but he couldn't see them yet. All he could see was a dusty road. In the past was a small town, a violent father. In the future was a war. It amazes Scott, the courage it took for him to go AWOL in the first place, but the courage it took to get off the bus, to turn around and face the future, takes Scott's breath away.

The night his father died, Scott sat alone in the dark, listening to the silence. His brother had just called to tell him. It was two-thirty in the morning. He remembers David's voice, the kind resignation.

"He died," he said. Just that.

Scott sat on the floor. He didn't know what else to do. It was the middle of the night. He couldn't get a flight out until morning. He had expected this moment for so long, it had stopped being real. The weight of it had hung over all of them for so many years it had become abstract. Death became an empty threat, like the monster in the closet. He paced his apartment. He stared out the window at the late-night traffic lights flashing red. Everything felt too bright with the lights on, so he wandered around in the dark. And standing in his kitchen, he pictured his father on that dusty road, standing in the tall grass, smoking a cigarette, waiting for his bus. Scott wondered if this was what death was, if at the moment of death you revert to someplace you've been before, some moment you've lived, and maybe this is where you stay forever. *Does time freeze when you die?* This thought has haunted him for months, the image of his father standing by the side of the road, waiting for a bus that will never come, alone, afraid, running low on cigarettes. He wants a better moment for his father, a kinder eternity. He pictures him sitting in a café on a New York street corner staring at the women he is about to fall in love with, the woman he will marry, who will mother his children. A moment pregnant with possibility, with hope. This is the moment he wants for his father, a happier time when he can throw off the shackles of sickness, when he can slip back into the beauty of a world where anything is possible, especially love. True love, whether you can prove it or not.

Scott stamps his feet, trying to get warm. He will come back when it's light and find a way to get into that yard. He will dig up that coffee can and find those tags. He will return what he has stolen, the piece of his father's past he took. The dog tags are a magic amulet after all, and his father needs them for the journey he is on.

He turns and heads up Greenwich to the D'Agostino's. Inside it is warm and bright. There is produce from California, impossible plums and hothouse tomatoes. The colors are fat, saturated. He wanders the aisles trying to get warm. He would eat something but all the food is protected by cardboard, plastic. He is afraid of the crackle he would make breaking into the packaging, that grating, synthetic alarm. Ahead of him, a beautiful woman pushes a baby carriage and a shopping cart. She is wearing clogs though it's the middle of winter.

"Hi," she says as he passes. "Sorry. Do you think you could—I'm trying to get those diapers off the top shelf."

She points. Scott stops. He feels as if she's woken him from a dream. There is that same disorientation, that same dizzy recalibration.

"This one?" he says, reaching up to grab a bag of Pampers.

"Thank you so much," she says. "Sometimes being short is a real bitch."

He nods, looks at the baby. It is bundled up for winter, swallowed by clothes, but peeking out are the most amazing eyes, these giant brown orbs. They stare up at him with wonder. He is hypnotized by them. He looks at the woman. She has the kind of beauty people describe as effortless.

"What's his name?" he asks.

"Sam," says the woman, lodging the diapers in the bottom of her cart. She is blonde, fresh faced. Any sign that she was ever pregnant has been erased. Now she is just another New York goddess in narrow, low-rise jeans.

"I can't really feel my face," says Scott. "And I'm wondering, is it still there?"

She smiles.

"Still there."

He nods, waking up further, becoming aware of where he is. Now that he has a plan, now that he understands his mission, he feels brighter, grounded. He is no longer a lost little boy.

"I just got off a plane from California. It's like Alaska outside."

"They say it's supposed to get worse," she says. "A cold front from Canada."

She puts a box of baby wipes in her cart.

"My husband's from California. He goes there a lot. Where do you live?"

"San Francisco."

"I love San Francisco. He's from L.A. Home of the brown air. I hate it, but it pays the bills, so..."

"And he left you here in the tundra? What kind of monster is this guy?"

She shrugs. She seems more relaxed than any mother of a six-month-old has a right to be.

"I don't mind," she says. "I was an only child. I get by just fine on my own."

Scott looks into her eyes. They are like her son's, bottomless, welcoming. He wishes he could have a woman like this, effortless, self-sufficient. He thinks, *If you would just put your arms around me for ten minutes, I could do anything. I could climb that fence. I could go to the memorial. I could drive to Maine and dump my father's ashes.*

"I'm Scott," he says, sticking out his hand.

She pulls off one of her colorful, striped wool gloves, sticks out her hand.

"Joy," she says.

Her hand is thin and warm. Her nails are pink.

"Just so you know," he says, "I don't usually troll the baby food aisle looking for women."

"Hey," she says, "we all have our fetishes."

"I'm usually more of a produce man. You can tell a lot about a woman by the way she picks a melon."

Joy smiles. She has a way of being that makes the room feel lighter.

"So what brings you here?" she says.

He thinks about this. The truth is like an avalanche. How

do you tell a stranger about your life if your words are boulders and you don't want to crush them under the weight?

"I grew up near here," he says, "on Bank. I don't know why, but every time I come back to New York, I find myself outside the old house."

"Nostalgia," she says.

"Maybe. It just—it feels important somehow, you know, to go back to the source. To see where it all started."

"I grew up in Oklahoma," she says. "My house is a shopping mall now."

"So you go to the Foot Locker," he says, "maybe tear up in the ladies' running shoe section."

She smiles again. He feels the ice melting in his bones. He is like a baby bird imprinting. Every woman he meets he looks in the eye, thinking, *Are you the one? Are you the one?* He thinks, *If I could just stand here in the supermarket making this woman smile for the rest of my life, that would be fine with me. That could be my death moment, my eternity.* He kneels and looks at the kid, Sam. He's wearing little booties and a tiny wool hat. Snot is running from his nose. Scott sticks out his finger, lets the baby grab it.

"My nephew is named Sam, too," he says. "All the old-man names are coming back, Max, Earl..."

"Earl?"

"Well, maybe not Earl."

"Sam was my dad's name," says Joy.

"My brother has three kids," says Scott, straightening. "He sells pharmaceuticals in L.A."

"Huh," she says, "so does my husband."

Scott puts his back to the baby food. All those bottles, rows and rows, all exactly the same, are making him nervous. Something about the number of days it would take to eat them all.

"How do you do it?" he wants to know. "Decide to be a parent? It seems so . . . big."

She brushes the hair from her face. In a little black dress with her hair down and makeup on she could end a war. She could lower the moon.

"It's like everything else in life," she says. "Sometimes you don't decide. Sometimes it just happens."

He nods. The feeling has returned to his fingers and toes. He is pretty sure that he and Joy have very different luck. That her life is this charmed escalator ride, while he is forced to scale the outside of the building using just the pressure of his fingertips for leverage. He wishes that just once in his life he could know what that was like, the path of no resistance.

"Well," he says, "I should probably get back out there."

He buttons his flimsy coat. In his dreams she would tell him not to be silly. She would invite him back to her house and make him soup. She would give him a blanket and a towel and show him to the guest room. She would say, *Stay as long as you like. You'll love my husband. He has a way with people.* But this is not the world we live in.

"Thanks for the diapers," she says.

He nods, starts to walk away, then stops.

"Would you promise me something?" he says.

She frowns, her body stiffening. This is not something strange men are supposed to say.

"What do you mean?"

He sighs.

"Nothing. Never mind."

He turns, then turns back.

"Just—don't stop. You seem so happy. Fearless, you know? Don't stop."

She narrows her eyes, her New York radar kicking in. He

wants to hold up his hand, to show her he is harmless, un-armed.

"No matter what happens," he says. He doesn't know what he's doing, but it seems vital somehow that this woman, this young mother, not turn into *his* mother. That she not fall somehow into despair. "It's—and I really think this—all in your attitude, you know? I mean, life's hard and, I don't know, things happen, and I just think it's important to be strong. Happy. It's so easy to give in to despair, to give up, but don't. Please."

He is flushed now, feeling giddy, reckless. It's like he's exposing himself to her, this stranger, all his weakness, his fear. He is unburdening himself here in the disposable baby-care aisle, like some kind of lunatic.

"Sure," she says. "I promise." He can't tell if she thinks he's crazy or not, and in truth he doesn't really care. All he wants is to connect, to feel human. He looks her in the eye. In a minute he will turn and walk back into the cold. In a minute he will hump his way uptown, teeth chattering, but right now all he wants is to feel like she *sees* him. So he looks at her and she looks at him, and for a split second he thinks she does, but, as always, time keeps going. The moment passes. Then they are strangers once again.

"Bye, Sam," he says and turns.

"Wave bye-bye, Sammy," says Joy, watching him go. The sound of her voice is so sweet Scott starts to cry. Nothing dramatic, just a few tears rolling down his face. In front of the sliding door he stops, puts up his collar. His reflection in the glass looks tired. He smiles at himself. *You're good*, he thinks. *You're a good person*. It's so important to him that somebody thinks so. Then, hunching his shoulders in anticipation, he steps out into the cold.

FIFTEEN HOURS AFTER meeting Joy, he is on the corner of Sixty-seventh Street and Lexington levering his mother out of a cab. It is twenty-seven degrees in the sun. David has gone around to the trunk to rescue the wheelchair. He is smiling a smile that Scott has never seen before. Doris, too, is uncharacteristically bubbly this morning. If Scott didn't know better, he would say she was actually in a good mood. She makes jokes as Scott and David help her out of the backseat, hoisting her by her scrawny, brittle arms. It is eleven-thirty on Friday morning. The sky is that frozen powder blue you see in David Hockney paintings. David rolls the wheelchair onto the sidewalk. Scott opens the door to the French bistro they've chosen (no stairs, not too crowded, and yes, they serve wine before noon).

"I'm going to have a salad," his mother says, "maybe a steak."

Something about the prospect of a civilized meal seems to have cheered her up. Scott feels relief. Maybe this won't be so bad after all. Maybe she'll rally and the trip will turn out to be a renewal, a rebirth. Maybe after all these years of demanding and wallowing and lashing out, she can be his mother again.

"Are you okay?" David asks him. "You look terrible."

Scott can only imagine what he must look like, wet hair

frozen in stalks, eyes baggy and dark. A zombie, maybe. Some kind of mental patient.

"I didn't get much sleep last night," says Scott. He has that hollow, jittery feeling that comes from sleeplessness. It is the kind of thing that coffee only makes worse. He wandered the city for hours after leaving the supermarket, plotting his ingress. He considered staking out his old home like a cop, waiting for the inhabitants to leave, then sneaking in and digging. He imagined ringing the bell and telling his story to whoever answered. At no point did he ever doubt that the dog tags would still be buried under that tree. He is on a quest, and quests are never fruitless. Walking the streets, he found himself fantasizing about single mothers and fresh vegetables. He was like Adam thrown from the Garden. Everything seemed hateful and filthy in comparison.

The waitress shows them to a table in the corner. They help Doris into a chair and the waitress rolls the wheelchair into the back. Cousins Florence and Alice aren't here yet. No one is. The restaurant is empty. *Who eats lunch at eleven-thirty?* Scott wonders as he and David slide into the booth. *Old people, that's who.* The leather booth is soft and welcoming against his body, and leaning back, Scott worries that he will fall asleep before the menus come.

"I had the most amazing night's sleep," says David. "I don't know why. Something about being back in New York, the winter air. What about you, Mom? Did you sleep okay?"

"I did, actually," she says and smiles a private smile.

Scott sighs. Why are they rubbing it in? He looks around at all the empty tables. They specifically chose this restaurant because it holds no memories. It is not a place Doris and Joe used to come. It is a neighborhood they never frequented. There are no ghosts here. No painful reminders. This is as close to neutral as it gets in New York.

"I've given up on sleep," he says. "I think it's overrated."

"Well, I had the strangest dream," says Doris. "We lived in the country and there were lobsters in the grass. What do you think it means?"

"Maybe your oxygen level is too high," says David.

The waitress brings bread and a saucer of olive oil. Scott is so hungry he could eat a blimp.

"Are you looking forward to seeing Florence and Alice?" David asks as Scott digs in.

Doris shrugs, still smiling her secret smile. David smiles back at her. The two of them are grinning like idiots. Scott watches them, crumbs on his lip, bread half chewed in his mouth. Did somebody make a joke? He looks around. Did he miss something? They're acting like the cat that swallowed the canary. *It's just mean*, he thinks, *to have a joke and not share. I could use a laugh. Are you kidding? Tell me something funny, for Christ's sake.*

Florence and Alice arrive, shaking their coats as if to clear snow. They both live out on Long Island. Florence's married to a dentist. Alice lives alone. Scott hasn't spent that much time with them. His mother has an uneasy relationship with all her relatives. She hates them, in other words. Well, not hates them, but she is suspicious of them. What do they want? What's their angle? She treats strangers with more respect. To Scott they are merely distant relatives, pleasant, but unaffecting. He has no idea they are really his mother's sisters. Really his aunts. Nobody does. Imagine the surprise when the truth comes out.

"Hi, hi," says Florence, swooping in for a kiss. She is fifty-six, the glamorous one, overly made up, wearing fur. Alice stands behind her, the spinster in her mannish shoes.

"Traffic was horrible," she says.

Scott stands, accepts an awkward hug. His mother is smiling her TV smile, that blank performance of cheer. She seems stronger today, much to Scott's relief. Last night coming in from the airport he was half worried she was going to pull some kind of last-minute dramatic collapse—a swan song, Blanche DuBois swoon—something to draw the focus from her husband's memorial. Something to place her firmly at the center of the world's attention.

Florence sits beside Doris, touches her arm, her face an approximation of concern.

"How are you?"

"How I am is an opera," says Doris. "It's Shakespeare."

Florence nods. She lives in Port Jefferson with her dentist husband. They have two children and a boat.

"Well, you look good," she says. "Doesn't she look good?"

Alice nods. She is looking Doris in the eye, her face measured and empathic. *Lean on me*, she seems to be saying. *I love you. I'm here.* The problem is, she's not. The problem is, she rarely calls, and when she does she tends to talk about herself. It's not that she's a horrible person. Like everyone else, she's just caught up in her own life. It doesn't help that Doris is so negative all the time. Who wants to listen to that? This is the problem with chronic illness. It's a slow-motion tragedy, and the closer you are to it, the more it takes over your life. Add a layer of removal, however, and the situation has the opposite effect. The sickness actually pushes you away. If you can't give your everything to it, if you aren't willing to be on call, then what can you really contribute? We all have lives, jobs, families. Everybody's good in a crisis. We drop everything, race to the hospital. But what do you do if the crisis lasts seven years? When do you get on a plane? How many times a month do you call? Once, twice, never?

So Florence and Alice try to fit all the time they should have been there over the last seven years into this one lunch.

"I'm just so sorry," Florence tells Doris.

"We both are," says Alice.

Florence clucks her tongue, pats Doris's arm.

"Maybe," she says, "and I don't mean to be callous, but maybe it's for the best. I mean, he suffered so much."

Scott waits for his mother to lash out, to say something biting, acerbic. Instead she just smiles her secret smile.

And this seems as good a time as any to talk about black swans. Soon Florence and Alice will get the biggest surprise of their lives. As humans we have a love/hate relationship with surprise. We like our world to be just so, predictable, organized. We take risks, but we don't like to be *at risk*. We hate when things happen that make us feel vulnerable, exposed, things that force us to drastically reassess the world in which we live. Why? Where does this need for control come from? To better understand it, picture a swan on a pond. It is beautiful. It is graceful. It is also white. All swans are white. This is what our experience tells us. But imagine one day you see a black swan. A black swan is, by definition, a surprise. Now take the notion of a black swan, and consider that there are events that happen in our world that lie beyond the realm of normal expectation. A terrorist attack. A tidal wave rising from the ocean and swallowing the coastal residents of four countries. They are events beyond the scope of our comprehension. Until they happen, they are literally *unimaginable*.

Because they are unimaginable, events like these are, by their very nature, *unpredictable*. The theory goes that the very unexpectedness of a black swan helps create the conditions for it to occur. In other words, *if you can predict it, it will not happen*. Let me repeat that. *If you can predict it, it will not happen*. And yet people are always trying to find explanations for these events after the fact. As Kierkegaard says, history runs forward but is seen backward. This is the human mind at work. We are always looking for patterns, formulas that make the things that happened appear more predictable and less random than they really were.

Time again rears its ugly head. For without time there would be no history, no need to forge stories from the past, to see faces in clouds, patterns. We wouldn't spend half our lives looking for meaning. We live and die on this Earth and it has to mean *something*. The universe is a story, isn't it? A novel? A movie? No. It's simply the unconnected mess of what happens. Unacceptable. We are literally incapable of letting things go. Our minds are designed to retain information that fits into a compressed narrative. In social science circles this distorted view of the world is called *the hindsight bias.*

If you can predict it, it will not occur.

This is the level of paradox we're dealing with here. We live in a universe that is becoming less ordered as it ages. Time, they tell us, is actually moving *backward*, and yet all we can see is what just happened.

What do you believe is true even though you can't prove it?

When Doris tells Florence and Alice she is their sister, when she pushes past their initial resistance *(You're kidding, right? Isn't she a scream?)*, when it finally dawns on them that they have lived their *whole lives* in darkness, the world will turn upside down for these women. They will rack their brains, going back. *Could we have known? Were there signs?* They will retrace their histories, look for clues, revisit every gathering, all the Passover Seders of their youth. That mousy girl in the ugly dress, she was our *sister.* When the unimaginable happens we look for answers. We turn to science. We turn to God. We hunt for understanding. When a tidal wave swallows a country, when two gunmen walk into a high school and start shooting, we look for meaning. We want to understand how it happened so we can stop it from happening again, but the whole point of these events is that they're unimaginable. We literally have to see them to believe them.

Lunch arrives. Scott has a hamburger. Florence and Alice eat salads. Doris has the cassoulet and eats a sum total of none of it. A strong wind and she would fly away like a piece of trash. When the waiter puts a plate of mussels in front of David, he says *thank you*, then bows his head slightly, closes his eyes.

"What are you doing?" says Scott, leaning over.

David opens his eyes, unclasps his hands.

"Nothing."

Scott stares at him for a minute, then turns back to Doris.

"Daniel is at the club," Florence is saying. "He's always at the club. I'm a golf widow."

Out of the corner of his eye, Scott sees David resume his pose, head slightly bowed. He whips around, catches David mouthing something.

"Are you praying?" he asks.

David shakes his head. The brothers exchange a look that contains the following exchange:

David: Don't do this right now. Just eat your lunch.

Scott: No way. Don't you flip out on me. You're acting crazy, and I'm not doing this by myself.

David: Calm down. Everything's going to be okay. I can see that now. You're not doing anything by yourself. None of us are. As the Bible says, *all is full of love.*

Scott: That's a Bjork song.

David: The point is, stop fighting. Let the world embrace you. You'll feel better.

Scott: Don't give me that Buddhist crap. You can't hide

behind some smug Zen nonsense. We're in the shit and in the shit we'll stay. Why should you have peace?

David smiles, turns back to his lunch. It worries Scott that he is being so calm. It makes Scott feel left out. Christians believe in the Rapture, in a day when God will call all the true believers up to heaven, leaving everyone else behind. This is how Scott feels. He has been abandoned to live out the end times with all the other hopeless cynics. As they eat, Florence fills them in on how the other relatives are doing. There's Rachel in Florida whose son married a crystal meth addict. There's Erica in Poughkeepsie who has *the cancer.* Uterine. Some of these people Scott knows. Some he doesn't. He listens to her monologue without absorbing the words.

He spent most of the night in the back of a dark club hatching a scheme. It was crowded and humid and he felt better just being there, just sitting at a table in the corner nursing a drink, surrounded. He drew diagrams on cocktail napkins. He wrote down details he remembered—where the tree stood in the yard, how many paces from the back door. The music was like a motor revving in his chest. He must have entered some hypnotic state. That's the only way to explain why it was eighty-thirty in the morning when he got back to the hotel, why he fell asleep in the elevator and woke up in the lobby with a bellman nudging him gently with the toe of his shoe.

"Everyone on our side is coming in for the memorial," says Alice. "Is Joe's family?"

Doris pushes food around on her plate. She is on her second glass of wine.

"Fuck them," she says. "Bunch of rat bastards."

There is a moment of awkward silence.

"Well," says Florence. "I'm sure they're not that bad."

Doris gives her that secret smile. It says, *Just wait. You'll see.*

"And then you're going to Maine?" asks Alice.

"We used to go there every summer," says David. "To the island. We thought it would be a good place for the ashes."

Alice nods, her face assuming that sympathetic frown. She lives alone in a condominium two towns over from her sister. She was a schoolteacher for twenty years. Now she knits and volunteers at the synagogue.

"It was so cold last night," says Florence.

"It was," says David. "I went for a walk, almost froze my ears off."

"I slept through it," says Doris. "The flight must have wiped me out."

Scott watches them, dumbstruck. *Are they really talking about the weather?*

"Maine will probably be freezing," says Florence.

"Don't remind me," says Doris.

"Last week," says Scott, "there was a woman on hold and she couldn't stop crying. She'd called the Hostess hotline. Maybe she wanted to report a faulty Ding Dong. All the operators were busy. She must have waited for twenty, thirty minutes, just sobbing. And I have no way to break in, no way to ask her what's wrong, so I just had to sit there and listen."

"That's awful," says Florence, making a face.

David gives Scott a look that says, *What are you doing? Why do you always have to be so dark?* Scott looks back. *Why don't you pray on it, God-boy? See what Jesus says.* He has this feeling in his bones that goes, *If you're not with me you're against me.* That's the point. They're supposed to do this together. *You get one end and I'll get the other.* That way the weight isn't too much. That way the burden is easy to carry. They used to hold each other in their sleep. When David was four and Scott was two, David would climb into his brother's bed and hold him. *My baby*, he told people on the street, picking him up. Scott would follow his big brother around the house laughing. Anything David did was magic. Now they hunch their shoulders and eat in silence. Now they circle their wagons and eye each other warily from the high towers of their castles.

Alice checks her watch. She has no idea what's coming. In twenty-four hours she will have to reassess her entire life, but right now she picks a piece of lettuce from her teeth, innocent, unsuspecting. If there was no such thing as time, there would be no surprise. Imagine it. No unexpected tragedies, no unforeseen disasters. There are statisticians in insurance company basements across the globe working tirelessly to devise formulas that will allow them to predict the unpredictable. They draw equations on blackboards. They compile data and crunch the numbers. If it were up to them, no one would ever be blindsided by life. There would be no acts of God, no random violence. Life would be 100 percent predictable.

"Do you like Portland?" Florence asks Doris.

"It's nowhere."

"The people are nice, I hear."

"The people are fine. They're soft. They believe in saving the trees. A bunch of bicycling fascists, if you ask me."

"Does that mean you're coming back to New York?" asks Alice. Scott can't tell if she welcomes this idea or is terrified by it.

Doris looks to her sons.

"If they don't want me."

Scott rubs his eyes. At this moment, family feels like weight and pressure. It is the sensation of sinking to the bottom of the ocean, the way the water squeezes you like a fist.

"I was happy in high school," he says.

"What?" says Florence.

"Who wants to see pictures of the kids?" says David, pulling out his wallet. He passes them around. The cousins *ooh* and *ah*.

"That's Christopher," he says. "He's ten. He plays shortstop for his Little League team. That's Chloe. She's eight. We're thinking of having her skip third grade."

"She's got tits," says Doris, signaling the waiter for another glass of wine. Florence makes a face but says nothing.

"And who's this?" says Alice. "Florence, look at those eyes. Isn't he just adorable?"

"That's Sam," says David. "He's seven months old. A real pistol."

"Sam," says Florence. "I like that name."

"All the old-man names are coming back," says Scott. "Ezekial, Methusala..."

David gives him a look. *You're not helping.* He glances at Doris. She's chuckling quietly to herself. Scott can see it on his brother's face—how he feels like he's going to have to carry the lot of them on his back. How he is their dad now, all of them. The waiter brings Doris another glass of Chardonnay. *Thank God she's got a wheelchair*, thinks Scott. He remembers the supermarket. It feels like a dream now, the bright white interior, like heaven with bulk candy. And there was that woman, Joy, that sweet-faced angel and her baby. What he wouldn't give to be back there now. They could barricade the doors and live for years feasting on box cereals and drinking Fanta. The baby would grow to be tall and strong and learn how to mop linoleum. At night they could quiz each other on the price of popular grocery store items. They'd make a game out of it. He would teach the child to read using the directions label on packages of soap, would teach him to add and subtract using a price gun.

"It's funny," he says. "I met another baby named Sam last night."

David looks at him.

"Where? At the hotel?"

"No. In the West Village. I went back to the old house, you know? And when I went into the D'Agostino's to get warm, there was this woman and her baby."

David blinks several times in rapid succession.

"It's a pretty common name," he says.

Scott shrugs. He is picturing his supermarket family. Outside the world would disappear under nuclear winter, but there they'd be, happy and secure, sleeping on beds of toilet paper and packing straw. He would build a nursery in the produce section and their babies (five, six, ten?) would lie on mats of green Astroturf. Overhead sprinklers would shower them lightly with mist every twenty minutes to help them grow. When they were old enough, they would play lime hockey in aisle 6 using brooms from aisle 9 for sticks. They would bowl cantaloupes into empty two-liter soda bottles in aisle 3. Every year Scott would surprise Joy on her birthday by making some tiny, precious jewel out of knickknacks from the kitchen-supply section in aisle 7 or the school-supply section in aisle 8. He would build dollhouse furniture for his daughters using toothpicks (aisle 2) and color them with shoe polish (aisle 13). He would make shoes from oven mitts (aisle 5) and hold dance parties by the pharmacy, blasting ABBA songs off K-Tel compilation CDs (taken from the magazine rack near the checkout counter) over the PA.

"Is this dance taken?" he would ask his daughters and they would giggle. He would pull them up onto the toes of his oven-mitt shoes and whisk them around in circles on lemon-fresh floors.

"Wake up," says David. "We're going."

Scott opens his eyes. Somehow the lunch has ended. He must have fallen asleep. He gets to his feet. The hostess fetches the wheelchair. When Florence and Alice see it they exchange a look. Concern returns to their faces.

"Oh, you poor dear," says Florence. She looks at Scott. Her expression says, *we had no idea it was this bad.* He stares back at her, stone faced, feeling oddly protective of his mother in this moment. *We may be freaks,* he thinks, *but at least we're freaks together. We don't need your sympathy, your condescension. Don't come in here with your last-minute apologies and dramatic gestures of solidarity and expect me to give a flying fuck. Where have you been the last seven years? A card at Christmas? Go fuck yourself.*

"It's just to be safe," says David about the wheelchair. "She gets short of breath sometimes."

Florence nods. She reaches out and squeezes Doris's arm.

"So good to see you," she says. "We'll see you tomorrow at the memorial."

Doris nods. She bares her teeth in what some might call a smile but what looks to Scott like an act of aggression.

"I've got a surprise for you," she tells them.

"A surprise," says Florence, bending down the way you would to talk to a child.

"For you, too," Doris tells Alice.

"What is it?"

Doris smiles her secret smile.

"Just wait," she says. "You'll see."

She lifts her feet onto the wheelchair rests.

"I will say this," she says. "Wear sensible shoes."

"Shoes?" says Alice.

"Flats. I wouldn't want you to fall."

The sisters exchange a look.

"Okay."

"And if you have heart medicine," says Doris, "I'd take it. They say a real shock to the system can do you in."

The sisters exchange another look. Scott sighs. He thinks his mother is drunk. Like Florence and Alice, he has no idea what's coming.

None of us do. That's the point.

DORIS HENRY WAKES at dawn on the big day. She sits on the edge of her bed and watches it snow. In the last three hours it's dumped eight inches on New York, and on the street below, for the first time she can remember, there is no traffic. Not a car. Not a pedestrian. The white streets glow orange in the light of the rising sun. On Park Avenue not a soul is moving. The cars sleep under blankets of snow. Doormen huddle inside warm lobbies, waiting for the plows to arrive. Soon the storm will pass and the salt trucks will emerge, and by noon the city will be back to normal—you won't even be able to tell the snow is fresh—but for now the city is hushed and still, like a woman holding her breath. It is a beautiful sight, even to someone as cynical as Doris, though the beauty only makes life seem that much crueler. But then this is how she is—a woman who can find the cloud in every silver lining. Outside the snow falls in a quiet hush. If Doris were to open her window and lean out onto the cold, wet ledge, she would hear only the breathy hiss of winter, the gentle creak of flakes settling. For some reason the words *born again* return to her mind. The Chinese wear white when someone dies. She doesn't know why she thinks of this, but she does. She always pictured blindness this way, not dark, but light, like staring into the sun.

She pours herself a glass of wine. Last night was bad. She hardly slept at all, even with half an Ambien in her. How do you say good-bye to the love of your life? If it was a funeral she could throw herself onto the coffin. She has always liked this idea, the passionate Mediterranean widow hurling herself into the hole after her husband, sobbing and tearing at her clothes. But as with most things, Doris likes the idea more in concept than in practice. She is not emotional that way, not demonstrative. She has to settle for subtler expressions of anger and grief, passive aggressions, a more Machiavellian approach. Besides, the whole issue is moot, anyway. How do you throw yourself onto a bag of ashes without looking ridiculous? No. She will show her loss, but in her own way. To cheer herself up, she pictures the look on Florence's face when she learns the truth. What a delicious thing a secret can be, a secret nurtured and polished for years. Some truths become more powerful with time. The tragedy of them increases. A bullet becomes a bomb becomes a mushroom cloud. If she had told Florence and Alice the truth when she was younger, say sixteen, they could have forged a bond. They could have become sisters. It would have been tough, but they could have overcome. There was still time to right the wrong, to fix what was broken. But now, fifty years later, it really is too late, and the thought of it is both wonderful and horrible. Horrible because for all those years she could have used a sister, could have used the love and support, but she was always too hurt and afraid to ask. She feared rejection more than anything. She had been rejected by her mother after all, and that is the most elemental form of denial on Earth. That level of unwantedness had fused with her bones, become part of her soul. Whenever she imagined telling the girls, she always pictured them laughing at her, cracking up over her longing, her need. *You want what? A sister? You? That's the funniest thing*

I've ever heard. This is what it's like to be an outsider. You learn to make do outdoors.

And yet now the thought of telling them is wonderful, because, here in her dying days, it is a sublime act of revenge. Now there is no time for reconciliation or apology. Not really. Now there is only enough time for the true magnitude of their mother's deception to sink in. Think of all the realizations it will trigger, the dethroning of that woman from her pious tower. Finally, Florence and Alice will know her as Doris knew her, as a liar. A selfish woman who would abandon her own daughter for the love of a portly man. A woman who would lie to her own children for decades, would deprive them of the comfort and strength of an older sister. This is Doris's true revenge, not against her sisters—because what have they ever been really except aloof and dismissive—but against her mother. Now, for the first time in her life, Doris will truly be seen. The thought of it kept her up all night, because to be seen is to worry about what you look like. Who you are. The thought of it makes her short of breath and jittery. Her husband is dead. Her children pretend to care for her, and today she will unmask them all and show the world the truth. For the first time in her life she will have the last laugh.

She rises from the bed and goes into the bathroom. Her bladder is the size of a penny. She has her clothes all laid out, the black turtleneck, the oversized silver jewelry, but standing in front of her suitcase she changes her mind. She chooses the white turtleneck and the white pants. She stands in front of the bathroom mirror putting on her makeup. She will have to drink white wine today. Red is too dangerous. She doesn't have the same control over her hands that she used to. She is always spilling things, always dropping them. Her oxygen line trails behind her as she walks around the room, stopping every few minutes to rest. Outside the snow slows. She remembers lying on a Brooklyn sidewalk when she was eight making angels in the snow. She was the quirky girl in glasses the other kids didn't talk to. Staring out at the gathering white, she pictures herself standing in the middle of the street. The air would be cold against her skin. She would walk up Park Avenue dressed all in white and for a moment she would be a young woman again. Her lungs would be healthy, her heart would be strong. The snow would stop falling and the sun would come out, rising above the tallest building. It would light her face, and in that moment she would be warm, despite the chill. She would close her eyes against the blinding bright. She would become a beam of pure light.

She has heard that people who die of exposure just fall asleep. The Eskimos put the elderly out on the ice, leave them to die. She tries to imagine what that's like, to step onto a block of ice and float off into the ocean surrounded by black water, killer whales, and time. It is a lonely image, and yet in those final moments how beautiful the world must be. She remembers the last time she saw her mother. It was at Florence's wedding. Doris didn't want to go, but there was part of her that needed to be there. She was a newlywed herself, and Joe had yet to meet any of her family. They had been married at City Hall with just two witnesses, strangers they had met in the waiting area. As the day got closer she got nervous. She tried to get out of it. Joe said *whatever you want, but I'm happy to go.* He had no idea of the truth, that her aunt was really her mother. On the day of the wedding they took the train out to Long Island. Everyone acted happy to see her. They all cooed over her handsome husband. All the relatives were there, even Cousin Jackie from California. Doris clung to Joe's hand the whole time. He promised not to abandon her, not even for a minute. He was such a gentle man, so patient. Doris watched her mother from afar, sticking to the periphery. She was like an antelope studying a predator from a safe distance. The ceremony was endless, one of those indulgent, narcissistic *me*-fests that Doris has always hated. Afterward there was a reception in the dining hall. Joe told her he had to use the bathroom.

"No," she said.

"I can't hold it forever, beauty," he said.

"Then I want to go, too."

They went looking for the bathrooms. She was fully prepared to use the men's room, to go in with him, but just as they got there her cousin Frank and his brother (what was his name?) walked past them and entered the men's room. She hesitated.

"Just use the ladies'," said Joe. "I'll meet you back here in three minutes."

He reached out and touched her chin. She made a pouty face. *Don't leave me*, she thought. He smiled, kissed her lips.

"If you can't find me, I'll probably be hiding behind that plant," she said, pointing.

"Okay."

He started for the men's room, but she wouldn't let go of his hand.

"Three minutes," he said.

Reluctantly, she let go. He went into the men's room. She went into the women's. Inside there were a half-dozen stalls. The walls were white, the floor. It was as bright as the snow is now glistening in the sun outside her hotel window. She went into a stall and sat on the toilet. This was a mistake, coming here. She didn't know these people. They didn't want her.

She was at the sink washing her hands when her mother came in.

"There you are," she said.

Doris thought of her husband standing on the other side of the wall. If she screamed would he come? She didn't know what to say. She dried her hands.

"What a day," her mother said. "I can't believe that's what you're wearing, though, pants."

Doris didn't speak. She felt as if her lungs were two birds flying away.

"And who are you with? Is that a wedding ring? Did you get married?"

Doris nodded.

"And you didn't invite me?"

"We didn't invite anyone," said Doris. "We got married at City Hall."

"Hmmph," her mother said, expressing her disapproval.

"Would you have come?" asked Doris.

"Well, we'll never know, will we?" This was her mother's way—to offer hope only after it was too late.

"I have to go," said Doris.

Her mother moved in front of the door.

"You haven't told him, have you? Your husband?"

"Told him what?"

"The truth. About me."

Doris felt like a bug under a magnifying glass. Her mother watched her.

"Not yet," said Doris.

"He doesn't really have to know. It was so long ago. And your aunt did such a good job raising you."

Doris nodded. She could scream and he would come. She knows this for a fact. She could open her mouth and let it all out, and her husband, her glorious husband, would burst through that door. He would take her away. He would rescue her. But she felt hypnotized by her mother's gaze. She was the mouse in an open field who freezes when the hawk descends.

Her mother reached out and touched her hair. She did it softly, the way a lover would, pushing a loose strand back behind Doris's ear.

"You look pretty," her mother said. "I like your haircut."

Doris wanted to run. She wanted to curl up.

"Maybe we could get a cup of coffee sometime," her mother said. "We'd have to find someplace quiet, out of the way."

The bathroom door opened. Cousin Julie from Trenton came in, almost running into them.

"Oops, sorry," she said.

Doris took the opportunity and fled. She pushed out through the bathroom door and ran into Joe. The mouse was in motion. Behind her the hawk circled for another pass.

"Whoa," said Joe. "Slow down."

"We have to go," said Doris. "Now."

Joe nodded. He didn't argue, just took her hand and led her to the closest exit. The wedding was at the country club in Port Jefferson, and as they pushed through the double doors, Doris could see the blue waters of Long Island Sound. She headed for the waterfront. Joe hurried to catch up. She lit a cigarette. He lit one, too, put a hand on her shoulder. He was a foot taller than her and solid. She pictured him grabbing her mother by the throat and squeezing. Her mother's feet would leave the ground. She would hang there in midair as the life was squeezed out of her.

"My father kept a belt on the wall," he told her. "When we were bad he would make us take it down and bring it to him. Or not even when we were bad. When he felt like it. He liked to threaten me. I was so stubborn. I used to go get the belt before he even asked, just to see what he'd do."

She smoked. Her hands were shaking. Her organs felt liquid on the inside.

"What would he do?" she asked.

"Hit me," he said. He dropped his cigarette onto the grass, ground it out with his toe. He was her mountain, her savior. "It's not the beating that hurts. It's the fear. If you can conquer the fear, then what comes next is just a matter of time."

Time. She sits by the window watching it snow and the past seems so far away. The good things. The bad things stay with you, but the good things recede. This is how it feels. Inside that country club her so-called family celebrated Florence's wedding, everyone smiling, laughing, dancing. Standing there by the water, she wanted to take her lighter and burn the whole place down. She has that same feeling now. Her savior is gone. She sits on the edge of the bed dressed all in white.

The past is a hammer.

The future is a sheet of glass.

AN HOUR LATER Doris sits in the restaurant at the Waldorf-Astoria with her son David and his family. Tracey and the kids flew in last night before the storm. They sit in a booth by a window. Outside the plows have come, pushing snow onto the sidewalks. Handymen from the outer boroughs emerge from the sheltered doorways of prewar Park Avenue towers to shovel the snow back into the street. The salt trucks arrive, spewing their corrosive payloads. Already the city has returned to normal. Traffic fills the streets. Pedestrians in overcoats and winter footwear vault across frozen puddles. They wade through snowbanks. Inside the restaurant, the children are having a hard time sitting still. They haven't seen snow in years, and then only in the mountains. Tracey tells Doris they've already been outside playing, throwing themselves into the powder. Her face is still flushed from the cold. Doris wants to like her, this woman, her daughter-in-law, but there is something about the girl that makes Doris think she laughs at her behind her back. David sits close to his wife, almost on top of her, his hand on her hand, as if now that she's here he never wants her to leave again. To Doris, it looks like he has returned to his hiding place behind his wife's skirt.

"Where's your brother?" she asks.

He shrugs.

"I don't know. I went by his room. He's not there. He's not answering his cell, either."

She thinks about this. Maybe Scott fled, took a taxi to the airport, and flew home. She can't blame him. She would, too, if she had a home.

"I like that sweater on you," Tracey tells her.

"Me, too," says David. "I didn't know you owned anything white."

"Ha-ha," says Doris. She is the kind of soldier who shoots at everyone, expecting even small children to be armed.

"Grandma," says Chloe, "did you know that aardvarks are nocturnal? That means they only come out at night."

"Knock knock," says Christopher.

David sees the distance on his mother's face.

"How are you doing?" he asks.

She shrugs.

"Ask me tomorrow," she says.

She sits there surrounded by family and she should be happy. She should feel comforted, but she doesn't.

"Knock knock," says Christopher. He scans their faces, looking for the one most likely to play. He is at that age where there is no place more boring than a restaurant. Soon he will start slipping sugar packets off the table. He will tear them open quietly and pour the sugar onto the floor.

"Who's there?" says Chloe.

David squeezes Tracey's hand.

"So the memorial's at noon," he says. "I figured we'd leave around eleven-thirty. Give ourselves plenty of time to get down there."

"Is anyone going to come?" Doris asks. "With this weather?"

"They'll come," says David.

"Orange who?" says Chloe.

Tracey gives the baby his juice in a sippy cup. *She acts nice*, thinks Doris, *like she cares, but does she ever call?* It is not unreasonable to think of this woman as her enemy, the opponent who stole her son from her, who turned him against her. It is a mother-/daughter-in-law story that is centuries old. Boys stay loyal to the ones they can fuck. This is the bottom line. Doris finishes her wine, orders another glass. Her son watches her with a worried expression on his face.

"People will come," he says. "Everybody loved Pop."

She nods. He says this, but what she hears is, everybody loved *him*. No one would come if it was just for *you*. All your relatives, your friends, they only ever really liked Joe. *You* were the one they put up with. She smiles her bitter little smile.

"Did you ever want to be more than just a mother?" she asks Tracey.

Tracey blinks at the question.

"When I was six I wanted to be a ballerina," she says.

"That's not what I—" says Doris.

"Then, when I was sixteen, I wanted to be a movie star, but I heard the hours were bad."

"Funny."

Tracey smiles. It is a mother's smile, the smile you give a brave kid as you put a bandage on his knee, a bath-time smile when you have to put your foot down and insist that your child *get in the tub right now!*

"Don't you like being a mother?" she asks Doris.

Doris looks at her son. A mother? To *him*? The question is a challenge, a caustic provocation, but thinking about it, Doris finds this wave of sadness wash over her, this fragile, sorrowful poise.

"I liked the moment when they were in bed," she says. "After the lights were out, but before they were asleep, and you could stand over the bed and watch them burrow down. The way their breathing would slow and expand. The looks on their little faces."

David watches his mother with something like awe on his face. This is the first time he has heard her speak of their childhood in a manner that is in any way reverential.

"You were good kids," she says, looking him in the eye. He nods, speechless. "You were. If your brother were here, I'd tell him the same thing. You were fun and you were smart."

"Thank you," he manages.

"And your father and I loved having you. Every minute. You made him very proud."

David sits there blinking, a father surrounded by his children, a grown man with a wife, and yet in this moment he is ten years old again, a boy who wants more than anything for his parents to love him unconditionally. "Maybe we should leave a little earlier," she says. "Make sure we don't get caught in the snow."

David nods.

"Whenever you want," he says.

The memorial is being held at the White Horse Tavern on Hudson Street. One last time back down to the old neighborhood. It is the center of their family myth. This is how it is with families. There is always one unspoken moment when a family is happiest, when everything is just right. You don't even know it's happening at the time. It is the kind of realization that only comes later. *Oh yes, that was the moment.* For the Henrys it was when they lived in the West Village. It was 1979, 1981. They had the duplex with the loft upstairs. The kids were old enough to walk to school by themselves. They came home and performed skits based on lessons they'd learned in class.

Once the kids got older, they started to pull away. Her husband started traveling more for work. By the time the boys went to college, Doris was spending more and more time alone. She hadn't counted on this, that her family would prove to be temporary, that motherhood would change. She hadn't realized that so much less would be required of her. That once her children were old enough, and her marriage had gone on long enough, they would all run efficiently on their own, like a factory that's been automated. By the time her sons went to college, all they required was the kind of routine maintenance that could be handled by a robot. She found herself caught in a nostalgia for a family she still had. This is the nature of time. You feel things slipping away from you before they're even gone.

David asks the waiter for the check. He has pulled himself together. As they stand to leave, he puts his hand on her arm. It is the first time she can remember him touching her unbidden since he got married. It is a loving touch, the protective hand of a son for his mother. Neither of them really know how to proceed, how to move forward from this point. They have been adversaries for so long. Their dynamic has become a dynamic of retreat, the tension of a rope being pulled in two directions. She can see on his face, for the first time in years, that he would like to bridge the gap, but he doesn't know how. He is her son. He will never have another mother, and yet she makes it so hard for him to love her, so hard to call her Mom.

She checks her watch. They have three hours. Three hours until the memorial starts, until the guests arrive and the testimonials begin. She has three hours left with her husband, three hours to love him as she has always loved him, protectively, divisively, alone. Soon he will be everyone's. They will stand and raise their glasses. They will offer their memories, their stories of youth, and in this way, retake possession of him. This, too, is the nature of time. You wait and you wait and it seems like forever and then the moment you've waited for, the moment you've longed for, the moment you've dreaded, finally arrives. And in those last remaining hours time moves at the speed of light, and you realize that what you thought would never come is now unstoppable. There is no way to put on the brakes, for the future you never thought you'd see is finally here.

PART THREE

KEYS

SCOTT HENRY RIDES the subway. He is wearing a black suit and carrying a shovel. A soldier going to war, a Navy SEAL on a rescue mission. People look at him with disinterest. A man in a suit carrying heavy tools is hardly the weirdest thing they've seen today. He has a black messenger bag across his back, slung over his shoulders. There is a pair of wire cutters inside, a set of work gloves. It is ten o'clock in the morning. He has two hours before the memorial. Two hours to penetrate the perimeter fence, to enter his old backyard, find the spot and dig.

He gets off the subway at Christopher Street, walks holding the shovel over his shoulder, like one of the Seven Dwarfs whistling his way to work. His shoes are made of a thin black leather that soaks quickly in the slush. But he doesn't slow or falter.

He is heading for his childhood home for what feels like the last time. After today he will not go back. It isn't healthy. A man must get on with his life, stop living in the past. He makes this promise to himself, even as he disappears into a city of memory and loss. Around him the city roars with life. It doesn't care who lives and who dies. It is bigger than everyone put together. Keep moving. This is what the city demands. Go on or we'll go on without you. Scott stands up a little straighter. He fixes his

tie. He stops at Greenwich Street, his eyes rising automatically
to the gap in the sky that used to hold the towers. They were
parents to all of us, mother and father. Even their destruction
didn't stop the city for long. Three thousand people died. The
streets were covered in ash. People took a deep breath, brushed
themselves off, and kept going.

At Bethune his pace quickens. It is a quiet street, mostly
empty of foot traffic. He reaches the fence and stops, lowering
the shovel. He does not look around, but bends and takes the
wire cutters from his bag. He is counting on the apathy of New
Yorkers, the fact that people are reluctant to question a man
who looks like he knows what he's doing. He has done the
math in his head. Thirty seconds to cut the fence, a minute to
walk to the tree, maybe ten minutes to dig up the can. The
whole operation should be accomplished before anyone has a
chance to think twice.

If it occurs to him as he cuts the first heavy wire fastener
that what he's doing isn't exactly rational, it doesn't slow him
down. After months of apathy and emotional navel-gazing, he
has decided that the key to his recovery is to commit entirely
to a course of action, no matter how seemingly insane. Make
a choice, see it through. He leans on his hands, squeezing the
grips of the cutters, and snaps through the two remaining fasteners. Then, before he has time to change his mind, he lifts
the chain link and, grabbing his shovel, slides through.

He is in a long alley that separates the larger apartment building on his left from the brownstones on the right. He moves
deliberately, shovel on his shoulder, to the side of his old home.
There is a small wooden fence around it and he goes up and
over. He stands for a moment scanning the windows around
him but sees no one. The view is the same as he remembers.
Brick walls with curtained windows, slices of New York liv-

ing with its overstuffed, overdecorated quality, which comes from staying too long in one place. Standing there he is at once thirty-five and seven. He is old and young. Standing there at this moment there is no past, present, or future. There is only this place.

He drops the messenger bag, walks over to the base of the tree. It has grown in twenty years, taller, wider. But to Scott it looks the same because he has grown, too, and so his relationship to the tree remains proportional. He may as well be the boy set to bury his treasure instead of the man come to dig it up. Snow is piled on the ground around the base of the tree. Scott takes the shovel and scoops it away, exposing the hard brown earth. His breath collects in front of his mouth in puffs of white. Overhead, a cloud moves in front of the sun, and Scott places the blade of the shovel against the earth. He sets the heel of his dress shoe on top of it. In his mind he says a silent prayer, again not to God, but fate. We get so few opportunities in life to correct the mistakes we've made, to fix the things we've broken. When those opportunities arise we must seize them without hesitation. This, too, is an act of faith.

With all his might, Scott pushes down on the foot plate and almost breaks his ankle.

The ground is frozen solid.

He lifts the shovel and brings the blade down hard. It makes a ringing sound. The concussion of the blow makes all the bones in his body jump one inch to the left.

"Fuck," he says out loud.

He brings the blade down again. This time he manages to chip a tiny spear of earth, making a hole about the size of a quarter. At this rate he'll be digging all day. He panics a little, raising the shovel and hammering into the earth a few more times with increasing recklessness.

He should have brought a pickax.

Sirens rise in the distance and Scott freezes, but it is just another New York drive-by. This is a city of emergencies, always someone in danger, in trouble, in pain.

He continues to work, sweat breaking out on his back and stomach. He takes off his suit jacket, lays it across a bush. Using the shovel like a hammer, he chips away at the earth, the cuffs of his pants getting dirty. He is ruining his shoes. Sweat soaks the collar of his shirt and freezes in the cold.

"What the hell are you doing?"

The voice comes from the apartment building behind him. Scott whips around, a guilty man caught in a spotlight. A man in an undershirt is leaning out of his window.

"I'm trying to sleep here."

"Sorry," says Scott. He turns back to the hole he's made. It's barely three inches deep. And just like that the nerve goes out of him. For the first time he realizes what he's doing, how crazy it is. He could be arrested. And for what? Some stupid childhood memory. A whim? So what if he stole his father's dog tags? Who knows if Joe even cared. He was probably glad to be rid of them.

Against his will, Scott remembers the last real conversation he had with his father. It was a week before Joe died. He went to dialysis and refused to get back on the transport. He was demanding to go home. He didn't like this new nursing home. He was sick of being institutionalized. All he wanted was to move back in with his wife, to be a normal human being again sleeping in his own bed. The trouble was he was too sick. He had broken his hip recently. He had trouble standing without help. He couldn't walk without falling. At the same time, the lung cancer was advancing rapidly. There were more medications than a layperson could keep track of. The dialysis center called Scott on a Wednesday afternoon. His father had plopped himself down in the lobby and was refusing to budge. They asked Scott what they should do. If his father didn't get on the bus they would have to call the police, and the police would take him to the emergency room. Scott told them to try bribing him with cigarettes. He asked to talk to his dad. The attendant handed over the phone.

"Hey, Pop," said Scott.

His father grunted. He was like a piece of luggage, a suitcase no one wanted.

"What's going on?" Scott asked him.

"I'm not going back there. Those people..."

There was a barely contained fury in his voice. Scott sighed. Joe had had a couple of strokes. His liver didn't process toxins that well. There were times when he wasn't exactly lucid. Was this one of those? Scott was at work. Everyone around him had the finely tuned hearing of a dog. He leaned down under his desk, spoke quietly.

"You've gotta go back, Pop. If you don't like the nursing home you're in, we'll find you another, but right now you have to go back."

"No."

Scott could hear the resolution in his dad's voice. You don't survive a dozen life-threatening maladies by being weak-willed. Stubbornness was what had kept his dad going for the last few years, a grim determination not to give death the satisfaction of having the last word.

"I won't," he said. "They treat me like an animal there. You have no idea."

Scott could feel his coworkers eavesdropping, all the cubicles filled with witnesses, all of them listening silently, judging.

"Look, Pop. I swear, if you don't want to stay there we'll

find you someplace better, but right now I don't know what else to do. I'm five hundred miles away. Just get on the bus and I'll come up this weekend and we'll straighten this whole thing out, okay? For me. Please."

His dad was silent on the other end of the line. Scott held his breath.

"One night," his father said.

"Yes," said Scott. "Absolutely. I'll call the social worker today and we'll find you a better nursing home."

He hung up and called his mother.

"I know," she said. "He called me, too. I told him he's not coming here."

"I hope you were nicer than that."

"I can't take care of him. It's too much."

Scott felt a surge of anger.

"We have to find him another place," he told his mother. "Start making calls."

His call waiting chimed.

"Mom," he said, "I'll call you back."

He took the other call. It was the dialysis center.

"We got him on the bus," said the attendant. "I told him I'd give him a pack of cigarettes. But once he got on he started yelling. He says he's not going back. He wants to go home. He's in the lobby again. What could I do? We don't kidnap people."

Scott felt dizzy. He sat there vibrating. His supervisor was staring at him. *Break time's over.* Scott chewed his lip. Maybe if he didn't speak, if he just put down the phone and hid under his desk, the whole thing would resolve itself. Maybe if he packed his things and went home, climbed under the bed, somebody else would have to deal with it. How many crises can one man handle? How many impossible situations can one man solve?

"Put him on the phone," said Scott.

There was the sound of the attendant putting the phone down, the sound of his father shambling over. His voice, when he came on, was defiant but defeated at the same time.

"Hello?"

"Hey, Pop," said Scott. "How ya doing?"

Silence.

"Look, we don't have a lot of options here. I'm not there. I can't come get you."

"I want to go home, to the apartment, your mother."

"She can't...you need more care than we can give you at home."

"I understand. She doesn't want me. None of you want me."

"That's not...We're just not equipped. You have so many needs."

"They put me in a diaper. I tell them I can go to the bathroom on my own, but they don't listen. I'm a grown man and I'm wearing a diaper."

Scott's supervisor made a *get-back-to-work* gesture. Scott gave him the finger and turned away. More than anything he wanted the angel of mercy to come and take him away, tell him he was free, that everything would be taken care of.

"Pop," he said, "we're going to figure this out, I promise, but right now you have to get on that bus. If you don't they're going to call the cops and the cops are going to take you to the emergency room. Is that what you want?"

Silence. He could sense his father's panic. Joe was trapped. His illness had trapped him. His lungs were dying. His kidneys were dead. He had a hard time walking on his own. He was making a last-ditch effort to regain control over his life, and yet how much control could he get?

"I want to go home," he said.

Scott took a deep breath. When he spoke his tone was icy, hard.

"You can't go home," he said. "You have two choices. Either you go back to the home or you go to the hospital. Which is it?"

He hoped that someday someone would forgive him for this, for bullying his own sick father, for strong-arming him. And yet what choice did he have? He, too, was trapped.

"No hospitals," his father said.

"Then get on the bus, and I'll call Mom and we'll figure this out."

"Come get me," his father said. *Rescue me. Take me away.*

Scott closed his eyes. For a moment he indulged the fantasy. He would fly to Portland. He would pick up his father and drive to the coast. They would live in a cottage. There would be peace and quiet. There would be dignity and love. Without dialysis or medicine his father would sicken gently. He would die in a rocking chair, sitting on the porch, looking out at the surf. If Scott were a better man, he would do this for his father, and yet even as he thought this, he knew it was just a fantasy. Without the medication his father would suffer. Pain would chew through his bones. Without dialysis his body would fill with toxins. His brain would rot. There would be no bucolic passing, just a slow, torturous ruin.

"I can't," he said. "You're too sick. You need to be someplace they can take care of you."

His father's voice, when it came, was small, vulnerable.

"You take care of me."

Scott couldn't breathe.

"Get on the bus, Pop," he said. "I'll be there this weekend and we'll figure this out."

His father was quiet. Scott could feel his abandonment across the phone line, could hear the realization sinking in. Joe Henry was on his own. He had made his play for control and it had failed. He would take his diaper and go back to the nursing home. He would hold his head high and return. His family didn't want him, and he wasn't about to beg. He would take the abuse, the mistreatment. He had survived worse and for longer.

"Okay," he said. "I'm sorry to bother you."

"No, Pop," said Scott, *you're no bother*, but it was too late. His father was already gone.

Scott lifts the shovel and brings it down on the frozen earth. He will do this for his father, return the things he's stolen, make it right. The shovel chimes against the iron ground, shovel handle blistering his palms.

"I swear to Christ," says the guy in the undershirt, "you do that one more time, I'm calling the cops."

Scott stands panting. It's no use. He'd need a blowtorch to dig this hole. He has failed. Failed himself. Failed his father. He throws the shovel into the bushes, grabs his coat and bag.

"Go fuck yourself," he tells the guy in the undershirt, and jumps the low wooden fence. The memorial was set to begin. He shrugs back into his jacket, every move an expression of fury. He stoops and slips under the chain link, but one of the cut fasteners hooks his coat and rips it.

He stands on Bethune Street, foiled. The wind has picked up, clouds blowing in across the Hudson. His shirt is soaked through from attacking the ground and the slice of the wind cuts through to his core.

"Fuck," he says again. It may be the only word he ever uses from here on out. His mind has seized up, like an engine without oil. The gears are grinding, motor racing, but no real thoughts come. He has failed, and for the life of him he can't figure out what to do next.

He takes off his work gloves, drops them on the sidewalk.
Shoving his hands into his pockets, he walks around the corner
to Bank. He stares up at his old brownstone, and then, because
he can think of nothing else to do, he sits on the stoop, his bag
beside him like a sad, lost dog. He is wearing a black suit with a
blue shirt and a striped tie. The stoop has been shoveled, cleared
of snow, but the temperature of the concrete, the constrictive
single-digit freeze, makes the step feel wet under his ass. He sits
with his knees bent, elbows resting gently on the caps. In one
of his jacket pockets he finds a package of Twizzlers and, but-
toning his coat against the wind, he peels off a spiral-red stick
and lifts it to his mouth.

How can he say good-bye to his father now? This is what
he's wondering as he sits in the cold. He watches people go by,
wrapped up in Gore-Tex and wool. He watches them walk their
shaggy dogs and carry their groceries in gloved hands. Every
twenty minutes a Puerto Rican kid with a red knit beanie comes
out of the supermarket and loads a stainless-steel delivery box
mounted to the front of a bicycle, then pedals off into the slush.

Women with comically long scarves push baby carriages,
navigating around snowbanks and sheets of black ice. He chews
his licorice and thinks of the bar around the corner where, fifteen minutes ago, his father's memorial began. He should stand
and go, but he can't. He's not ready. His parents used to take
them to the White Horse when they were kids, park them at
a table with a coloring book or a Jumble. They would have a
drink and watch the city go by.

On the street a young woman in a bright yellow coat and
hat with a baby carriage passes.

"Hey," she says, "I know you."

It is Joy from the supermarket, and little Sam, bundled up
like a hot dog in a bun.

"Hi," he says, coming out of his daze. "It snowed."

She adjusts her bright yellow hat. She looks like a sunflower.

"Yes, it did."

She looks up at the brownstone behind him.

"Is this it?" she says. "The old homestead."

He nods.

"Thirteen years. That's how long we lived here. Me and my brother and my mom and dad. We played stoop ball on this stoop and watched the Halloween parade go by. I went to P.S. 41 and Grace Church School. My brother got his skateboard stolen by a kid with a Swiss Army knife, took him five minutes to find the blade. He kept pulling out the corkscrew, the screw-driver, the tweezers."

"You're making it up."

"I wish."

He holds out his package of licorice.

"Twizzler?" he says.

She shakes her head.

"You know what they say about taking candy from strangers," she says. "What kind of example would I be setting for young Sam?"

Her cheeks are red from the cold, the tip of her nose. He wants to put his lips to it and warm her with his breath.

"But we're not strangers," he says. "We met the night before last. You're Joy and I'm Scott."

From his carriage, little Sam watches the cars go by. Scott wonders what it would be like to be a baby again, to see everything for the first time. Would the world be simpler or more complex? Joy reaches out, takes a piece of licorice.

"Well," she says, "if we're not strangers..."

He smiles, watches her take a bite. Her lipstick is the exact color of the licorice. He wants to take the baby from the stroller and climb in, fasten the little seat belt and fall asleep to the gentle rolling of the wheels.

"How's your husband?" he asks.

"Far away," she says and sticks out her lower lip.

"But you're fine, right? Aren't you this sturdy frontierswoman, the only child, self-sufficient in all things?"

She paws a strand of hair from her face, tucks it back up under her hat.

"It gets cold at night," she says. "Even us frontier women need a husband to warm up the bed sometimes. Not to mention fight off the Indians."

He watches the Puerto Rican kid pedal up on his delivery bike. Rain, shine, snow, or sleet, people need their groceries. Looking at him, Joy notices the dirt on Scott's pants, the ripped jacket.

"I don't mean to pry," she says, "but what happened to you?"

At first he doesn't know what she's asking—everything? The story of his life?—but then he sees where she's looking, and for the first time notices what he's done to his suit.

"I was digging," he says.

"Digging. In a suit."

"It's a long story."

She looks at him. She is learning what everyone else already knows, that Scott is not a particularly casual person, that he doesn't know how to make small talk, to smile and talk about the weather.

"You're not one of those crazy people, are you?" she says. "Who seem normal, then mail you packages of human hair?"

"No. I'm just the regular kind of crazy. Standard maladjusted, issues with authority, a healthy amount of denial and self-destructive instincts. Plus all the grief."

She looks at him. There is something in his face she recognizes, something familiar, something that makes her want to help him. He reminds her of someone. An old boyfriend? She doesn't know, but she feels the need to reach out, to help him. She pulls the baby carriage to the foot of the stairs and sits down next to him.

"Hi," she says.

"Hi," he says. Now that she's this close, he can't look at her. It takes all his strength just to hold himself together.

"I'm Joy," she says.

"I know."

"And you're this crazy guy I met in the supermarket, and I don't mean to be forward, but there *is* something really wrong with you."

He nods. His face is burning and he is blinking to keep from crying. He feels like if he relaxes, even for a second, he will fall apart. He will start to leak like a dam, and then he won't be able to stop. Joy takes a deep breath, puts her hand on his arm. She reaches out to him in sympathy, one human being to another, a stranger bridging the gap. The feel of her hand, the warmth, the firmness of her touch, is all it takes. He is a house of cards.

"My dad," he begins. She waits. "Died."

"I'm sorry."

"And, uh . . ." Tears are forming in the corners of his eyes. "His, um, memorial service—like a party—is today." Everything around him is liquid now. The egg of sorrow has cracked, and it is worse than ever, making a tragic, sticky mess of everything. Sorrow coats the street, the girl, the baby, like glue, sticking Scott to this stoop, to this place, this moment.

"What time?" Joy wants to know.

"Now," he says. "It, uh, started about a half hour ago."

"You should go."

"I know."

"You should go."

He nods.

"Where is it?"

"Around the corner. The White Horse Tavern." His voice cracks. He is twelve years old again, going through changes. Together they watch the delivery boy ride off into the slush.

"My dad died when I was sixteen," says Joy.

He nods. She is saying, *You're not alone. We are all part of this secret society, the whole human race. It is a culture of death and loss, a secret club of grief.*

"I can't go," he says. "Not without them."

"Without what?"

He looks her in the eye. There is a part of him, internal, subterranean, that embraces failure, because it is easier to give up than to persevere. Easier to see the world as a place where malevolent forces conspire to keep a good man down, where quitting isn't just an option, it is the *only* option. Because the alternative is complete and utter annihilation. And yet what kind of man would he be if he didn't try?

So he tells her. Everything. His dead father, the dog tags. He explains his plan, the clipped fence, the shovel, and the setbacks; the frozen earth, the man in the undershirt. When he's finished she doesn't know what to say.

"How do you know they're even still there?" she says.

"Because I'm on a quest."

She thinks about this.

"You are a little crazy, aren't you?"

"I'm usually not this bad, but I think I'm going through a rough patch."

"Yes. I'd say you are."

She stands and brushes at the seat of her pants.

"Wait here."

She takes her baby from the stroller and climbs the steps to the front door. He stands.

"What are you doing?"

She rings the bell.

"Let me do the talking," she says.

He considers bolting, turning and racing down the street in his ruined dress shoes, a half-frozen man, arms pumping, heading God knows where. But he doesn't.

The door opens. A man is standing there, early fifties. And there is a little girl behind him, peering through his legs.

"Hi," says Joy. "I'm Joy."

"Stay inside, honey," the man says to his daughter. To Joy he says, "Can I help you?"

"I live around the corner," she says, "and this is going to sound weird, but my friend grew up here."

"I can't let you in," he says quickly.

"No," says Joy, "we were just... my friend buried something in the yard when he was a kid, something of his dad's. And it's his father's memorial service today. He wondered..."

"The dog tags," says the man.

They stare at him. The man puts his hand on his daughter's head.

"We found them when we were redoing the yard a couple of years ago. My son thought they were the coolest thing ever."

Scott's heart is in his throat.

"Do you still have them?" asks Joy.

He nods, looks at Scott.

"My dad died last year, too," he says.

Scott nods. He, too, is in the club, the secret society of lost fathers.

"I'm sorry," he says.

Scott's throat is dry. The words are almost a croak.

"What's your father's name?" says the man.

"Henry, Joe Henry."

The man nods.

"Wait here."

He closes the door. They hear him climbing the stairs.

"I don't know what to say," says Scott.

"We need these things," says Joy. "These rituals, memorials. They help us say good-bye. Otherwise it just lingers. People die and we pretend they're just missing, and it drags on for years, this level of denial, waiting for them to come back. Trust me."

Scott closes his eyes. He is remembering how every year on January 2 in San Francisco, businessmen throw the pages of last year's paper calendars out the window. For half an hour the downtown streets fill with a flurry of white, dates and appointments all floating to the ground. It is a moment where time literally flies, all of last year's activities filling the air, the highs and lows, the pithy aphorisms, all the words of the day, the major holidays, professional milestones. If you stand on the street and look up, all you see is time. It descends gently from the sky, fluttering in the breeze. It fills the gutters, the detritus of another year, all the days and nights now gone. Getting rid of it makes people feel lighter, cleansed. They are casting off the weight of what came before. This is what Scott thinks as he stares out at the blanket of white. But what about the things you don't want to let go of? What if letting go of the past feels like a betrayal, an abandonment? Doesn't he owe it to his father to never say good-bye?

Overhead, the sky is cloudless and so brilliantly blue it hurts. In the cold everything feels sharper, like each breath he takes cuts him in some way. *You are alive*, thinks Scott. Right now, in this moment. In *this* one. He wants to stop the clock, to hold on to this feeling, this crazy, beautiful, flushed agony, but he can't. It, too, is destined to recede. Years from now he will remember that there was a moment here, but he will not remember what it felt like. Right now, though, standing on a New York City street corner, everything is crisp and real. This woman is his woman and this baby is his baby, and he is a man in the prime of his life in a black suit with dirt on his pants and blisters on his hands from trying to burrow down into the frozen earth. Any second now the door will open and his Grail will appear. It will happen because it has to.

The door opens and the man and the little girl are standing there.

"My son is going to be upset," says the man, "but he'll understand."

He holds up the dog tags. They've been cleaned, polished. Scott reaches for them.

"There's a shovel in my backyard," says the man.

Scott freezes.

"It looks like someone tried to dig a hole in packed earth in February," says the man, his body language hostile now, guarded. "Bad idea."

Scott looks at the dog tags, then at the man's face. It is a moneyed face, nice skin, gray hair well cut. The next few seconds are critical. Scott takes a deep breath, tries not to panic. He is on a quest and a troll is testing him. He must not fail.

"That was a mistake is what that was," says Scott. "An error in judgment."

"He hasn't been himself recently," says Joy. "Has he, honey?"

She coos to the baby. The man watches her, a young mother with a beautiful child, happy, smiling, and softens. His daughter is behind him in the hallway spinning in circles, making herself dizzy.

"I stole them," says Scott. "He was my father and I stole from him. I have to bring them back."

The man takes a deep breath, sighs.

"You're lucky I understand grief," he says, "or you'd be talking to the cops right now."

And then, just like that, he tosses the dog tags to Scott and closes the door.

Scott's heart surges. The dog tags are smooth in his hand, worn. He holds them up, reads his father's name. It is there, worn but readable. *Joe Henry.* Proof. The man lived. He was here. He mattered. Scott starts to cry. He did it. He is not a fuckup. He is a good son.

"Amazing," says Joy, because she is always amazed by the kindness of strangers, the small heroic things they do every day.

"What time is it?" he asks, wiping his eyes, the tears already freezing against his skin.

Joy checks her watch.

"Twelve fifty-five."

Scott panics. He is so late. The day has gotten away from him.

"I have to go."

He starts down the stairs.

"Wait," says Joy. "Are you gonna be okay?"

"Thank you," he calls, his feet pounding against the pavement. He will be running soon, tripping into full speed. The quest isn't over. He has found the Grail, but now he must deliver it.

"Thank you so much," he shouts, leaning into the wind. "I mean it."

Joy watches him go, shaking her head.

"What a strange man," she says to her baby. Sam smiles at her with those big brown eyes. For the thousandth time today she falls in love with her baby all over again. He is her man, when her man is away, which is always.

"What a strange, strange man," she coos, trying to make Sam laugh.

Then she sees Scott's bag on the stoop, a black messenger bag to be worn over the shoulder.

"Wait," she cries, turning to look for Scott, but he is already gone.

She picks up the bag, not knowing. What is her obligation here? To a man she barely knows, an emotionally unstable man on his way to a memorial? Already she has done more than most. Already she has crossed lines that most New Yorkers wouldn't even look at. But deep down she is a small-town girl, a woman with manners who believes in helping people. A woman who believes that the good things you do in life come back to you. So she lowers Sam into the warmth of his carriage, hangs the bag over the handles.

The White Horse Tavern, she thinks. It is four blocks from here. She will bring Scott his bag and then take the baby home. It is bath day and she will peel her son like an onion, pulling off his tiny coat, his gloves and mittens. She will lower Sam into the warm water of the kitchen sink, will anoint him with hypoallergenic shampoos, gently washing every nook and crevice. Then she will dry him with terry cloth, as if he is royalty, a tiny king to be pampered and inspected. She will powder his bottom and sing him to sleep.

She releases the brake on the baby carriage, heading east.

"Come on, Sam," she says. "Good deeds are always rewarded. Remember that."

This is what Joy believes is true, even though she cannot prove it.

Except in this case she is 100 percent wrong.

THE WHITE HORSE Tavern stands on the corner of Hudson Street and Eleventh. The ghosts of a thousand poets drink inside. Set against the new-fallen snow, its black-and-white facade is a tonic of clarity and precision. Here, it seems to announce, is a place where the truth can be told, where understanding can be had. Inside these walls there are none of the multicolored complexities of the outside world. There is only alcohol and bar food. There is only black and white.

In the final moments before the guests arrive, David Henry wanders the segmented rooms of the pub, going over last-minute details with the caterer. It gives him something concrete to focus on, something mundane and manageable, something to distract him from the other thought that's going through his head, which is this:

He's with God now.

This is what he thinks as the guests begin to arrive, the uncles and cousins, the nephews and aunts. *My dad's in heaven.* It is a thought he is trying on like a pair of glasses, seeing if the world becomes clearer or less focused. In his mind, heaven is a magnificent cloud city, like the one from *Star Wars: The Empire Strikes Back*. The palace where Lando Calrissian lived. David had the poster when he was a kid, Luke and Leia standing together, light saber raised against the malevolent black of Darth Vader's helmet. *Fathers and sons*, thinks David, *this is what it all comes down to.* He looks around at all his relatives, old men in black suits with ear hair, women with stretch girdles and too much makeup. They are drinking the booze he paid for, eating his snacks. He greets them as they enter with a squeeze of the shoulder, a kiss on the cheek. The White Horse was not his choice. He wanted to have the memorial someplace classy, but his mother insisted that they do it here. She didn't want some soulless ballroom. She wanted someplace earthy and significant. Under his instruction, the bar has been transformed into something elegant. The tables have been covered with white cloths. Waiters pass crudités around on delicate platters. Ten pounds of shrimp have been flown in from the left coast and assembled into towers. The place looks good, regal even. He owes it to his father, he thinks, to spend money, to elevate the tone. This isn't some trailer-park get-together, some AA send-off with its jittery, coffee-black decor. We are saying good-bye to a titan, not an ex-con in a speakeasy under a paper banner that reads *Bon Voyage, PeeWee!!!!*

Christopher is sprawled out on the floor near a plate-glass window playing with Cousin Eddie's boys. Looking at his son in this place, David sees himself. He is standing where his own father once stood, a beer in hand, and in the repetition he sees connection. This is the other face of time, not a straight line, but a circle, a cycle of days and weeks, of seasons. Everything comes around. It is disconcerting sometimes. We find ourselves repeating moments our parents lived, echoing their triumphs and mistakes. We try so hard not to become them, not to live blindly by their examples, not to fall into their patterns. It is something David thinks he has accomplished. He is not an alcoholic, not a victim to his vices. In his family, he thinks, he alone has broken the cycle.

He has been reading the Bible recently. Ever since his gutter revelation the other night, he has taken every spare minute to familiarize himself with the word of God. After the Hudson Street miracle (after he was hit by a speeding cab and emerged unscathed) he hurried back to the Waldorf-Astoria. In his bedside table he found a Bible (even at the Waldorf-Astoria apparently there is the chance for redemption). It had the flimsy leather binding and tissue paper pages he remembered from the private-school chapel of his youth. He opened to the first page, traced the words with his fingers—*in the beginning God made the heavens and the Earth*—the tiny royal font, all those numbers and colons, the ancient proper names: Moab, Barnabus, Gemeriah. It felt sturdy to him, this volume, substantial, and yet simple somehow. Here, in six hundred–odd pages, was the history of the universe, the explanation for everything. He read about Adam and Eve and the expulsion from the Garden. He read about Noah and the drowning of the world's sinners. He stayed up all night studying the text. When his family arrived, he had the Bible in his coat pocket. As Christopher came running down the airport concourse, David put his hand on it, drawing strength from the binding.

Now Tracey stands beside him wearing a tasteful black sheath, greeting people. She is doing exactly the right thing, as always. He is a lucky man. He sees this now. Blessed, really. We are put on this earth to take care of each other. This is what his father believed, how he lived his life. And this is how David wants to live. He has made a mess of everything. He knows that. But, God willing, he will make things right. It is simply a matter of follow-through, commitment.

Last night at the hotel, David excused himself and disappeared into the bathroom. He did this every half hour, taking the Bible with him. Tracey asked if he was feeling all right. He said it must have been something he ate at lunch. He sat on the toilet with his pants up flipping the rice-thin pages. The children played loudly in the room outside, jumping on the beds and rifling through every piece of candy in the minibar. In the midst of their chaos, Tracey talked on the phone to her mother. David turned on the sink faucet, creating a soothing rush of white noise. Don't get him wrong. Having his family around him again was a relief. They were his oxygen. His sanctuary. But at the same time there was a need in him for peace and quiet. It was important. He was on the verge of an essential awakening. He was trying to see the world in a new way, and every time he felt close, there was a shout from a child, or the baby would cry, or Tracey would ask him something and he would lose his train of thought.

The truth he sought felt like one of those multicolored posters you stare at. In plain sight is one image, but if you squint, if you cock your head at just the right angle and unfocus your eyes, you can see a second, deeper image. This is what he was doing in the marble-tiled bathroom of the Waldorf-Astoria, reexamining everything, trying to see the world with a different eye.

Sitting on the toilet, he read the following passage, *Genesis 11:1–9:*

[1] And the whole earth was of one language, and of one speech. [2] And it came to pass, as they journeyed from the east, that they found a plain in the land of Shinar; and they dwelt there. [3] And they said one to another, Go to, let us make brick, and burn them thoroughly. And they had brick for stone, and slime had they for mortar. [4] And they said, Go to, let us build us a city and a tower, whose top may reach unto heaven; and let us make us a

name, lest we be scattered abroad upon the face of the whole earth. [5] And the LORD came down to see the city and the tower, which the children of men built.

[6] And the LORD said, Behold, the people is one, and they have all one language; and this they begin to do: and now nothing will be restrained from them, which they have imagined to do. [7] Go to, let us go down, and there confound their language, that they may not understand one another's speech. [8] So the LORD scattered them abroad from thence upon the face of all the earth: and they left off to build the city. [9] Therefore is the name of it called Babel; because the LORD did there confound the language of all the earth: and from thence did the LORD scatter them abroad upon the face of all the earth.

David read this and felt hollow. He pictured the tower, a spiraling brick obelisk, winding up into the clouds. Was it really hubris that built it, or hope? He imagined all the people of the world working in harmony, aspiring to a greater knowledge. This was the first, the original tower. What must it have felt like to stand at the top looking down? To be the first human to stare out at the plains, the sea? For the first time, from a brand-new vantage point, men had a sense of perspective, of clarity. They saw their lives in context. They looked upon the world they inhabited and understood themselves in relation to it. Why was this so threatening to God? Why was his reaction so severe? Reading the Bible, David began to worry. He had only reached page twenty, but already the Bible was full of expulsions and recrimination. The God of the Old Testament didn't seem very kind at all.

He takes Tracey's hand and squeezes. She squeezes back reassuringly. Last night after the kids had fallen asleep, he lay in her arms. Snow fell outside the window, lit from below by the streetlights. Lying next to her, feeling her skin on his skin, he started to cry. She stirred beside him, touched his face, only half awake.

"Poor baby," she murmured, the way she would to one of her children. She thought he was crying because his father was dead, but that wasn't it. Not entirely. He was crying because he was a sinner, because he had hurt so many people, but they didn't know it yet. He was crying because he knew the first step toward redemption involved telling the truth, owning up to his mistakes. Only in repentance is there forgiveness. But he was scared. He had gotten in so deep. It seemed impossible that he could be saved.

"I'm a bad person," he said.

She mumbled into his shoulder.

"Oh, sweetie," she said. "No."

"You don't know," he said. The world was crushing him. All he wanted was to throw off the weight he had been carrying. Sitting at dinner earlier, playing word games with the kids, watching Tracey cut Chloe's food, it had hit him. *What have I done?* He felt the blood drain from his face, the floor shift under his feet. As if from a tower he saw his life. He saw the mess he'd made, the people he'd hurt. He saw his hubris. He was a selfish monster. He didn't deserve to be happy. In that moment he had decided. He would tell Joy it was over. She was his weakness, his pathetic attempt to fill a void that only God could fill. From here on out, David needed to be strong. Tracey was his wife, the mother of his children, his first and only true love. He owed it to her to come clean, to recommit to their family. He had made a vow in front of God and everyone. He had broken it out of fear and sorrow. His father's illness had made him crazy.

He could see that now. For years he had been living in some evil fog. He had acted out of selfishness and need, even as he told himself he was fine. Not only had he lied to everyone he cared about. He had lied to himself.

"I have to tell you something," he said. The room was dark, just a sliver of window exposed, and through it the glimmering reflection of moonlit snow. Tracey had her hand on his chest. Her head was on his shoulder. She was breathing deeply, almost asleep, unaware that the moment was pregnant with danger, unaware that her husband was poised to ruin everything, to upset the delicate balance he had worked so hard to maintain. He could smell her shampoo, and under it the slight musk of her body. It was a smell he knew in his bones. *I love you. I love you. I love you*, he thought. *Don't leave me. I promise I'll change. I swear. God strike me dead where I stand if I don't.*

"Hmm," she said. "It's late. Could we—maybe tomorrow?"

Relief. He kissed her scalp. He would kill himself if he lost her, cut his own throat. He deserved it. Everything was so clear now. It was like a fever had broken. The lie was a Band-Aid he had to rip off, exposing the raw wound below. He should do it now, fast, while the courage was in him, but he was afraid and she had given him an out, and he took it. He lay there under her familiar weight. The Bible was in the bedside drawer. He should take it out, slip from under her, and retreat to the bathroom. More than anything, he needed guidance, and yet deep down he knew what he had to do. He had to tell Tracey everything. He had to get down on his knees and beg for her forgiveness.

Tomorrow.

But this morning, with the kids and the blizzard, there had been no time to talk. And by ten-fifteen it was time to get ready for the memorial. The kids escaped from the room. They ran down the halls in their underwear and had to be captured. The baby felt hot. Everything was so close and there was no time for confession. He could have pushed it, but he didn't. Every time he felt the words move to the front of his tongue, he froze. It felt like drawing a gun and not pulling the trigger. He told himself it was for the best. This was a conversation that needed space, time. It would have to wait. He would tell her when this trip was over, would sit her down and in his calmest voice lay out for her the mistakes he'd made. He would beg her forgiveness, the way he had begged God.

Standing in the White Horse Tavern, he looks around for his brother. *Come on*, he thinks. *Where are you?* Families are supposed to help each other. They're supposed to stick together, and right now he could use the help. His mother has been acting weird since they got here. She disappeared into the bathroom for twenty minutes, and when she came out she sat on a bar stool near the front door and greeted people. She was warm, bubbly even. She has yet to order a drink. Nobody knows what to think. David himself is hard pressed to explain it. Maybe this is her final step into madness. She is like his Bizarro World mom, dressed all in white, smiling, telling people how nice they look. Having grown up with her, he is waiting for the other shoe to drop. It feels like the setup to a joke, and it is, but it's a joke he won't get until it's too late, and it will be on him, on all of them.

Across the room, his daughter sits on a table. She is surrounded by grown-ups and she is holding court, entertaining them with facts and figures. *When the new Messiah comes*, he thinks, *she'll be a little girl. She will make everyone see the futility of war. She won't be vengeful. No one will have to strap explosives to his or her body in her name.* As he walks around greeting relatives, he thinks about Joy, his sweet, effervescent second wife. There is rubble in his heart. What did she ever do except believe his lies? What did she ever want except to be happy? What will he say to her? How will he explain? On the ride down from the hotel he was excruciatingly aware of how close to her apartment he was getting, how dangerous this excursion was. *The only chance I have,* he thought, stroking Tracey's hand, *is if I can control the way the story breaks.* Climbing from the cab, helping his mother onto the curb, he glanced around in a manner he hoped would be perceived as nonchalant. *Please God*, he thought, *don't let her see me.* Inside he tries to keep his back to the window as much as possible. The last thing he needs is to be recognized from the street. He has come this far without discovery. Another twenty-four hours, and he'll be out of here. Another twenty-four hours and he can resolve this all from the road. Standing there, he makes a deal with God. *If you let me make it through this trip, then I promise I will fix this. I will stop lying. I will be a good father to my children, a good husband, a good son.*

He approaches Tracey, takes the baby. He wanders the room thanking people for coming. He is the host, the oldest son, the boy, now a man, who has replaced his father. Sam is warm and sleepy in his arms. Everyone who approaches gushes and coos. *Look at the baby. He's darling.* They are mostly older relatives, peers of his mother's, her younger cousins. Their own children are nowhere to be seen. This is how close David's family was to their relatives. The cousins feel no connection whatsoever, no allegiance. David shakes hands. He kisses cheeks and talks about the pharmaceutical industry. They all have questions. At their age, pills are a major focus. Everyone wants to know how they can get them cheaper. Can he send them samples? He discusses pending legislation, talks about political lobbying. He reassures them that drugs are getting less expensive. It's not true, but this is what they want to hear. He tells them not to bother going to

Canada or Mexico. It's a myth that you can get the same drugs cheaper there, he says. They are generic knock-offs, filled with God knows what substitute chemicals. *You'd be better off praying for your arthritis to go away.* He says this and he thinks it might be true. He has been praying for the last twenty-four hours and today he feels like he just might have a chance.

"Your mom looks good," says Uncle Albert.

"She's had a rough time," says David, "but I think she's starting to come out of it."

"How are *you* holding up?"

He bobbles the baby in his arms.

"We're good," he says. "It's been tough, but I think it'll be really helpful to have this memorial. To say it out loud."

From the corner of his eye, David sees his Uncle Jack arrive, carrying a large piece of poster board. Doris greets him. David excuses himself, walks over.

"Hey, Jack," he says.

Jack gives him a hug. He is Joe's youngest brother, gray haired, stocky.

"I didn't know if you guys did one already," he said, stripping the brown paper from the poster board, "but I thought we should have it."

He turns the poster board around. It is a photograph of the family blown up. The four of them, Joe and Doris and the two kids, taken in Maine. In it they're all sitting on the front porch of the house they used to rent. Joe has his arm around Doris. He is wearing a checkered, snap-front shirt. His beard is wild. He has a broad, effortless smile on his face. Doris is in jean-shorts and a T-shirt. She is in her thirties, skinny, with long hair, freckled legs, and a cigarette jutting out from between two fingers. The two kids sit on the step below them, smiling. They have bowl haircuts, two boys having an out-of-city adventure.

Happy. They look happy.

Seeing the photo, David feels a strange kind of vertigo take hold of him. Everything slopes and winds up around him. The room spins like a twister, drawing into a knot, and then unfurls, settles back down again. He wonders: *Is it the father who is dead, or the family?*

Tracey comes over with Christopher and Chloe, and David hands her Sam.

"See?" she says pointing to one of the kids in the picture. "That's your daddy when he was your age."

David touches their little heads, trying to ground himself.

"We were in Maine," he tells the kids. "See your uncle Scott. He was younger than you are even. Six, maybe."

"Who's that?" his son asks, pointing to Joe.

"That's my dad, your grandfather. You remember him."

But they don't, not the way he looks in that picture.

David remembers the last words his father spoke to him, hollow-cheeked, morphine-addled, lying on his deathbed. *Stop it.* He said, *Stop it.* What did it mean? David glances at his mother. The photo has moved her off her stool, like a magnet to a piece of metal. She is subdued in the face of such evidence of better days, stares hypnotized at her husband's beaming face.

Stop it.

David takes her arm.

"Why don't you sit down, Mom? You look a little shaky."

He leads her to a table. Jack takes the photograph and props it up on a table by the bar. Once again, David searches the crowd for his brother. It would be just like Scott to miss this. He is so selfish sometimes, so caught up in his own navel-gazing. David takes a deep breath, exhales. He doesn't want to have anger in his heart. He is tired of all the negativity. He wants to forgive, to let things go. He looks at his wife. She

smiles at him sympathetically, bobbles the baby. He will be a
better man for her. He will start over. He swears. He has made
his deal with God. Standing there, he is willing to cut himself,
if that's what it takes, to sign the deal in blood. He will simplify
his life. He will be true to his word, the kind of man his father
would be proud of.

Stop it.

Cousin Florence and Cousin Alice come in. Florence is with
Daniel, her mustached husband. She is wearing mink. There
is lipstick on her teeth. She has had work done. David can
see it now, an eye job. The wrinkles around her mouth have
been smoothed. Who does she think she's fooling? God sees
the truth and so does everyone here. Seeing them, Doris stirs,
comes out of her daze.

"Florence," she says.

He nods.

"I have something to say," she tells him.

"To her?"

"To everyone."

"Maybe we should wait for Scott."

"Is he coming? I got the feeling he wasn't coming."

David squats down in front of her.

"I don't know. I haven't talked to him."

And at this moment, in this place, he loves his mother with
a burning ferocity. He wants to protect her. Maybe it's the onus
of the day, the fact that finally, after all these years, there is
nowhere left to run. Maybe it's the recognition that after seven
years they have come to the end of their long journey, that all
the fighting and resentment, all the unmet needs, are redundant
now, pointless. Now, what matters is that they stick together.
It's what his father wanted, what David promised. A boy should
take care of his mother.

"I love you, Mom," he says.

She looks at him.

"No matter what?" she says.

"No matter what."

She nods, looks around the room. So many memories, so many ghosts.

"I have something to say," she says.

He nods.

David helps his mother up. Among the sea of black suits and dresses she looks like a tooth, the first hint of a smile. He leads her over to the bar, to a space near the photograph. He picks up a glass and taps it lightly, the way you do when you want to make a toast.

"Excuse me," he says. "Hi."

People settle down, stop talking. Traffic sounds bleed in from the street. Next to David, the photograph offers its nostalgic wink. It is evidence of the unstoppable nature of time. Moments can be captured, frozen, but only in two dimensions. We can seize an instant and look upon it, but it only serves to remind us how fast the universe is moving. David puts a hand on his mother's arm. His wife is behind him, shushing the kids.

"Thank you for coming," he says. "All of you. We've had a hard few years. This isn't the way any of us wanted things to go. But I'm sure my dad, wherever he is now, would want me to thank you for being there, for supporting us. Every little bit helped and for that we're all grateful."

His mother is staring at him like he's talking Chinese. He wishes she could forgive people the way he has, that she could forgive herself. He never took her harsh view. He always felt that their friends and relatives were generous with their emotions, their time. How much can you ask? It's not their job. The bulk of care falls to the wife, the children. This is the way it goes. For everyone else, a visit is great, a phone call, maybe a little more in a crisis. For David, looking out over his relatives, there is a sense of unity. He is a big believer in family, a strong proponent of reaching out to people, including them. Looking around now, he sees only friendly faces. He is warmed by their presence, their support.

"Before I turn it over to my mom," he says, "I just wanted to offer a little prayer. I know most of you aren't religious, but I think times like these bring us face-to-face with what we believe. I know I've struggled with it over the last few months. What does it all mean? Why are we here? In the last few days I feel like I've come to an understanding, a place of acceptance."

He looks down and sees his son, head bowed. He *believes in me*, thinks David. He wants his son to love God always, to never stop seeing the wonder in the world. No doubt, no fear, no heartbreak. *Every night*, he tells himself, *I'll kneel beside him. We'll pray together. I'll tell him, Don't be like me. Don't give in to weakness, fear.*

"I'd like to think that there is a heaven," he says, "and that my dad is there now, and he isn't sick. He isn't in pain. That there is a place after all of that suffering that is healing. I'd like to think he's at peace, really, and looking down on us and feeling happy that everyone who loves him has come together in this"—he looks around—"*bar* to remember him and keep his memory alive. And for that I say, Thank you, God. Please bless my father and keep him safe. Amen."

People are crying. A few say Amen, but not many. They are irreligious Jews and lapsed Protestants, reluctant to pray out loud. No one wants to look like a fool.

"Okay," he says. "My mom would like to say something. But before I let her, I just want to say how awed I am by the love my parents had for each other, by the strength and longevity of their marriage. There are very few things you can do in this life that actually mean something, and being married for forty years is definitely one of them."

People start clapping. Looking out at them, Doris is reminded of the soldiers in the Los Angeles airport, the way people applauded as they rolled off the plane with their missing limbs. She looks out at all the familiar faces and where David saw friends, she sees sharks. She steps forward shakily. David puts a hand on her arm to steady her. In his mind she is about to deliver a powerful, moving speech, a sweet-tempered acknowledgment of the good times. She will be gracious, forgiving. She will bring a resolution to all the years of infighting and defensive posturing. More than anything he wants her to find closure. He wants healing—the kind you would find in a movie.

He has seriously misjudged the nature of her wounds.

"This is all bullshit," she says. "I mean, whatever, you came out. You got in your cars and drove down from Poughkeepsie, flew up from Boca, like aren't you heroic? But you know, my husband never liked most of you. Some. Jack he liked. And you, Erik. He liked his sister Lois in small doses. It's a joke, really. He was better than everyone in this room, and now he's dead. And don't give me that five-stages-of-death shit. Am I angry? You're fucking right. I never wanted to do this, to get everybody together. It was my kids' idea, and one of them couldn't even bother to show up, so I don't know what you want from me."

Everyone is frozen. David stands next to her, a look of horror on his face. She is getting her closure, just not the kind he expected. The love he felt before dissolves into a pool of anger. He is mortified, ashamed. *That's it*, he thinks. *She has finally flipped her lid.* But he is wrong. Doris is stone-cold sober, maybe for the first time in years. Soon it will all become clear. Soon

he will understand: Sometimes the path to healing runs straight
through retribution.

"I have something to tell you," she says. "A secret I've kept
for sixty years. My husband knew, but he was the only one. And
I've been keeping it for too long. Why should I suffer? This
is the kind of world we live in. I want to say nice things. You
think I don't want to say nice things? You think I don't want to
get up here and talk about heaven and how we all get justice in
the end? The trouble is I don't believe it. The trouble is I think
it's a crock of shit, so instead I'm going to tell you the truth.
I'm an old woman. What do I have to lose?"

She looks around at the faces. Everyone is staring at her,
stunned. They all look old to her now, like dinosaurs, on their
way out. She zeroes in on Florence and her dentist husband, on
dowdy, superior Alice.

"Girls," she says, "I want to talk about your mother. You
think she was such a goody-two-shoes, such a nice little old
lady? Well, guess again. She was a liar and a thief. All she could
ever think about was herself. How do I know? Because she was
my mother, too."

There is a ripple in the audience. She can see it on people's
faces, shock, doubt. Her son squeezes her shoulder. She pulls
loose.

"When I was five years old," she says, "Ruth met Artie, but
he didn't want a woman with baggage, so she gave me away.
She gave me to Zelda to raise. She said *you aren't my daughter
anymore*, and she went off to start her own family. If you don't
believe me you can look at my birth certificate."

She opens her purse, takes out a folded piece of paper. Her
hands are shaking. This is her trump card, dug up from stor-
age and carted around with her for the past week. She holds it
up in triumph. She can see it on their faces: Nothing is what

it's supposed to be. The family scandal has been dropped like a bomb and now they are all casualties.

"Mom," says David. "Mom, for God's sake."

She pulls away from him and moves into the center of the crowd. She is holding the birth certificate up and turning slowly so that all can see. The room is throbbing. Everything seems so bright, as if a light has been turned on behind the scrim of the world. David watches her, his heart pounding. He is afraid. He realizes that he has no idea who she is. All these years she, too, has been a stranger. She, too, has had her secret life.

"I'm your sister," she tells Florence and Alice. They are staring at her, horrified. Their day of reckoning has finally arrived. Doris's heart is racing. She feels light-headed, euphoric. Her husband's ashes are hidden in her tote bag. She has hauled them down from the hotel. It gave her strength to know that he was here, that she was not alone. He would never leave her alone. He is her husband and he loves her. He accepted her when no one else would. *Give them hell*, he is saying.

Take that, she thinks. *Take that*.

This is the moment Scott walks in. There is a screech of tires outside and everyone turns to look, and there he is, Scott, the black sheep, and appearing behind him, out of breath from running, is some woman, and the woman has a baby. Inside the bar the scene is one of chaos. Everyone is talking at once. It is a white noise of confusion. Doris is still spinning in the center of the room, oblivious, caught up in her moment. Seeing them, Scott stops in the doorway, daunted. He wants to turn, run. Joy is behind him, stopped beside Sam's stroller. She reaches for Scott's arm, his messenger bag hanging on the baby carriage in front of her. From across the room, David sees them. He turns white. Here it is, just like that, the moment of his undoing.

Stop it.

And right then something catches Scott's eye, a photograph. He steps into the bar, drawn in by the giant picture of his happy family. He sees his parents, younger, stronger, happy. He steps toward the image, hypnotized, oblivious to the noise, the confusion. He is overwhelmed by the sight of himself as a child, his own smiling face. It seems impossible that he was ever that young, that carefree. In the center of the room, Doris stumbles, dizzy from spinning. Someone catches her, leads her to a chair in the corner. She is like a box of pencils, a brittle bag of bones.

"Did you see them?" she says. "Did you see the looks on their faces?"

Joy steps warily into the bar. She is still wearing her sunflower-yellow hat. Her cheeks are flushed from the cold. The baby, suited up in yellow and black, looks like a bumblebee. David stands frozen. He literally can't believe what's happening, can't believe his brother has shown up accompanied by his other wife. A city of eight million people. What are the odds? And yet at the same time he feels the rightness of this moment, the inevitability. He tried to make a deal with God. He promised to be a better man, but God doesn't make deals. This is proof of that. David has sinned and must be punished, but it isn't easy. Like his father he is a fighter. He looks around for Tracey. She is near the bar, just a few feet from Joy. He believes but cannot prove that if the two women ever meet, the world will cease to exist. Matter and antimatter will collide and they will all be destroyed by the blast.

Stop it.

Scott steps toward the bar, eyes locked on the photograph, lost in his own private reverie. Joy stays close behind him. She has yet to see David, yet to realize that her whole life is a lie. Watching her cross the room, David has the urge to run, to leap through a plate-glass window and escape.

So close, he thinks. *I was so close.*

"Scott," says Tracey.

He looks at her. She steps forward.

"You missed a hell of a—I don't even know what to call it," she says, then notices Joy standing behind him. "Hi," she says. "I'm Tracey."

"Joy."

David watches as the two women reach out and shake each other's hands. He raises his arms as if to shield himself from the blast. Next to him Uncle Jack is trying to get his attention, but David can hear nothing, see nothing, except his brother, his self-involved, fucked-up excuse for a brother. *It's too much*, he thinks. *The final straw.* That's how dysfunctional this family is. *We are supposed to help each other, but all we ever do is fuck each other up.* He feels a fury fill him. It is a bright and shiny dagger, a flame of such overwhelming heat, he feels scorched.

The final revelation hits him with the power of ten thousand suns. He is not the survivor he thought he was, the escapee who made good. He, too, is a freak. He has tried so hard to distance himself from his family's malfunction, to tell himself he was different, but now he sees that lie for what it is, delusion. God looked down from heaven and saw the hubris of man. The people of the world spoke one language. They communicated easily. They cooperated. Each knew the mind of the other, and because of this they were building a tower to heaven. So God reached down and made a mess of their minds. From harmony he created Babel. David used to think the story related only to the misunderstanding between nations, to their different languages, but now he sees that the confusion goes deeper. What God did was not just make it impossible for men of one country to communicate with men of another. He made it impossible for anyone to communicate with anyone else, even if you spoke the same language. He doomed us all to misunderstand forever the will and intentions of others. Why would he do that? Why would he want us to live in chaos, to endure the endless frustration of ignorance, the solitude it brings?

We're all strangers—brothers, mothers, sons. Nobody makes sense.

This is what it feels like to David. He had dared to hope that his family could unite, that they could speak the same language, but now he sees this hope for what it was, hubris. The tower has toppled. He looks at his brother, his mother, and his two wives. They might as well be speaking Chinese, Arabic, Greek. Around them the room boils in chaos, all the cousins, the uncles, the nieces. Everyone is talking at once, but nobody is making any sense. No one is listening. Nothing is getting through. The world has gone mad. And realizing this, David renounces God. The fragile heart of his faith crumbles and disappears. It's too much. He refuses to worship a God who would let people live in such agony. A God who would let fathers sicken and die. A God who would offer no comfort, who would deprive people even of the ability to take comfort in one another. Being thrown out of the Garden of Eden was not the mortal blow, thinks David, because Adam and Eve still had each other. It was the moment that God set the human race against itself. The moment he took away our capacity to communicate, to speak and listen and understand. This was the moment of ultimate isolation. And a God who would throw his flock to the wind like that does not, in David's opinion, deserve to be worshipped. So David takes his faith and breaks it like a board, and by doing so, by casting away the one stone remaining in his crumbling foundation, he leaves himself with no grounding at all. He is now free to finally, and for the first time in his life, totally lose his shit.

Stop it.

He charges across the room. Scott turns at the last moment, sees David and raises the dog tags, a look of triumph on his face.

"Look," he says. "I found them."

David grabs Scott by the collar, raises his fist to strike.

And here we have come to the defining moment, that diamond-hard interstice of worlds colliding. Now is the time when everything happens at once, and too quickly to accurately recount. We have traveled so many miles, have journeyed so long to get here, but it will all be over before you can take it in.

Stop it. Slow down.

Let us consider this moment—the moment of instantaneous velocity—the moment before everything collides. Let us freeze the room, the world; David with his fist raised, Scott turning, still hypnotized by the family picture. Let us freeze Joy at the moment of recognition, her eyes widening, seeing her husband materialize from thin air. Let us focus on Tracey, that loyal and beautiful mother of three, her hands rising, trying yet again to stop her husband from doing the wrong thing. See the children huddled at her feet, their oversized eyes and pinchable cheeks. Picture all the relatives frozen in clusters, mouths open, distorted by emotion. Imagine Doris sitting in a corner, leaning forward, feeling dizzy, short of breath, her birth certificate still clutched to her heart, proof, finally, of who she is.

In a second we will all be moving. In a second the world will resume its chaos. Everything will happen too fast to be taken in. Later, people will tell their stories, give their perspective, but no one will be able to say for sure, definitively, what really occurred. We could hold congressional hearings on national television. Law firms could hire outside vendors to program computer simulations, calculating in three dimensions the positions of all the major players, the angles of impact. Senators from Southern states could stand and offer magic-bullet theories. But there is no way to know for sure what will really happen when the world begins to move again. Joy, in telling her side of the story, would focus on the moment she first recognized her husband, the drastic, life-altering shock of it, her mixture of confusion and understanding as she put the pieces together, as the black swan showed its beautiful, malevolent wings. She would describe the visceral pull she felt in that moment to protect her baby from her husband's sudden violence. David would talk about how, in a world without faith, everything turned red, how for some immeasurable period of time he lost control. He went insane. Scott, who is soon to receive an unanticipated blow to the head, would be hazy on the details. His impressions would be sensual, the sound of the punch, the way the room tilted at a crazy angle, the weightless feel of falling.

See them now all frozen in time at the black-hole center of this story. It is one-eighteen-and-sixteen-seconds in the afternoon, Eastern Standard Time, on February 14, Valentine's Day. Outside the snow has given way to blue skies. Sunlight spills in from windows on two sides. It fills the main room of the bar, which is about twenty feet wide and ten feet deep. To the left is a second room with a dartboard and two audacious piles of shrimp. There is a short hall with two bathrooms. Inside the men's room were once written the words *Go home Kerouac*. Near the main bar there is a plaque on the wall commemorating the night in November of 1953 when Dylan Thomas downed his eighteenth and final shot of whiskey, staggered out of the bar, and collapsed on the street. After falling into a coma at the Chelsea Hotel, he was taken to St. Vincent's Hospital, where he died. St. Vincent's, by coincidence, is the hospital Scott and David will find themselves at in less than an hour, a broken hand and a broken nose. Cause and effect. They will sit there bleeding, in pain, bombarded by piano music.

There is a long bar stretched across the rear of the main room. The bartender is a fifty-one-year-old man named George Hennessy. He lives in Brooklyn with his mother. At this precise second he is drawing a pint of Boddington's. The blond-amber beer hangs in midair. Behind him the hands of the clock are frozen in a disapproving stare. In front of him the surface of the bar is an obstacle course of drips and spills. Look around. See Cousin Florence (now Aunt Florence) stuck in the act of angrily shrugging on her mink coat. Her husband, Daniel, is helping her get it on. Florence is as mad as she's ever been. She never liked surprises and she never liked Doris and she is about to walk out in a huff. Beside her Cousin Alice (now Aunt Alice) is frozen in mid-turn. She is looking behind her, trying to catch a glimpse of her new sister, Doris, who is seated in the back of the room, looking pale, feeling dizzy. Alice is torn between leaving with Florence (who has always demanded absolute allegiance) and staying, reaching out to Doris. She has always wanted another sister. Florence can be such a bitch.

See Uncle Jack, with his overgrown eyebrows. He is frozen in conference with his brother Calvin and Calvin's wife, Claire. Jack is divorced. He has been in love with Claire for six years, but he is too modest to ever say anything. He lives alone in a ramshackle house in New Hampshire and reads books about the Spanish American War. Like his brother Joe, Jack will die in a hospital, but in his case the cause won't be lung cancer. It will be a head injury sustained from falling off his roof.

See them all, every one with their secret lives, their secret worlds. They stand inches away from one another, but they might as well be miles apart.

It is one-eighteen-and-sixteen-seconds in the afternoon on February 14, Valentine's Day. In Karbala, Iraq, an American soldier on foot patrol has just realized that he has triggered an improvised explosive device. It is the last thought he will ever have, for as soon as the clock starts moving again, he will disintegrate in a hail of shrapnel. In Mexico City the rain has finally stopped after two days and the sun peeks through the clouds, throwing a rainbow against the mountains. And at this moment all around the world, thousands of babies are being born, thousands of graves are being dug. People are kissing and fighting and laughing and crying in numbers too large to imagine. If you step back far enough, the world becomes a blur. If you pull away from this bar, this story, if you retreat out of this city, out of this country, off of this planet, if you rise up out of the galaxy, out of the universe, into the black void of space, everything stops being specific. All you can see is time. And then, if you rush back in, if you drop like a bomb from a plane and rush down toward Earth, toward a target, a single set of coordinates, in that last moment before impact, you can see exactly what it is you're destroying.

Everything, all at once.

And in that moment, we're all the same.

For a split second, everything stops, stutters, then, inevitably, it starts to move again.

David pulls back his fist. Tracey reaches out to stop him. Joy recognizes her husband. Scott comes out of his daze in time to register the anger on his brother's face, to see his fist come up, swoop forward and connect with the side of Scott's head, knocking him to the ground. As Scott falls, David drops down on top of him, unaware of screaming from both Tracey and Joy, unaware of the shouts and general chaos of the room. Thirty-seven hours ago he was running down the street chasing the idea of God. He was hit by a cab and emerged unscathed. And now everything has gone to hell.

He pulls his hand back and throws one last punch, connecting with the bridge of his brother's nose.

Bull's-eye.

And there it is, the beginning, middle, and end of everything. In terms of our story, this is the big bang, time, light, energy, the universe spinning, expanding. The puzzle is assembled. The picture is revealed. It is a photograph of the Henry family, a blown-up poster of better days. The father and mother sit on the top step of a rustic house in Maine. They are arm in arm, smiling. At their feet are two little boys. They are happy and whole forever.

Or maybe it is a different picture, a picture of a broken family in a bar, the two brothers now at each other's throats, the father reduced to ash in a box, the mother forgotten in a corner. We take the puzzle and break it apart, dump the pieces back in the box. Years from now we will find it forgotten in a closet. The picture will be faded, pieces will be missing. We will put it out on the lawn and sell it with the shoes we no longer wear.

One thing is for sure. No one in that room has any idea that the big picture has finally revealed itself. Our moment of true understanding watching them from outside is their moment of absolute confusion. They are all caught up in the fractured chaos of broken promises, of things not working out as planned. They are all stuck irreparably in the narrow focus of their own lives. Scott falls to the floor. David drops down on top of him and, without an ounce of mercy in his heart, breaks Scott's nose.

And in the orgy of aggression that follows it is ten minutes before anyone notices that Doris Henry is dead.

THE GIANT STEPS

THERE IS SNOW on the beach. The ocean is a cold gray sheet. Underfoot, there is no sand, only rocks, the beach a three-mile horseshoe curving outward, flanked on one side by towering clay cliffs. When they were kids, Scott and David would collect beach glass from among the pebbles here. They would bring the faded gems home in their pockets and dump them out onto the kitchen table. They would wash them in a colander and present them like jewels. Their parents kept a jar on the mantelpiece, a treasure chest of broken beach emeralds. This was Bailey's Island, Maine, the opposite of New York City—sleepy, bucolic, slow. It was their escape, their Fresh Air Fund. Every summer for a month they left the confines of New York. They escaped the concrete labyrinth and drove north. For four weeks the boys lived outdoors among the poplars and saplings, crouched down in the lanky seaweed, hunting for crabs. They went barefoot. Their hair grew long. They went days without putting on a shirt. When you're young a month can seem like a lifetime, all those lazy days stretching together. When you're young, time is irrelevant. There is so much of it, it spills from your cupped hands and tumbles to the ground. They would lie in the grass and stare up at the sky, listening to the sound the wind made rustling the tops of the trees. In the afternoon they would ride their bikes from one end of the island to the other and back. They would sit in the shade of a tree and read Tarzan books, Robert Heinlein, *The Stainless Steel Rat*. There was a hidden fortress next to the house, a womb in the trees, inside which, if you climbed under the low-hanging branches, you found yourself in a shaded hollow, completely hidden from the outside world, the floor a musty weft of pine needles. This was where their wars were planned, their secret mission, mapped out in the dirt—dreams of enemy soldiers in their bunkers, and then the stealthy deployment, two boys crawling through the tall glass, reconnoitering the nearby houses.

Their parents sat on the back porch and read. The pace of the world was the resting heartbeat of a sleeping dog. They listened to the radio, then went inside to fix lunch. In the stillness of the country there was nothing but the sound of the breeze, carrying with it the distant cries of seagulls. From the porch they could see the ocean. It lay just a few hundred feet away, down the winding path through the blueberry patch, and then left through gnarled crab apple trees to the sloping dirt path that wound down twenty feet to the rocky outcroppings of Pebble Beach. You could be there in minutes, seconds if you ran, if you kicked up your ten-year-old heels and took off, the tall grass whipping at your bare legs, the salt air burning your lungs. There were gardener snakes out there and tennis balls they had lost. Birds hopped through the weeds, hunting for worms. Once the brothers had stood at the edge of the cliff and thrown fish heads into the air. In seconds they were descended upon by seagulls. Their parents watched from the porch, drinks in hand, as their sons disappeared into a fluttering cloud of white. It was a feeding frenzy, an orgy of indeterminate character. Were the boys in danger? Were they being absorbed into some exotic avian tribe? Watching, their parents waited for them to break free, to take flight.

If you ran in bare feet, scanning the ground for rocks and pricklers, if you scrambled down the grassy hill and stepped gingerly onto the vertical shale outcroppings, the stone sheered and jagged like the teeth of a comb, you could jump the last few feet into the hot sand (which existed only in tiny pockets between wave-smooth rocks). You could stand panting on the beach and listen to the crashing waves. In front of you was a field of seaweed floating in the middle tide. It was a verdant, blackish green, all tentacles and bulbous air pods. Under it lay all kinds of life, hermit crabs and barnacles and periwinkles. Flip the seaweed back, turn over a rock, and all manner of crustaceans would scramble forth. Scott and David's parents would send them down here sometimes in the evening to collect seaweed for the lobster pot. If you walked far enough, there was a rock shaped like a boat that you could stand on and pretend to be captain. There were boulders you could climb, digging your naked toes into worn pockets and pulling yourself up by your fingertips. From the top you could pretend to be a giant. You could stand on the beach and know in your heart that the summer would never end. That you could be a kid forever. It was true because you would make it true.

This is what Scott thinks as he climbs down the rocky path today. It is twenty-plus years later. He is a thirty-five-year-old man making the trek one last time with his thirty-seven-year-old brother. They are both carrying cardboard boxes. It is February 18. The air is a creaky, low-pressure gray, clouds hanging just out of reach. They have spent the last few days in a daze. There have been hospitals to visit, funeral homes. There have been forms to sign, decisions to be made. What should

they do with their mother's body? Should they continue their
journey or fall back, regroup? After everything that had happened, it would have surprised no one if the two brothers had
given up and parted ways, if Scott had gotten on a plane and
flown home, leaving David to deal with the mess he'd made,
but instead the two brothers clung together. After the emergency room, after the endless wait for a verdict—a stroke, their
mother had a massive stroke and died where she sat, still clutching the paper record of her birth—the boys returned to their
hotel, where Scott packed his things and moved into David's
room. Tracey had already been there, had already packed up
and left with the kids. There was no note, no bitter farewell
jab. In her wake she left only judgment and silence. David and
Scott sat in that silence for two days. What was there to say?
Their mother had died. David had proven to be a polygamist.
Scott had shown up at their father's memorial with his brother's
second wife, and now it was over. It was all over, and they
thought if they just sat still and didn't say anything, if they didn't
hope or dream or wish, then nothing else would happen. No
more calamities, no more asteroids falling from the sky, no more
self-inflicted wounds. If they just sat still and didn't try to do
anything, then maybe the world would let them be.

For twenty-four hours they didn't leave the room. They
stayed in bed and slept. The world had proven to be bigger
than they could handle. It had risen up over them and crashed
down with deafening thunder. They lay on their beds in the
climate-controlled stillness of their room and stared at the ceiling. They were exhausted. They were in shock. They turned
off their phones. They had been humbled by the magnitude of
their tragedy. It literally took their breath away, so they made
themselves very small and burrowed down into their bedding,
and they waited for the worst to pass. In the middle of the night

Scott could hear his brother crying. He didn't try to comfort him. There was no comfort. This was the world they lived in. Their parents were dead. Scott and David had gone mad with sorrow and stumbled into mayhem. Here was the ruin they had found. To look for comfort would be a further sign of madness. Instead they tried to accept the things they'd experienced, the crimes they'd committed, the pain they'd suffered.

On Wednesday they got out of bed and packed. They did so without speaking, both knowing somehow that it was time to go. When David picked up the phone to call the front desk and arrange for their rental car, it was the first words he had spoken in thirty-six hours. His voice sounded weak and apologetic. He wouldn't speak again for six more hours. In silence they rolled their suitcases to the elevator. Scott dragged his mother's valise, red scarf still tied to its handle. He hauled her black turtlenecks and her smuggled packs of cigarettes. He carried her pants and shoes, her jewelry and glasses. They put them in the trunk of the rental car and drove west across the park to the funeral home. There they picked up the box that held their mother's ashes and put it in the backseat next to the box that held their father's. It was a twisted variation on the family vacation, children in front, parents in back. David slipped the car into gear, pulled out into traffic. He took Tenth Avenue north, got on the West Side Highway. They drove up through the Bronx, past the Cloisters. They were heading for Maine. It was a seven-hour trip with no traffic. The road was still icy in places, the trees loaded down with snow.

Somewhere around Connecticut, Scott spoke for the first time.

"I feel like one of us should smoke a cigarette," he said. "You know, for old times' sake."

David put on his blinker, changed lanes. He had a hard time

looking at Scott without feeling waves of shame. There was the cut on Scott's cheek, the tape on his nose, his two black eyes. David knew he could never make it up to him, to anyone. It is a humbling feeling to realize you've ruined everything. Such utter destruction is no mean feat. It must be worked at with intensity and perseverance. The follow-through it takes to destroy your own life is enormous. Driving north, David revisited all the opportunities he'd had to take a different path. So many moments he could have turned back, but he didn't. The thought kept him awake last night, tossing, turning. Scott was snoring gently in the next bed. As quietly as possible David turned on the TV. They were playing *Close Encounters of the Third Kind*. It was the scene at the dinner table where Richard Dreyfuss keeps putting more and more mashed potatoes on his plate. The shape they make reminds him of something. He is crazed, obsessed. He smoothes the potatoes into a mountain, takes his fork, and slices off the top. His daughter starts to cry. He still has a sunburn on one half of his face. His children are afraid of him. His wife doesn't understand him. David watched the scene without sound. He thought, *I know exactly how he feels.* He recognized the husband's fevered state, saw in his sculpting the true sign of his own madness. A man who would take a second wife, who would, as the walls closed in, try to recycle himself through God, to skip the reckoning and go straight to forgiveness, he is a true lunatic. David thinks about Tracey, his children. All they ever wanted was to love him, and yet living among them, he felt so alone. His family was right there reaching out and he couldn't feel them. And he thought the problem was them, but it wasn't.

It was him, all along.

He drives the speed limit. It feels good to get out on the open road, to leave New York behind. He is afraid to think too far ahead. There are craters up there, dark tunnels with no light in sight.

"Are you okay?" his brother asks.

"Compared to what?"

Scott doesn't answer. This is how it goes. For the next few hours they make brief attempts at conversation, neither of them pushing too hard. In Massachusetts, Scott turns on the radio, finds a rock station, and for a few miles this feels good, to have something aggressive and quick blaring from the stereo, but then the music begins to feel like an assault and David turns the radio down, then off.

"I liked her," says Scott.

"Who?"

"Joy," says Scott. "If you're gonna have a second wife, I mean, she seemed like a good choice."

David winces. He can't bring himself to think about that moment, that nauseating instant of recognition, his two families' tragic, all-at-once collision. The chaotic clusterfuck of it flashes through his mind from time to time like rape and he has to cover his eyes. **Tracey:** Your *husband? He's my husband.* **Joy:** *What do you mean? David, what is she talking about?* At the White Horse Tavern, the whole thing unfolded with such painful clarity, such clean precision, he was struck mute by the awful beauty of it. He knelt on the floor of the bar with his brother's blood on his hands, staring up at their stricken faces, his wives, his children. *David? Daddy?* All they wanted was for him to explain, to tell them that what seemed like an epic betrayal was really just a bad joke. But what could he say? The words just wouldn't come. And then, in some sick reprieve he will revisit for years in therapy, a scream came from the back of the room, and he turned to find his mother dead. Punishment. It felt like punishment. In one second he went from having two wives and a mother to being womanless, childless. And he can't even be mad. It's all his fault.

"I am such an asshole," he mutters.

Scott nods.

"I am such an asshole," David repeats.

"Louder."

David yells.

"I AM SUCH AN ASSHOLE!!!"

Scott studies his brother. He finds, in David's ruin, his humiliation, a kind of relief. He loves his brother more for his flaws, accepts him. Now that he is human. Now that he is fallible, weak. This was all Scott was looking for. A correction, a lessening, an unmasking. The emperor has no clothes. He is human and hurting just like the rest of us.

"Feel better?" he asks.

David doesn't answer. He adjusts the rearview mirror so that he can see the boxes that hold his parents' ashes. The whole thing boggles the mind. There are no metaphors, no advice books. They are past the point of no return. Everything is white now, empty.

"Hungry?" he asks Scott.

Scott shrugs. They haven't eaten more than a packet of peanuts between them in two days.

"Should we stop at that seafood place in Portsmouth," David asks, "like in the good old days?"

"We could hit the liquor store in New Hampshire."

David shakes his head.

"I was thinking more clam chowder than beer."

Scott looks out the window. One year when they showed up at the house, there was an egret standing on the back porch, a tall, white bird with spindly legs. It betrayed no interest in leaving. They would go to bed at night and wake up in the morning, and there it'd be, standing on the back porch drinking water from a dish. After two days they put it in the car and drove to the marshes. Only there did it remember it was a bird and fly away.

"You should call Tracey," he says.

"I'm afraid to," says David after a minute.

"You should call, anyway."

David nods. "I'm sorry," he says.

"Not to me. To her."

"I meant for the"—he gestures—"hitting."

"Whatever. You've hit me before. You'll hit me again. We're brothers. You're just lucky you sucker punched me. If I'd seen it coming, I'd have knocked you into Sunday."

David switches lanes, accelerates around a station wagon.

"How is it possible," he wonders, "that you found her? The one woman?"

Scott thinks about it.

"Just lucky, I guess."

David sighs. Just because he doesn't like the way God operates doesn't mean he has completely given up his faith. If you'd asked him two days ago he would have said, *absolutely, I'm an atheist again.* But last night, like a flower in a lava field, his faith started to blossom, rising from the ashes. No one was more surprised than him. The thought that fed it is this: *You don't get to choose the God you believe in. You don't get to decide to be reverent based on whether things are going poorly or well. You have been selfish for too long. You can't control your God. You don't get to dictate under which circumstances you will believe. God doesn't make deals, and he doesn't like to be threatened, especially not by someone as arrogant and fault-ridden as you.*

It is only in recognizing your true powerlessness that you can restore your hope.

Faith is a promise you make to yourself.

Because, lying in the rock-bottom abyss of his despair, he finally realized what his father meant when he said, *stop it.* He meant stop hiding. Stop pretending everything's okay. He meant stop putting up walls and acting like none of this is affecting you. Stop lying. Stop running. *Stop it,* he said, his eyes flaming, and what he was really saying was, Stop shirking your responsibilities, even as you claim that it's your responsibilities that make it impossible for you to help us. Stop fighting so hard. Stop pretending to be invulnerable.

We're your family. We are all you have.

"Thank you," David tells Scott. He doesn't have to say for what. They both know. *Thanks for not leaving me. For being here. For seeing this through.*

"No problem," his brother tells him.

For both brothers it feels like a huge storm has finally passed. They can't bring themselves to say it out loud, but the truth is *it's over.* They will not have to carry their mother through her long, dying years, will not have to watch as she falters and slowly suffocates. It has been seven years, and for the first time they can remember, there is no sickness ahead of them. There are no agonizing decisions, no brutal sacrifices. If they think about it too long, they feel giddy, a dizzying mixture of joy and sorrow brewing in their hearts. There is that buoyant, unreal feeling that comes from finally dropping the heaviness you have carried all these years. You feel unbalanced, fragile. You walk with your arms out. Scott and David are still reeling from the speed of it, the suddenness. But the reality is slowly setting in: They have reached the end of the road here on the East Coast, back where it all began, and now all that's left is to say good-bye.

They drive north through tree-lined states, reaching Bailey's Island at four P.M. They rise up over the great stone bridge from Orr's Island, having made the turn-off near Brunswick. Everything looks familiar. There is the sensation of driving into the past. Neither of them has been here since they were teenagers, and yet both of them could close their eyes and retrace every road, every field. They can picture the walk to the General Store, past the church that had the rummage sales every Sunday in the basement. You take that road back past Cook's Field and there on your right is the jolting blue of Mackerel Cove. Keep going and you reach Land's End and the turn-off for the Great Steps, a natural rock formation that looks like the staircase of a giant. It is here where they stood when they were kids watching the waves pound the stone, imaginations engaged, picturing the colossus that must have strode from the sea, climbing those stairs onto dry land. They could imagine him stepping from island to island, his massive head way up in the clouds. The crash of the waves echoed the jarring concussion of his footfalls.

Coming over the rise of the bridge, seeing the lobster boats bobbing in the water, Scott feels unexpectedly small. They are here suddenly, back at the place where their adulthood first emerged from the sea. *It will all be different.* He knows it before he sees the new town houses that dot the landscape. This place has not survived intact. In two decades the economy has boomed and busted, and in that time people from New York and Boston and Portland have built their dream vacation homes. They have installed swimming pools and cluttered up the open spaces. The sleepy coastal island with its small-time lobster trade has become just another weekend retreat for city folk. In order to have the moment they have envisioned, David and Scott will have to do this with their eyes closed, living in their memories.

David drives the island's main road. Everything is different and the same at once. It's spooky, and though they had planned to stay the night, seeing it, they both decide independently to push for a return to the mainland. Once they have done what they came to do, they will head back. This is not a journey for reminiscence, after all. It is a bon voyage, and though you may stand around on the dock watching once the ship has pulled away, those who have been left behind do not linger. They do not stay the night.

"Here?" asks David, and Scott says, *Yes.*

David turns left, climbs the short hill. It is the middle of February and most of the vacation homes are empty, driveways abandoned, houses locked down for the winter. The short street jogs left at the rosehip bushes. David slows, pulls into an asphalt driveway. Theirs was the house second to the end. A thin layer of snow covers the earth around it, crunching under their feet as they climb from the car. The air is chilly, the sky gray, and they can see the white clouds of their breath. They stand for a minute listening to the silence, the quiet ticking of the engine, and the far-off echo of the waves.

"They put on an addition," says Scott, looking at the house. He remembers the wicker rocking chair that used to creak in the living room in the middle of the night, as if a ghost were shifting, trying to find a more comfortable position.

"Let's go," says David. He leans into the backseat, pulls out his father's ashes. Scott opens the rear passenger-side door, grabs his mother's. They walk around the side of the house, and suddenly there it is, the ocean. It is like walking straight into a photograph, a memory. They stand for a minute, staring out— the angled field, the sudden cliff, and, beyond it, the flat plane of the Atlantic. Everything else may have changed, but this moment, this view, is just as they remembered.

"What do we do now?" David asks, and the question seems

somehow larger than the immediate future. It is a question about life. What do we do now that our parents have died? What do we do now that the women we loved have left us? What do we do now, as men in our late thirties, who have been suddenly left out in the open, exposed? How do we start again?

"To the beach," says Scott.

They descend through the brittle grass, stepping over crusty piles of snow. It is the first time either of them has been here in the winter. There is a grandeur to it, a majesty to the landscape, the angry, roiling ocean. Scott imagines what it must have been like for women to watch the seas, waiting for their husbands to return. The wind picks up. He tightens his collar, stumbles down the hill.

Behind him he can hear David humming, but he can't make out the tune. They wind down through the woods, ducking under frosted spiderwebs, and emerge onto the hill overlooking the beach. The waves are louder now, pounding in rhythm. They are two men in suits carrying boxes, like Bibles. It is a funeral procession, but also an act of trespass. They are boys who don't know how to cry, who have taught themselves to be strong, and in their blind delusion of strength have driven headlong into walls. They are humble now, regretful. They have come here, to land's end, to the edge of the ocean, carrying the remains of their past in boxes. All they want is a chance to do it over, but time doesn't work that way. You cannot go back and do things again. All you can hope for is improvement in the future. All you can hope for is change. *Please let things change.* It is madness to make the same mistakes over and over and over again. And yet what if this is the only way you know how to live?

They climb down the shaley outcroppings, jumping and slipping to the rocks below. They can feel the cold of the ocean emanating from the water. It fills the air, tightens their skin. Somewhere out there predators lurk under the dark surface waiting to be fed. Below them is a bottomless black. *The ocean is where we all end up sooner or later*, thinks Scott, *sinking down into oblivion.*

"Here?" says David, holding up his box.

Scott looks around. It is all happening so fast.

"Let's walk a ways," he says.

They tread along the coastline, scrambling over broken rocks. Everything feels familiar, the sea, the beach, the cliff. It is they who have changed. Scott is the first to spot some, a piece of beach glass, glinting at his feet. He stops, reaches down, picks it up.

"Fifty cents for blue," he says.

"A dollar for red," says David. This is what their father used to pay them. Green glass was everywhere, brown. It was blue and red you never saw. They would spend hours scouring the beach, trying to raise money for comic books, candy bars.

Now, as they walk with their parents' ashes, they find themselves watching the beach. They are looking for the smooth remains of bottles, shiny coins of broken glass worn smooth by the sea. This is what happens when things break. The pieces separate, scatter. They are battered by the elements, buffed and polished smooth, then deposited on far-off beaches. All your hopes and dreams. The boys walk along uneven ground hunting for treasure. Dried seaweed crackles under their shoes. Driftwood lies where it has washed up, jagged Styrofoam buoys and the frayed webbing of busted lobster traps. There is an earthy stink to the muddy clay that Scott thought he had forgotten. It takes him back. He is six, he is seven, he is eight. They are both of them reliving those idle days of summer roaming, afternoon turning to evening without the sun ever going down. They would run wild over the island, lost in some invented adventure, waiting for their parents to call them home.

Now look at them, cold and shivering in their matching black suits. They are neither young nor old. Instead they hover somewhere in between, like a ball tossed in the air—in that moment when it is no longer rising but has yet begun to fall—that moment of instantaneous velocity when the ball hangs motionless. This is how they are, no longer boys and yet not fully men, though what else do you call a boy who has survived his father, his mother? What else do you call a boy with children of his own? Who is a man if not him?

David bends and picks up a rock. He tosses it out into the waves. It falls with a satisfying *plunk*. He is trying to imagine how he can fix things, get his family back. He is trying to formulate a plan. If he thinks about it too much, he feels dizzy, overwhelmed. There is still so much healing left to do. He knows this, though: It will require humility and perseverance. It will take time. And yet what else is time there for, if not to slog through the lonely act of reestablishment, if not to work piece by piece to rebuild the things you love?

He will do whatever it takes.

"Do you think...," he begins, then stops.

"What," says Scott, hunting for a good throwing rock.

"Do you think you could call Joy?"

Scott thinks about this. If he called her, what would he say? He could ask her if she still planned to keep her promise. He could tell her that what happened in that bar didn't matter. He could tell her not to let it make her bitter. She could laugh in his face. He could say the words that lay hidden in his heart, which are *I will love you. I will be your supermarket man. I will make things right.*

You helped me, he could tell her. *Now let me help you.*

He finds a good rock, fist sized, heavy. He puts down his
mother's ashes, takes a few quick steps, and hurls it into the
ocean. The wave-head explodes, as if from a gunshot. David
lays down the box he carries. He finds a bigger rock, throws it.
Scott scours the ground. The challenge has been given. They
stand there for an hour throwing weight into the ocean. The
stones get bigger, the splashes deeper. Soon they are working
together, lifting fifty-pound stones and dropping them into the
surf. Their shoes are wet, their pants soaked to the knees. They
are returning the rocks to the sea. *Take it back,* they are saying,
as if they could reassemble the fortress from which the rocks
have fallen, as if they could rebuild something massive just by
putting the stones back where they belong. They throw their
shoulders into the side of a boulder and try to roll it. It is unspoken, this mission. They will gather the hardness from beneath
their feet. They will clear the beach of its wounded. Their suits
fray and tear. The air around them fills with the deep hiccup
of weight descending into water. They will stay here until they
return every stone to the sea, until they erect a wall between
themselves and the hurt. They will build a tower into the clouds
and then, carrying their parents' ashes, they will climb to its
highest point. They will stand in the air, swaying miles above the
Earth. Birds will pass below them. Planes will fly in the down-
ward distance, and still they will climb higher, ascending into the
stratosphere. They will keep climbing until they reach the after-
life, and there they will deliver their burdens. They will tell the
gatekeeper, *Take them. Love them. They were good people, despite
their vices. They were our parents. Their weakness was their beauty.
Their longing, their hunger, their fear. Do not leave them by the side of
the road. Do not judge them just because they didn't believe in God.
They believed in each other and that was enough. They believed in us.*

The boys will build their tower. They will climb high into

the sky and there they will finally let it go, all their pain and grief, all their guilt and anger, and when they come back down, they will be so much lighter that they will float like feathers on the breeze. They will fall like laughter and settle gently to the ground. They will lie there breathing in the soothing calm of the ocean air, the waves lapping gently at their feet, and the water will be warm and the sky will be blue and it will be summer again, summer forever.

This is all any of us can wish for, to be unburdened, to forgive those who have hurt us, to set ourselves free.

ACKNOWLEDGMENTS

Thank you for reading this book. I understand you have choices when it comes to your entertainment and I appreciate your choosing *The Punch*. Thanks to my wife, Kyle, and my daughter Guinevere. Happiness and contentment are two different things. Who knew? Thanks to my agent, Jane Gelfman, and my editor, Jay Schaefer, for their wisdom and insight. Thanks to my family, without whom none of this would have been possible.

ABOUT THE AUTHOR

Noah Hawley is an Emmy, Golden Globe, PEN, Critics' Choice, and Peabody Award–winning author, screenwriter, and producer. He has published four novels and penned the script for the feature film *Lies and Alibis*. He created, executive-produced, and served as showrunner for ABC's *My Generation* and *The Unusuals* and was a writer and producer on the hit series *Bones*. Hawley is currently executive producer, writer, and showrunner on FX's award-winning series *Fargo* and on *Legion*, from FX Productions and Marvel Television.